# RECKLESS

### Saskia Walker

HEAT | NEW YORK

**THE BERKLEY PUBLISHING GROUP**
Published by the Penguin Group
Penguin Group (USA) Inc.
375 Hudson Street, New York, New York 10014, USA
Penguin Group (Canada), 90 Eglinton Avenue East, Suite 700, Toronto, Ontario M4P 2Y3, Canada
(a division of Pearson Penguin Canada Inc.)
Penguin Books Ltd., 80 Strand, London WC2R 0RL, England
Penguin Group Ireland, 25 St. Stephen's Green, Dublin 2, Ireland (a division of Penguin Books Ltd.)
Penguin Group (Australia), 250 Camberwell Road, Camberwell, Victoria 3124, Australia
(a division of Pearson Australia Group Pty. Ltd.)
Penguin Books India Pvt. Ltd., 11 Community Centre, Panchsheel Park, New Delhi—110 017, India
Penguin Group (NZ), 67 Apollo Drive, Rosedale, North Shore 0632, New Zealand
(a division of Pearson New Zealand Ltd.)
Penguin Books (South Africa) (Pty.) Ltd., 24 Sturdee Avenue, Rosebank, Johannesburg 2196,
South Africa

Penguin Books Ltd., Registered Offices: 80 Strand, London WC2R 0RL, England

This is an original publication of The Berkley Publishing Group.

This is a work of fiction. Names, characters, places, and incidents either are the product of the author's imagination or are used fictitiously, and any resemblance to actual persons, living or dead, business establishments, events, or locales is entirely coincidental. The publisher does not have any control over and does not assume any responsibility for author or third-party websites or their content.

Copyright © 2008 by Saskia Walker.
Cover art by Don Sipley.
Hand lettering by Ron Zinn.
Cover design by George Long.
Text design by Kristin del Rosario.

First edition: July 2008

Library of Congress Cataloging-in-Publication Data

Walker, Saskia.
    Reckless / Saskia Walker.—1st ed.
        p. cm.
    ISBN 978-0-425-22138-9
    1. Auctioneers—Fiction.   2. Art—Collectors and collecting—Spain—Fiction.   3. Artists—Spain—
Fiction.   I. Title.
    PS3623.A35956R43 2008
    813'.6—dc22                                                                              2008014757

PRINTED IN THE UNITED STATES OF AMERICA

10   9   8   7   6   5   4   3   2   1

*Reckless* is dedicated to my agent, Roberta Brown, my dear friends Barbara Sabin and Wendy Wootton, and to the wonderful man in my life, Mark Walker.

Thank you all, for your support, for your encouragement, and for everything else you bring into my life.

# 1

LONDON, ENGLAND

*Katrina Hammond wanted to be reckless, and it looked as if* the opportunity to do so might just have presented itself; he was drop-dead gorgeous, he was interested in her, and he was right there on the other side of her desk. "What you're asking me to do, Mr. Teodoro, is way beyond the scope of my job."

"I'm aware of that, but it's you that I want."

She took a quick intake of breath. He was so direct.

"Can't you make an exception, for me?" Sergio Teodoro smiled, and it gave the impression that—for a man like him— nothing in this world would ever be impossible. Right from the moment he'd entered her tiny garret of an office in the eaves of the old Victorian building, he'd overwhelmed it with his presence. Handsome, self-assured, and a quintessential charmer, he made her want to live dangerously.

"I'll ensure that you enjoy every moment of the task," he

added. He watched her across the desk while he opened his suit jacket and adjusted the fine, white linen cuffs on his expensive shirt. Beneath the suit, his body was strong and groomed, the epitome of suave. His cuff links glinted in the mid-September sunlight that poured in from the window, his physical presence at odds with the tiny office space, where reference books were stacked high on the shelves and a desk fan did little to stir the air. This cramped space was not the right setting for Mr. Suave. No, and she would dearly like to observe him in his own world.

"You make it sound very inviting." She responded with a slow smile, attempting to return her attention to the notes she'd been making while he spoke about the family art collection he wanted her to value for auction.

"Let me take a look at what we've got here," she said, "and then I can take your proposition to my boss." She studied him surreptitiously as she reviewed the list. It would feel good, being under that body. The urge to be wild was right there, eating away at her composure, making her hot in the most specific way: sexually.

Sensation raced over her skin as she considered what might happen. It wasn't that she was a sexual ingenue, she was plenty sassy in bed. She just hadn't been sassy *out* of bed, and she wanted to be. She wasn't that sort of woman, part of her insisted.

Or was she?

Perhaps she was identifying with his blatant sexuality. He came across as an archetypal Mediterranean lothario, and it had the unexpected effect of making her want to match up to him. Once she took that step outside her normal patterns of behavior she knew there would be no holding back. One moment of recklessness could change her life forever. And, oh, how that idea excited her.

"I will of course cover your travel expenses," he added, drawing her attention back to him, his rich Spanish accent washing over her, all soft rolling syllables and seductive tongue strokes.

It was far outside of the usual scope of her job. She undertook valuations in-house, and within a one hundred mile radius of London. He wanted her to fly to Catalonia, a region of northern Spain where tourists flocked for the beautiful beaches and distinctive Mediterranean culture.

"And you will enjoy the most intimate hospitality I can offer you at the Torre del Castagona, our country home, while you undertake the job."

The deliberately seductive look in his eyes left her in no doubt he meant a kind of hospitality that she wouldn't normally associate with work. But this was about work, she reminded herself, attempting to shelve the arousal she felt. He might be a compelling man, but he was also a potential client, and an important catch for her, business-wise.

"I'm positive we will find time to enjoy each other's company." Exactly how they would enjoy each other's company was reflected in his eyes. He made her feel his meaning as surely as if he had been holding her down over her desk, working into her body with his.

Katrina blinked. She lifted her shoulders and took a deep breath. "Mr. Teodoro—"

He held up his hand and smiled. "Sergio, please."

"Sergio. Our company undertakes valuations in England. Potential clients from Ireland or the European mainland usually bring the objects that they wish to have valued for sale here, to Pocklington's Auction House. It would be a somewhat unusual procedure for one of our company representatives to travel out of the country to undertake valuation work."

He opened his hands in a relaxed, dismissive gesture, kinglike in his manner. "We have a rather large collection of late-nineteenth-century art and artifacts, largely French. Your specialist area, yes?"

She nodded.

"It makes more sense to have you come to us. I read about your expertise on your company Web site. I decided that you were the ideal woman for the task."

Again, his gaze raked over her speculatively. His eyes were so brown they were almost black, thickly lined with lashes, as glossy black as his hair. His mouth moved in a contained smile, as if he was pursuing private, deviant thoughts about what he was suggesting to her. The man exuded sexual charisma.

Beneath her fitted shirt, Katrina felt her breasts tightening in response to him. Her usual British reserve was crumbling by the moment. "I'm flattered, although I have to point out that several of my colleagues are more experienced with large collections."

*Why am I trying to put him off?*

It wasn't as if she didn't find the job attractive. An all-expenses-paid trip to Spain while she valued the collection for auction was an attractive prospect. Pocklington, the company owner, might look favorably upon her willingness to take it on, not to mention the commission that would go against her name, and she could do with that boost right now. She'd been in Henry Wallace's shadow for far too long, both personally and professionally. This was the break that she needed.

Sergio shrugged her remark off, continuing to observe her with a suggestive glint in his eyes.

"May I ask why you don't auction the goods in Spain?" she asked, trying to focus on the business at hand, difficult though it was. The room felt increasingly warm. As a junior member of staff, her office was in the attics of the building. The tiny garret with its sloped walls and rooftop view tended to heat up quickly, especially on a warm day like this.

"Of course. I wish to keep the sale low profile at home in Spain. This is my father's collection, and he has approved the sale. My brother has, however, raised an objection with our solicitor." His expression grew resigned, as if he were disappointed by his sibling's actions.

"My brother likes to make trouble. My father disinherited him over two years ago. His complaint grows out of his bitterness. He is liable to make a drama out of this event if the sale takes place in Spain . . . his way to get back at my poor father over their feud."

He sighed heavily, shoulders lifting in a regretful shrug. "He craves the attention. He is . . . *artesano*? You would say, maybe, a minstrel?"

"Ah, he's an artist?"

"Yes." His expression was filled with regret. "No sense of responsibility, and I think he sees this as a way to get his name known. I like to keep things more personal than to have our family business appear in the newspapers. I'm sure you can understand."

Katrina nodded, her mind working quickly through the situation. It made sense. If his brother had been disinherited, that meant that Sergio also had the sole responsibility for his father's chain of convenience stores, an extensive business that covered the north of Spain.

"I should perhaps confide that my father is frail. He has been very ill and was recently was moved to a hospice." He put one hand to his chest and paused, as if seeking her understanding. "We are selling the collection in order to make sure he is kept comfortable. The best care that money can buy. You understand the situation."

Katrina murmured sympathetically. It was a familiar scenario. There was usually a serious reason why families decided to sell off their beloved collections.

"Of course. I need to get the company director's approval on the job, but I should be able to speak with Mr. Pocklington later this afternoon."

If Sergio had requested her as his valuation expert of choice, it might be possible. Henry Wallace would have been the obvious candidate. Not only was he senior to her, but he also had the requisite knowledge, and he spoke Spanish as well as French, which would make things a bit easier in general. She didn't. She understood only a smattering of Spanish. Her languages were French, Norwegian, and Latin. That was all stated on the Web site, too, but for some reason Sergio Teodoro had come to her. Perhaps he preferred working with women?

*And when did work stop and play begin?* she found herself wondering as she considered his classically handsome face. Would the erotic promise she found in his eyes be fulfilled if she went to Spain? Arousal fluttered in the pit of her belly.

His eyes narrowed, his smile widened. He knew what she was thinking, and he was responding to her signs of interest.

She looked away, unnerved, and as she did, she caught sight of Henry—her ex-fiancé, as well as her senior at the auction house—hovering outside, visible through the small glass panel in the door to her office. He was pretending to use the photocopier on the landing while eyeballing her with Sergio.

*How dare he?* Annoyance flashed through her. She'd been the dutiful little fiancée, and he'd dumped her for a slimmer, younger model, a woman he'd apparently been sleeping with on the side. While she proudly wore his antique engagement ring and dreamed of their wedding day, he had humiliated her in front of all their friends and colleagues. The fact that he was now watching her with some sort of possessive, insistent curiosity riled her to the max.

Glancing back, she saw that Sergio was still observing her as if planning how best to devour her. A heady sense of purpose hit her, her motivation to change strengthening. Where had being a well-behaved woman got her, after all? She knew what she wanted to do. For once she wanted to act on her instincts, and that meant taking this fledgling flirtation with Sergio a step further. Pushing back her chair, she stood up.

*I'll give you something to look at, Henry Wallace.*

Her heart rate went up, but she was taking control of this situation right now. Walking around the desk, she stepped over to where Sergio's long, limber legs stretched out toward her. Sitting on the edge of the desk, she crossed her legs high on the thigh, one ankle brushing against his leg as she did so. The very act of touching him that way, deliberately, gave her a frisson of pleasure.

Sergio's eyebrows lifted, and his smile grew. He eyed her legs appreciatively for several long moments.

Oh yes, he was attracted to her, and the physical contact made her blood race. She slid one hand over her thigh, smoothing her skirt, smiling at him invitingly when he lifted his gaze to meet hers.

"You've made the job sound very . . . tempting," she whispered.

"Good. I hoped it would be."

He was so self-assured. Is that how he would be in bed, undeniably confident and oozing pure machismo? Between her thighs, she clenched at the very thought of it. She ran her finger inside her shirt, dipping one finger into her cleavage where the skin was humid.

He watched her movements, blatantly enjoying them. He didn't even try to pretend he was doing anything else. Something fluttered inside her, a sense of growing freedom and the certain knowledge of feminine power within her reach.

His lips moved slightly, his hands tightened on the arms of the chair. He glanced up from her cleavage, locked eyes with her. "I will be anticipating your arrival."

"When do you want me?" she breathed, wondering if it was really her own voice that she heard issuing that unmistakable invitation. How she wished that Henry could hear as well as see the exchange. She'd never done anything like this before, but she'd seen other women acting this way, and she'd often wondered how it would feel. Now she had gone for it and, oh, boy, did it ever feel good. A decadent sense of being a woman—a woman who knew what she wanted and went after it—blossomed inside her.

His smile was rich, and his dark eyes narrowed, his gaze growing intense. His hand moved from the arm of the chair to her leg, his fingers clasping her ankle possessively. "Come as soon as you can. I'll be ready and waiting for you."

*Now,* her body cried, *I want to do it now.* She pictured him over her, pinning her to a bed, riding her hard.

The sound of the door opening snapped her out of it.

"Katrina," an uptight voice interrupted, "can I help with your client at all?"

It was Henry, and he was twitching with annoyance. Next to Sergio, everything about him looked pale and weak. She used to be attracted to his schoolboy appearance. Now he just seemed immature and unsophisticated.

Sergio swung around in his chair and gave the intruder a dismissive stare. "Ms. Hammond is handling me very well, thank you." He emphasized the word *handling.*

Katrina's body hummed with pleasure.

Henry glowered at Sergio and then at her.

The atmosphere in the room was instantly charged with animosity. Part of her, the part that was fundamentally bruised and needed to heal, reveled in it. Two male egos were vying for her attention. In that moment, she felt powerful. It was a heady feeling, and it spurred her on. She stood up and, resting one hand on Sergio's shoulder, she gave Henry a cool smile.

"You're not needed here, Henry."

Her ex stared at her, disbelievingly at first, his eyes filled with surprise as he took in the sight of her touching the other man, a client.

*Yes, Henry. You're witnessing the birth of a new me; get used to it.*

"If you're sure?" he mumbled, looking positively stunned at her response.

She nodded, her grip automatically tightening on Sergio's shoulder.

Sergio moved beside her.

She rocked on her heels and withheld a gasp when she felt him touching her. He had reached behind her to run his hand up the back of her thigh, underneath her skirt. She felt the fabric shifting and rumpling against her leg as his hand curved around her leg from behind. His hand was solid and warm against her skin, the thin barrier of her sheer stockings only heightening the electricity in his touch. Her nerve endings danced, sensation rattling up her thigh, making the pulse in her groin thud wildly. She felt dizzy, positively light-headed.

"Well, I'll be around," Henry gestured outside the office, "just in case you change your mind."

Gathering herself, she shooed him with her hand and then moved, reluctantly pulling away from Sergio to shut the door behind Henry.

Henry flapped about by the photocopier, pretending to program it while glancing back over his shoulder. Annoyance had got the better of him, and he pursed his lips and glowered at her in the most unattractive way. It made her want to laugh. Yes, she was finally starting to get over him, and throwing off past history fed into her current, wayward mood.

She heard Sergio's chair shifting.

He'd stood up and was closing on her with deliberation. Instinctively she turned to face him, watching as his tall frame blocked out the light from the window, casting her in shadow. He was a good six inches taller than she, and broad shouldered. And right up against her.

"I like your style, Katrina." He moved his fingers into her hair, running them through it slowly and lifting it up as if to examine it in the light. "If I may call you Katrina?"

"Yes, of course, please do." Her reply was breathless. She wasn't used to men looking at her quite the way he did, and it was doing strange things to her.

He was so close she could smell his cologne, a subtle but masculine scent. He was clearly acting on her advances. Like a red flag to a bull, she thought with amusement, feeling giddy at the idea of it.

He drew her away from the door, his hands on her shoulders, turning her as he examined her. "I find you a very attractive woman."

"Once again, I'm flattered." She reminded herself to breathe. *Match him,* she urged herself. "The attraction is mutual," she added.

Lust flared in his eyes. He backed her up against the side of the filing cabinet, his eyes locked with hers. Even through her clothes, the metal was cool against her back, and she pivoted her torso against it. With one sure finger, he lifted her chin. Breathing her in, his eyelids lowered. She felt as if a jungle beast had cornered her, and he was considering whether he wanted a meal or a mate.

Uncertainty flashed through her when his hands roved over her. *What is he going to do? Kiss me? Surely not? Not here in the office, with Henry watching?* Flirting, the casual, intimate touch, yes, but more than that? And yet, if that was how he did things, would she really want to object?

*No,* her body cried, wanting him badly. *Let him kiss me. Right here, right now.*

She gasped aloud, her spine tensing. His free hand had moved to her breast, and he was deliberately measuring the outline through her shirt, sending skittering sensations over her skin. Apparently Mr. Sergio Teodoro wasn't waiting for her approval. Her body clamored with need.

Instinctively, she moved and pressed her breast into his hand. He squeezed it firmly. That small act felt so good, she moaned aloud. He leaned down, ran his nose along her cheek, then bent to kiss her lips, quickly prizing them open and tasting her mouth.

Resistance was not even a possibility. Her thighs trembled. Forgetting that they were being observed, she closed her eyes—forgetting everything except the sheer sexual aura, the physical strength and will of this man who had her pinned there. Her hands clutched at his jacket, welcoming the kiss; then she gasped and pulled back, eyes flashing open, shocked. His hand was under her skirt again, at the front this time, lifting it as his fingers moved high enough to touch her underwear.

*He can't mean to touch me . . . here, now?*

"Mr. Teodoro—"

"Sergio," he interrupted, and gave a dark laugh. The look in his eyes was so self-assured. He was fully aware of the affect he was having on her.

Her objection died on her lips when she felt his finger brush over her lace underwear. Her legs quivered. She breathed in so hard it was audible. She shook her head. "I shouldn't really . . ."

"Why not?"

*Yes, other people do things like this,* her inner voice insisted, reminding her of the secret fantasies she had: the sexy daydreams she had never shared with anyone and never fulfilled. She knew she should break away from him, for decorum's sake, but she couldn't, because she did not want to.

Sexual tension emanated from him, magnetizing her. She whimpered when he cupped her mons, boldly squeezing it in the palm of his large hand. Her legs felt weak. It was only her shoulder blades angled on the top of the filing cabinet that were holding her up—that, and his hand grasping her, right there in the juncture of her thighs. As he bent to bite her earlobe, she turned her head, looking over his shoulder, and caught sight of Henry. He was still hovering outside, neck stretched, head bobbing, clearly rattled by the sight of them in a clinch. He was staring at Sergio's back as he arched over her, his hand buried between her thighs.

She took a deep breath and arched one eyebrow at him.

*Eat your heart out, Henry.*

Emboldened, she moved her hips, rolling them, pushing herself into Sergio's hand. Offering herself. No longer reliable, professional Katrina Hammond, she embraced this new blatantly sexualized, confident woman that she wanted to become.

A woman who wanted to kick down her own boundaries like there was no tomorrow.

Sergio responded quickly, pushing his knee between her legs, one finger pressing her underwear into the damp groove of her sex. She felt the size of his growing erection through their clothes, where it was now embedded against her hip. Her sex clenched, need echoing through it. She felt the wetness there, and knew she was growing slicker by the moment. He moved against her, letting her feel the size of him.

His fingers had found their way inside her underwear. He was touching her naked pussy. "You arouse me," he whispered against her ear.

"I can tell," she blurted, breathless, disbelieving laughter escaping her.

He drew back to watch her when she shivered and moaned under his assault. "You will come . . . to Cataluña?" Humor lit his eyes as he confidently massaged her clit.

"I'll come," she breathed, one hand clutching at his jacket, the other braced against the filing cabinet at her back. She was right on the precipice of coming, in fact.

"I'm glad we understand each other," he responded and applied more pressure, his finger pushing down and into the groove of her sex, the heel of his hand wedged against her clit.

She heard a small ping, then another, as the elastic of her underwear gave way under the pressure of his hand, and then his finger was inside her, and her body clutched onto it, automatically welcoming the hard intrusion. Sensation raced the entire length of her body. Like wildfire, out of control, she was anchored to the moment and yet undeniably lost to it.

"Good?" His fingers made a slight slurping sound as they moved on her damp flesh.

A hot tide of embarrassment washed over her, but she couldn't deny it. She managed a nod, squirming against him, desperate to find that release.

"Good, yes," she blurted. Her voice sounded high and warbled as she got the words out.

He pushed deeper.

Pleasure bolted through her. Outside her office she could hear voices in the corridor, but she didn't care. Henry was out there, but she didn't care. Sergio was watching her with an inquisitive stare, a stare that sent a shiver under her skin, and she didn't care. Because it felt so good, and she was riding it out, plunging onto his hand, ramming her swollen clit against his palm, and biting her lip to save herself from crying out loud as she came.

# 2

*Once safely out of earshot of anyone in the auction house, Sergio* reached into his inside pocket for his phone and flipped it open, scrolling to the number he wanted as he moved into the crowds swarming on the busy London pavements.

Elaine answered quickly. *"Hola, Sergio."*

"I'm on my way back to the airport now."

"How did it go?"

He couldn't restrain a smile. "Señorita Hammond proved to be very agreeable."

Elaine laughed. "I knew that you would have her eating out of your palm within moments."

"Absolutely," he replied, wondering what Elaine would think if she knew how literally Katrina Hammond had been eating out of his palm. The scent of her desire still lingered there.

"She's very attractive, too, blonde, with bright green eyes. I believe you would call her an English rose, and she is just coming into bloom."

"You can be so charming when you choose to be." She sounded wistful. "Don't get too smug, my dear. There's many a slip between cup and lip."

"But you, my darling stepmother, will be there to rein me in if I do," he said, daring her to try.

"Indeed I will," she purred down the phone.

Elaine liked to think she was the one in charge of this situation, which wasn't the case. He wanted to put her thoughts back on a more secure path, in case she did something stupid before he got back to Castagona. "All our . . ." He hesitated to describe the situation. ". . . family troubles . . . will be over soon."

He hailed a passing taxi. "*Adios, Elaine.* I will be home soon." Smiling to himself, he snapped the phone shut and darted to the taxi.

*Mr. Pocklington peered at the list Katrina had made through* his half-moon spectacles, sucking on his teeth thoughtfully, as was his way. He'd always looked like a dusty headmaster to her, complete with baldpate and bushy sideburns. Even though it was hot, he was wearing his trademark three-piece pinstripe suit, with salmon pink shirt and a burgundy bow tie. Savile Row tailored, of course, but à la mode of a different age, just like his taste in art. He was impressed by the list, she could tell. A little light gleamed in his pale blue eyes, the light that always flickered on when he sensed a notable collection.

He mumbled into life. "I think it would be worth your time." He glanced over his spectacles, drawing his heavy gray eyebrows together as he looked at her. "Often these private collectors want to set a high reserve on the asking prices because they are reluctant to sell. If he leans that way, talk him out of it. It's not worth working with an overseas collection if we don't actually shift half of it."

Katrina nodded, stifling a smile.

"How long do you think it will take to value the collection?"

"Mr. Teodoro estimated four days, maybe five. If you approve the job, I would request a flexible ticket and hope to complete the appraisal and return sooner." She nodded at the piece of paper in his hand. "That's not the full list. That's just the larger items I jotted down during our discussion. Apparently Mr. Teodoro's father had an interest in obtaining series of work from a sculptor's earliest maquette through to the final version, and the same with sketches and finals. Such series might draw interest from major museums worldwide. He also has a large collection of documentation, including the correspondence of European artists who were active in the late nineteenth century."

"It's definitely a meaty collection," Pocklington agreed. "We wouldn't want it to go to a competitor." He let out a sudden chortle. "You know, Katrina, I wasn't sure how it would work out when I took you on here. I did it as a mark of respect to your dear departed father. But I hoped you'd learn to take the initiative in your own time, and I can see that might be happening here." He prodded the sheet of paper with one finger and looked at her with a compassionate smile.

He meant well, but Katrina shifted her feet, always made uncomfortable when reminded of how she got here; her mother had approached Pocklington asking him to employ his old friend's daughter. Katrina was mortified at the time but couldn't turn the post down. As a student it was her dream to work at a respected city auction house, just as her father had done. Her mother had jumped the gun, and Katrina had tried to forget the favor, but it still undermined her confidence at times.

"I appreciate all you've done for me, but I've always wanted to be here because of my performance in the job. This valuation project is notable and would give me the chance to prove myself."

He nodded and returned his attention to the list.

At one time, being employed by this man was her pinnacle of achievement. Now she wanted to excel and to try different things. It was strange how one's goals shifted over time. Her life had followed an orderly, linear pattern: grammar school, where she had studied hard and made it into university. She wasn't genius standard—far from it—but with a lot of hard work she made it through her degree course. She'd then gained a position as a valuation assistant at a provincial auctioneers. When she was taken on at Pocklington's Auction House, she was unhappy at how it had come about, but she was also thrilled to to be there at all.

Henry had also seemed to be a good move on this linear passage. Her mother was proud of her when they had announced the engagement, and that was no small achievement in itself. Then their engagement had all fallen apart, leaving her feeling on shaky ground both personally and professionally. At work she felt excluded. Partly, she knew she made herself feel that way; she wanted to disassociate from their shared environment. Her mother was still upset about the whole thing, convinced Katrina must have done something wrong to lose "such a good catch as Henry Wallace."

Katrina couldn't bring herself to tell her mother exactly what had gone on. Reflecting on it now, she cringed inside. Henry had turned out to be nasty, disloyal, selfish, and rather a bore. Was that why she felt so restless? Why she felt the need to shake things up? Because she'd played it safe for so long? Or was it because she was fast closing on her thirtieth birthday and feared she hadn't yet lived? She had the urge to laugh aloud when it occurred to her that one good orgasm had set her free from predictability. Now she wanted more, maybe even a hot affair with a sexy client.

Pocklington tapped his fingers on the table thoughtfully. She wanted to convince him, to say the right thing to push him along. A few days ago, she wouldn't even have risked it. Her mother had been so strict with her, drumming into her that good girls were "seen and not heard." Perhaps that's where she'd gone wrong. Being demure and agreeable meant Henry had easily trampled on her. It had got her nowhere in life. She didn't want to be aggressive, but she did want to find ways to express herself more.

Pocklington was frowning. He could so easily insist Henry take the case, which would thwart her in every way.

"I'm sure you're questioning whether I am ready for a job like this."

He looked up, surprised.

"I'd really like to undertake the valuation; in fact, I'd like to handle the whole process myself, if you are willing to give me that responsibility." She gave a little shrug, following her instincts, trying to gauge how best to sell it to him. "This is a great opportunity for me to demonstrate how much I've learned since I started working here. I'm ready to take on a project of this importance, and I'd like to prove that to you. If I have any doubts about the client or any part of the collection, I can be in touch with you for advice."

Pocklington put down the piece of paper and steepled his fingers under his chin. He looked pleased with her remark. "That seems like a fair compromise. I'm pleased with your initiative."

"Thank you, sir." She beamed. The last thing she wanted to have to do was to inform Sergio that someone else would be flying over to do the job.

"When's the client thinking of having the valuation carried out?"

"He'd like me to begin as soon as possible. I can be ready to fly over within a week, and we could certainly aim to wind up the inventory stage by the beginning of October. I would estimate we're looking at sending the shipment people in mid-month, with catalog distribution late October for an early November sale."

Turning to his desktop calendar—businesslike, now that he had authorized the job—he quickly cast his eye over it, noting when the goods might be shipped back for sale, scribbling details onto the calendar in pencil. "E-mail details through to Lucy as you inventory the goods, and I'll be sure to look them over. You'll also need to collect detailed provenance for each item. That might be the most time-consuming part."

She nodded, glad he wanted her to e-mail Lucy, his PA, for him to oversee. Pocklington was an old-fashioned man and didn't use e-mail, but that secondary connection would help a lot.

Pocklington paused in his scribbling. "In view of the situation with the father being ill, you'd better ask Lucy to prepare you a specific set of ownership release documents for our own security."

"Will do."

When he wound up the meeting, Katrina stood and reached out to shake his hand, anticipation lifting her spirits high. "Thank you, Mr. Pocklington. I won't let you down."

*What a difference a day makes,* she mused as she left his office. That morning, she'd been feeling depressed. She was over Henry but still had to face him every day at work, which was awkward. Not to mention the embarrassingly sympathetic glances from their mutual friends. In a few days' time, she'd be working on a prestigious valuation project in another country. She needed this, something completely different. Work wise, and play wise. Sergio's attention had made her feel good, and it had shown Henry a thing or two.

Lucy looked up and smiled when Katrina knocked and then ducked into her office, adjacent to Pocklington's.

"Did you get the go-ahead?" Lucy asked. A woman in her early fifties, she personified practical efficiency. She wore flat shoes, the minimum amount of makeup, and a no-nonsense short haircut. Even so, she had a caring, motherly approach and often took an interest in the staff above and beyond her duty.

Katrina nodded and smiled. "He said I should e-mail you my inventory as I go through the collection; he's going to over-see my work himself."

"Good. That means you won't have to deal with Henry on this one." Lucy nodded her head in approval. "Anything you need while you are over there, just let me know."

"Thanks, you're an angel." Leaning on the desk, Katrina jotted down the full name of the collection owner on her note-pad. "I need a set of ownership release documents made out in this name. I'll be heading off sometime next week. Is that enough time to prepare the paperwork?" She tore the page from her notepad and handed it across.

"Plenty." Lucy looked past Katrina as she popped the piece of paper into a tray on her desk.

Glancing over her shoulder, Katrina lifted her eyebrows when she saw that Henry was standing in the doorway, appar-ently waiting for her. She turned back to Lucy and lowered her voice. "Excellent. Just let me know when it's done."

"Will do. Leave it with me."

In an unspoken agreement they curtailed a conversation that might otherwise have gone on. Lucy had an amused look in her eyes. It was obvious that Henry was dying to find out what was going on.

Katrina smiled and turned to leave the room, stepping past him as she did.

As she strode across the landing, Henry was hot on her heels. "Katrina, I'd like to speak to you about this rather un-usual valuation project—"

"My, my, good news does travel fast," she interrupted. She'd only mentioned it to two other people before her meeting with Pocklington, and yet he'd found out already.

Henry ignored her remark, plowing on as he followed her up the stairs. "I have my doubts about whether you're ready to take on a project this large, on your own."

"Of course you do." She glanced back and gave a soft laugh, which she was pleased to see perturbed him. "But there was always going to come a time when I matched up to you at work. Move over, and let someone else have a go at the juicy stuff."

Annoyance flashed over his face.

She stopped outside her office door, turning her back against it and barring the way. "Oh, and next time you come to my office, I suggest you knock."

"I'm just concerned about you," he snapped.

"Don't be. That's not your job anymore. You resigned from that position."

"I'm sorry," he mumbled.

"No, you're not. Be honest for once. You're just jealous that I've been approached by a client."

He peered at her in disbelief.

*Where was this coming from?* She would never have said things like this to him before, when the old stiff-upper-lip attitude had prevailed. His behavior had been eating away at her for a long time, and unburdening herself felt hugely rewarding. It was time for some honest home truths. She might even call her mother, put her straight on a few facts about golden boy here.

Henry had adopted an incredulous expression. "You can't

just go to this man's home. You don't know the first thing about him."

"What do you think he's going to do, sell me to the white slave trade? Get real, Henry. He's a respected Spanish business-man with a reputation to keep."

Henry's eye twitched in annoyance. "I'm concerned about whether the client was acting appropriately toward you."

Now they were getting to the point. "Oh, but he was . . . acting appropriately, that is."

He gesticulated through her door and in the direction of the filing cabinet. "Katrina, I saw him touching you."

She shook her head at him. He had philandered right under her nose while they were engaged, but he just couldn't take it when she was with another man, even though they were now apart. "Henry, get over it. He's attracted to me, and I'm attracted to him. We're both consenting adults, and I'm looking forward to exploring our relationship further in Spain."

The look on Henry's face was totally priceless. Bewilder-ment haunted his eyes. "You never used to be like this," he mumbled.

"No, but maybe I was being held back. I'm free now, and I'm feeling better already. Thanks for the helping hand, Henry. If it hadn't been for you and your not-so-subtle affair, I wouldn't have found out what I really needed—and that was my free-dom."

He didn't like hearing that at all. Scowling, he backed away without another word, reaching blindly for the banister to re-treat down the stairs.

Katrina couldn't help smiling. Ahead of her, she had an exciting job and the company of a sexy host, but the look on her ex's face right at that moment was the absolute icing on the cake.

# 3

BARCELONA, SPAIN
One Week Later

*Nicolas Teodoro looked up from his desk when the sound of the* phone ringing broke his concentration. As he did, he noticed that the sun had moved from the small balcony outside the window. He had been so caught up in work he hadn't noticed how late it was, well past midday.

He dropped his pen and moved aside the travel grant application that he'd been working on for a group of his students, in order to answer the call. *"Sí, Nico Teodoro. Hola."*

He'd barely issued the greeting when a familiar voice broke into a disgruntled tirade at the other end of the line.

*"Raimunda . . . sí."*

He frowned as he tried to follow what his father's housekeeper was saying. Raimunda was a woman of extremes, swinging from stoic silence to fast-moving diatribes as a matter of course, and it was practically impossible to follow her when she was in one of her fumes. At such times she often slipped from Spanish into Basque and—despite having grown up with her as a constant in his life, and being her favored son of the house, the one to whom she would pass the little treats and show rare moments of affection—even he couldn't follow what she said. This was one such time.

He gave a soft sigh, interrupted, and tried to calm her down. *"Más lento, por favor."*

The voice at the other end of the phone stopped dead, and then she apologized and took a deep breath.

Something must have happened up at the house to set her off this way. Raimunda hated using the telephone, but she'd been calling him almost every day with some new development. After he'd confronted the family solicitor, Ciro, the week before, he thought Sergio would abandon his latest plan to sell their father's art collection and simply concentrate on their father's welfare and running the company. Apparently not.

Raimunda had begun to speak again, and this time she managed to slow herself down enough for him to catch most of what she was saying. Sergio was bringing in an outsider, an overseas agent, to auction the art collection. Nicolas's mood darkened.

Sergio's latest actions perplexed him. This surely was an act borne of his need to prove his power over the family. Their family solicitor had agreed the collection couldn't be auctioned while their father was ill and had reluctantly promised to inform Nico of his father's welfare and whereabouts and of Sergio's moves. But now Sergio seemed to be taking another route, presumably outside of the solicitor's knowledge.

"Is it for me?" a sleepy voice said behind him.

Nico glanced back at his tenant—a genial American student called Kent—and held up one hand to quiet his friend, urging Raimunda on.

Kent scratched his head, grabbed a carton of orange juice from the counter between the living area and the kitchen, and skulked over to the sofa, depositing himself there in sprawl of long limbs and underwear.

From what Raimunda was saying, an English auctioneer was traveling in, and soon. She'd overheard Sergio and Elaine talking about it. Nico frowned. No doubt some stuffy *inglesa* who'd whisk the art away without even considering their father's intentions. He fought the urge to crush something.

"*Una señorita?*" he quizzed when he heard Raimunda mention a name. He scribbled the details on his blotter and asked Raimunda to keep him informed.

"*Una señorita,*" Kent repeated after Nico had put the phone down, and waggled his eyebrows suggestively. His American accent added even more implication to the phrase.

"Not what you think. My brother is up to something again."

"Bad news," Kent responded, rubbing his face.

Nico's thoughts had gone to his father. It had been over two years since he had seen him, over two years since their last argument. Their relationship had begun to fracture long before then, though. His father had never approved of Nico's choice to pursue a career in the arts. He'd wanted his son to study business, not performance art. He'd laughed when Nico apprenticed himself to the masters of Spanish performance art, but when

Nico announced he was going to work for the city, to run a theater program for kids who might otherwise end up on the streets, his father had practically disowned him. Nico couldn't fathom it. Perhaps his father had thought all along that Nico would come around and grow out of it. Not the case. Nico was determined to live his own life, be his own man. He refused to work for the family business.

It was the last straw in their fragile relationship. His new stepmother, Elaine, had helped that final fracture along—and Sergio, of course. They'd leapt on it as a chance to push him out once and for all.

Nico had moved out of the family house, removing himself from the poisonous atmosphere Sergio had nurtured since their mother's death. Nico had encouraged Raimunda to leave, too, and offered to help her. Raimunda was devoted to his father, just as she had been to his mother, and even though Jorge had changed over time, she wouldn't abandon him. When did it all start? Nico tried to pinpoint the exact time. Was it when his mother had died, or when Jorge had met Elaine, or before that? Long before, he thought, but Elaine had hastened the change.

His father hadn't been in perfect health when he'd last seen him, but it had come as a shock to hear he'd been taken to a hospice rather suddenly. It wasn't Nico's concern; he'd hardened his heart a long time ago, when he'd found his father's love and approval had come with a proviso—that he work in the family business—but it annoyed him that Sergio seemed to be using his father's failing health as an excuse to wield his power.

"What is it, the art collection again, or something else?" Kent yawned as he spoke. Kent was a student on exchange, studying languages at the local university. He liked to live fast, go days without sleeping, and then make up for it with sleep marathons.

Nico nodded and pushed back the thoughts of his father, the insistent image of him showing them part of the collection being prepared for shipment to a major exhibition when he and Sergio were barely school age. That enthusiasm for art hadn't extended to his son becoming a practitioner, however. Nico had to unclench his teeth to reply to Kent. "Yes, he's going ahead anyway, trying for an overseas auction house."

Kent gave a wry laugh. "You gotta hand it to him; he's getting good at sidestepping you to get what he wants."

"He hasn't sidestepped me yet, though, has he?" Nico gave a wry smile as he considered how annoyed Sergio would be if he knew that the housekeeper was keeping him up to date with information. He liked the thought of annoying his older brother. Long before Sergio had encouraged their father to disassociate with Nico, they had been at loggerheads, two brothers who competed with each other, seemingly destined to do battle to the end.

"He's been waiting for this for a long time."

"Yeah, why?" Kent came from a different kind of background and had been intrigued by the reasons for the Teodoro family split. One of his university professors had told him he was renting space from the family who owned the biggest chain of convenience stores in the region. Kent had asked Nico outright if it was true, suspecting it was a different Teodoro.

Nico was continually amazed at people's capacity for gossip, but he'd answered Kent's questions and found himself telling far more about his family than usual. Kent proved a sensible listener, though, and Nico had appreciated the audience. He realized he'd been holding the story inside for many months, and somehow the telling of it was therapeutic. In fact, he'd almost put it all behind him and forgotten his father's coldness toward him and the age-old feud with his brother, when Raimunda had called him with the news about an ambulance at the house, his father's removal to a hospice.

"My brother is motivated by his greed for power and control. Even though he has it all, he wants more, to prove a point. According to the family solicitor, he claims that he needs the funds for my father's care. Why not take it from the business or the personal accounts, if that is the case?"

Kent nodded, rubbing his closely cropped hair as he did, coming fully awake. "So, do you think he's doing this to annoy you?"

"Perhaps, yes." Nico wasn't sure on that point, but he would find out.

Kent took the final swallow from the orange juice carton. Nico watched him absentmindedly as he scrunched the empty carton between his hands.

Kent gave him a cheeky smile. "I owe you rent . . . and orange juice. I'm going to the bank tomorrow to transfer some funds. I'll be able to pay you your back rent then."

Nico's mind had been moving in a different direction, and he reached for a piece of paper on his desk. "If you've got time to make a few phone calls for me, and practice your Spanish"—he winked—"we could forget about the rent this month."

Kent's eyes lit. "Sure. Sounds like a good deal." He grinned and reached out his hand for the list. "What is it that you want me to do?"

"You remember I said my father was taken to a hospice last week, and the solicitor told me my father's condition had deteriorated."

Kent nodded, glancing at the piece of paper as Nico passed it to him.

"I compiled a list of all the possible places he might be: hospices, private hospitals, care homes. I'm trying to find him . . . without my brother knowing." He glanced at Kent to see his response.

"You're looking for him? I thought you said you and your father would never speak again."

"Yes. And we probably never will. I just need to know how he is, you know." He shrugged, determined not to feel remorse or emotion. All of those things had died in him a long time ago, replaced by anger and a relentless self-reliance that made him stubborn and disagreeable at times. "And, if he's happy about the collection being sold, fine. Personally, I don't think he would be."

Kent looked as if he was about to say something and then thought better of it, simply nodding. He looked thoughtful for a few moments while they sat in silence. "And what are you going to do about Sergio and the auctioneer?"

"I'm not sure yet. I can't go up to Castagona right away, I'll be working with the kids most of the day tomorrow."

"You could try to get to her first, the señorita."

"That's what you'd do is it, Kent?" Nico laughed. Kent was working on making Nico into more of a ladies' man.

Kent shrugged and gave him a wicked smile, as if to say, "Of course."

"It's a good suggestion."

Kent stretched his arms out, hands upraised. "Hey, I'm not just a pretty face."

Nico glanced down at his blotter and the details that Raimunda had given him. He could call this woman, put some doubts into her mind. But then Sergio would hear about it, and that would defeat the purpose. No, he could handle it with more subtlety than that. He smiled to himself, relishing the thought of challenging his brother, his old adversary. Maybe he hadn't left their rivalry behind. Maybe he didn't want to.

"You gonna check her out?" Kent asked.

Nico nodded. "Yes, and if Sergio is resorting to subterfuge, then I can, too."

# 4

*Katrina stood at her Barcelona hotel window wrapped in a towel,* still damp from the shower, breathing in the atmosphere of the city. Barcelona was a vibrant place; passion and mystery were heavy in the atmosphere. She'd flown in earlier that day to make the most of her short stopover there before going out to Castagona in the morning, the village outside of which the Teodoro country house was located.

Something about the historic heart of Barcelona made her feel more alive. The city's passions spilled onto the pavements and narrow cobbled streets from houses that were characterized by their shadowed doorways and shuttered windows, trailing foliage, and art-encrusted walls. Seduction of the senses waited at every turn. And now, on the edge of the evening, the place hummed with expectancy, its normally vibrant culture intensified by the festival that was in progress.

La Merce was a yearly event held during the final days of September, when the inhabitants of Barcelona celebrated the end of summer with a bang. With parades and fireworks, hundreds of revelers danced and performed in the streets on the Sunday evening. The festival was held to greet the cooler months of autumn, but this year the city still baked with late summer heat as it took place. The sound of music and mayhem rising from the narrow streets below her window lured her to join in as she pulled on her undies and slipped into a filmy summer dress that she'd bought especially for the trip. The dress was feminine and scarflike, with delicate layers of the fabric floating in around her shins.

When she'd arrived at the hotel, chilled cava, chocolates, and flowers were waiting in her room, with a note from Sergio saying that his driver would collect her at ten o'clock the next morning. She picked up her glass, taking another sip of the heady, sparkling wine he'd sent for her to enjoy. It chased her nerves away, nerves that sprang up if she thought too long about walking into Sergio's home after what had already passed between them. She applied lipstick, grabbed her shoulder bag, slipped on her strappy sandals, and headed out.

Walking along the dimly lit interior corridor of the hotel, with its marble floor and solid, dark wood doorways, she noticed the tranquillity in contrast to the buzz of the street outside. The hotel was an old building and cool, even without air-conditioning. High ceilings, marble floors, and shuttered windows kept the light out. She stepped quickly down the wide, marble steps, her hand running lightly over the oak balustrade that was set upon coiling black wrought-iron Art Nouveau spindles.

As she walked across the reception area, she could already see the moving procession outside on the street. The tinted glass of the main doors barely muted the color of the spectacle. Excitement bubbled inside her. She'd never traveled alone like this before. Previously, she had holidayed with friends, with her mother, or with Henry. There was something liberating about being in a strange and beautiful city alone.

The hotel wasn't far from Las Ramblas, the main avenue in the city, a cultural thoroughfare over a mile long, where city folk and tourists alike gathered every day to see performance art or buy goods at the market stalls. La Merce spilled out beyond Las Ramblas, though, into the areas of the surrounding streets and squares, flooding the city. Twilight was near, and the fireworks displays would begin soon. Excitement barreled through her. She headed past the reception desk toward the door and was startled when she heard her name called.

"Ah, Señorita Hammond, excuse me." The receptionist waved at her from behind her marble counter. "I have a message for you." She pulled a folded piece of paper from the wood mail slots on the wall behind her.

"Thank you." Katrina retrieved the note and opened it, wondering what it could be.

*Enjoy the festival.*

The handwriting didn't look the same as on the note in her room, but this one was written in capital letters, so she had to assume it was from Sergio as well, even though it felt a little odd. She turned the page over, but there was nothing other than her name written on the front.

*Señorita Hammond.*

*"Gracias,"* she said to the receptionist and dropped the slip of paper into her shoulder bag before continuing on her way.

As she pushed through the heavy glass doors a wave of humid warmth hit her. The sound of music—overlaid with drums and whistles—filled the narrow side street. She stared as a man on stilts strode by, waving down at her as he passed. Smiling up at him, she was startled when another figure darted out from the periphery of her vision and stepped right up against her. She exclaimed in surprise, then her hand went to her throat and she let out a relieved laugh. Dressed from head to toe in black, the man had a closely fitting red satin eye mask covering half of his face, and a trident in one hand. Bloodred horns jutted from his thick black hair. He was *el diablo*, the devil himself.

Demons were among the most popular figures during the festival, but to be approached so suddenly by one had startled her. The man continued to stand in front of her, his attention fully on her, his eyes dark and inscrutable behind the mask. He was tall and noticeably fit, and his posture alone held the suggestion of limber power. He lifted his trident, moving fluidly like a mime artist. When he moved, she could see just how fit he was, his body outlined in the skintight black outfit he wore beneath the cape that rested over his back.

He peered at her, his movements and gestures exaggerated in mime. He created a space between them, and he used it to point his trident at her, running the pointed tips of it down from her collarbone to where her dress began at her cleavage, sending a delicious shiver under her skin. Her breasts immediately tightened, her nipples lifting the sheer fabric.

"*Bonita, señorita,*" he announced, with a wicked smile.

Her body trembled. He was complimenting her. "*Gracias.*"

She was mesmerized, couldn't drag her gaze away from him. The outfit he was wearing showed his body to perfection. Inside the dark fabric of his top, his chest was firm, his waist tapering to lean hips. His thighs were long and strong; they made her want to run her hands over them, made her want to check out his backside. She looked back at his face, not trusting herself to pursue her examination further. She was already far too stimulated. But it didn't help, because the man's mouth was attractive, firm but beautifully sculpted. There was a subtle cynicism to his smile that made her yearn to touch his lips, to soften them.

Removing the trident, he bowed, flicking back his cloak when it slid forward over his shoulders. As he straightened up, he beckoned her with one hand, as if calling for her to follow him onto the street and into the parade.

*Why not?* she mused. There was no particular path through the city that she intended to follow; she'd planned to meander and see what she could see. She had no one to answer to. This was her evening, and if she wanted to follow and watch the *diablo*, she would.

His lithe figure moved into the exotically dressed crowd, at first easy to spot. As the distance between them grew, it was harder to pick him out, and she jolted into action, following him at a safe distance, hanging back about ten feet, keeping him in her sight. The smell of food cooking among the street vendors quickly reached her, and she breathed it in. One of the vendors caught her eye and gestured as she walked by, so she paused to shake her head. When she looked back at the crowd, she had lost the *diablo*.

She darted on, disappointed, then laughed when he stepped out of an alleyway and crossed her path again. Her heart raced. He'd been waiting for her, watching to see if she followed. The deliberate way he let her know that excited her immensely.

Watchful, he headed on again, weaving in and out of the parade, never going far and never breaking eye contact with her for very long. She meandered along the edge of the crowd of exotic dancers at a safe distance behind him, swaying to the music, an up tempo that demanded her body respond.

*"Señorita,"* a voice called out from a doorway as she passed, and she saw a woman beckoning to her. The woman was dressed in tight designer jeans and a brightly colored, embroidered blouse. There was a trailing sash tied around the waist, its fringe reaching almost to the ground. Long hair scrolled over one shoulder to her waist, heavy jewelry weighting her fingers and ears. Her image was a curious mix of modernity and historic ethnicity. She spoke in Spanish, then paused and spoke again in English. "Fortune-telling here, very cheap, let me tell your fortune for just a few euros."

Katrina paused. Part of her wanted to go with the woman, to hear her fortune. She glanced back and saw that the *diablo* was weaving among the parade, treading water while he watched what she did. He wanted to wait for her; he still wanted her to follow him.

No, she didn't want her fortune told. The element of surprise was what interested her now, the excitement in not knowing which way the path would lead. She shook her head at the woman, thanking her, and moved on, following where he led.

After a while the parade cut through a plaza. The old square was dotted with tall palms and overlooked by large stone mansions surrounding the square at its center. There, the party music did battle with the sound of other musicians. A flamenco display was taking place in the center of the square. A young couple danced, while a man played guitar and an older woman sang. A circle of people had gathered round to watch.

Drawn to the display, she glanced around for her mystery man. Did he have to move on with the parade, stay with the crowd of exotic dancers that he was with? As she wondered, she saw that he had noticed her pausing. He had obviously seen her observing the flamenco display and was moving toward it, as if in silent agreement to stay nearby. Her heart raced. He'd made a connection and was now maintaining eye contact across the crowd, his smile across the group of flamenco dancers for her alone. A dark thrill ran through her. He was moving with her now, flirting with her in a seductive, private dance.

*What would he look like without the mask?* she wondered, alternating between watching the dancers and following where he moved around the circle of onlookers. His eyes rarely left her. Her most recurrent secret fantasy was to be pursued by a mystery man, a dark stranger who had eyes only for her. The fact that he was the embodiment of her fantasy unnerved her but made her hot, too. Hellishly hot.

And now he was coming closer.

Focusing on the display, she watched the guitar player. He sat on a small stool, his deft fingers playing out the quick rhythm for the dancers. Dusk was falling fast now, and someone had lit a fire in an old tin drum. The woman dancing was beautiful, a dark-skinned Madonna with exquisite posture. She wore traditional dress and thundered her heels against the concrete, her hands open as if to channel her overflowing energy. Her partner was a slim, agile dancer who moved around her, seemingly speeding her pace all the time with his dramatic, passionate gestures. As she moved faster, so did he, as if they were beating out an interchange of passion and power through the dance.

Beyond them, the *diablo* paced around the crowd toward her. She glanced away, looking at the older woman who stood by the guitar player, singing her accompaniment, her eyes fixed on an invisible image in the middle distance, as if seeing the images of her song there.

It was then that Katrina felt movement against her back, warm breath on her neck. She shivered. Fingers closed on her shoulder. "The beat of their heels gets into the blood, yes?"

The husky words were whispered close to her ear. Glancing over her shoulder, she already knew who it was. Her heart hammered wildly in her chest, the thrill of his direct approach holding her riveted, speechless. He had closed on her fast, touched her and spoken to her. He knew she was English. Did she look that much of a tourist? She gave a breathless laugh. "Yes, it does."

Up close he was devastatingly attractive. Dark stubble on his chin made her long for the rough touch of it on her naked skin. Everywhere. His glossy black hair was unruly, inviting her to sink her fingers into it as she moved against him in a dance of their own, a dance of sexual desire and fulfillment. Her body ached for sexual release; now that he was close, the sense of physical need almost overwhelmed her.

*What did he look like without the mask?* Her fingers itched to reach for the mask, to remove it and reveal his face.

This time she followed him without hesitation when he beckoned. He led her away from the center of the plaza toward a quiet side street, between the massive Gothic mansions that lined the square. There, gateways led onto hidden courtyards at the rear of the buildings. Although the sound of the music still reached them, it was quieter here in the dark, narrow street, where a single lantern at the back entrance to one of the courtyards nearby shed light on them.

It was dangerous to follow a stranger down here; she knew that, and yet she pressed on. Her feet simply refused to stop following him. Drawn on an invisible thread—a thread of lust and curiosity—she couldn't resist.

Ahead of her, he paused, just when they were far enough away from the crowded plaza that only the faint sound of the music and song still reached them. As she approached, he began to circle her. A lone lantern that jutted from a nearby wall spilled a small circle of light, and beyond that, the moonlight far above. She was reminded of the flamenco. Her heart was beating fast, her body hot with anticipation. She wanted him to touch her again, and she knew he was about to do just that.

Stepping closer, he reached around her, holding her from behind, his body hard and strong. The rush that hit her was almost too much to bear. Instinctively, she moved with him, her hips circling with his, her bottom nestled against his hard hips. She was dizzy from desire, from the heady, elated feeling she got from moving with him.

He urged her toward the nearby wall, quickly pushing her against it, turning her body to face him with commanding hands. Her bag slid from her shoulder when her back met the wall, and she heard it fall to the ground. White jasmine trailed over the wall from the courtyard beyond. The scent of it filled her nostrils when she gasped for breath.

His mouth met hers again when he thrust close against her, locking her against the wall. Her back was crushed against it, her heels shifting for balance. Like that time in her office, she remembered. But not. The rough surface against her back felt shockingly good, but his mouth was so hungry on hers it made her squirm for more.

His hands were all over her, exploring her outline. Then he gripped her hard and held her hips fast against his for a long moment. She felt the need in him, the sheer force of his desire. Her breasts tingled with awareness, and she rubbed them against the hard surface of his chest, welcoming the needles of sensation that shot through her nipples. He brushed her lips again, and then kissed her hard and fast, passionate and hungry.

Her mouth opened, letting him in, wanting him. Her thighs were hot, sticky, her underwear damp and clinging to her intimate places. She felt the swish and sway of her skirt around her knees, realized he was lifting it and moving his hands underneath. Trembling, her breath caught when she felt skin on skin, his hand stroking the outline of her thigh and hip.

Cool air wisped in around her legs, and then he was right against her, hands on her bottom, practically lifting her off her heels. His body was hard and demanding against hers as he rode her against the wall. He murmured something in Spanish against her throat. It sounded passionate, the words rolling to-gether on his tongue, his voice husky. Then she felt his cock through the thin barrier of clothing, and she understood.

*He wants to mate.* The thought echoed through her mind, the recognition both primal and instinctive. *And so do I.*

She wanted to feel that glorious erection inside her, feel it push her open and possess her thoroughly, his body riding hers until they both came. He kissed her throat and jaw and then came up for air, holding her captive with one strong hand on her hip, capturing her skirt within it. The other he lifted to slowly trail his fingertips across her cleavage. His hips were still pressed against hers. She shivered with arousal, a low whimper rising in her throat. He laughed softly, and she joined him, the mutual pleasure echoing between them.

*If it weren't for the clothes,* she thought, longing to fling them off entirely. She wanted to see his face. She reached for the mask.

With a lightning-quick response, he captured her wrist, holding her hand aloft. Tension emanated from him; she felt his scrutiny. The moment seemed weighted, as if in removing the mask she might spoil the mood. She swallowed. It didn't matter. She still longed to see his face.

Reluctance poured from him, but he seemed to understand that she needed to know what he looked like. He released her hand, immediately creating a space between them, her dress falling back into place.

She pushed the mask up and over the horns he wore, lifting it free of his head, holding it in her hand. The light from the lantern hit one side of his face, etching a stark profile. He watched her reaction, his gaze intense.

"You look like . . ." Disbelieving, she stared at him, the name frozen on her lips. Yes, it was as if Sergio Teodoro stood before her, only leaner, a younger version, perhaps. Different. Less polished and formal, more wild, perhaps.

He gave a wry, rueful smile and shook his head, his dark eyes narrowed and watchful. "I know what you are thinking. You have met my brother, Sergio. I am Nicolas Teodoro."

The simple statement sent her thoughts reeling. This was Nicolas? The troublemaking brother that Sergio had mentioned was the man who had been teasing her all evening. As her thoughts raced, it all began to fall into place.

"Bloody hell, you really *were* stalking me," she accused, folding her arms across her chest defensively.

His brow furrowed. "Stalking? No, I only meant to meet you."

She moved one hand to the base of her neck where she felt hot and cold all at once, like a fever had hit her. She was mortified. She felt as if she had been duped and should have known. "What is this, some sort of trick? Did Sergio send you?"

"No," he responded quickly, almost vehemently. He sighed. "Please . . . accept my apologies."

His face relaxed, and when he made the request it was thoroughly charming, just like his brother. "I wanted to find out who you were, to understand more about the woman my brother is bringing to our family home."

Reaching his hand under her chin, he lifted and stroked it gently as if to soothe her, then slid his fingers around the column of her neck and into her hair.

Oh, but the way he touched her was so delicious. Even though she bristled, her body responded, her pulse tripping, her thighs moving against each other as she forced herself to put distance between them, to break the contact.

"But then you seemed so willing to play along with my little game . . ." he added, reminding her of her earlier, more willing responses to his touches, "it was hard to end the game." He flashed dark, sexy eyes at her, his eyebrows lifting.

Heat flushed her face. She didn't want to think about that, but she couldn't deny it either. What if her client found out she'd been canoodling in an alley with the very man he'd warned her about? "The note at the reception desk, you left that for me, didn't you? So that you would see who picked it up?"

"Your mind is sharp, señorita." His smile was so enticing. "Yes, I left you the note. I wanted to meet you, but I didn't realize it would be quite so enjoyable." He laughed softly, a seductive, almost wistful sound that lifted on the evening breeze.

"How on earth did you know where I was staying? Surely Sergio didn't tell you."

"Sergio didn't tell me," he replied simply.

In the distance, fireworks lit up the sky behind him, backlighting his outline, shimmering off the red horns he wore.

"Nicolas, the devil."

He bowed in response to her comment, his cloak falling forward.

Her mind was still racing, arousal and confusion vying for her attention. He was Sergio's brother. He had left the note, not Sergio. That was how he had known who she was, that was how he'd made contact. The disinherited son had been keeping a watchful eye on the situation, her included. It was devious, underhanded. Her annoyance grew. She felt used, but in what way she wasn't quite sure. Sergio had indicated that his brother felt he had a claim and that he was trouble, but she never expected to be approached by him.

She was about to quiz him again, when he placed his hands either side of her head on the wall, backing her against it again and pinning her there.

She gasped, tried to escape the cage he had made for her, but he moved quickly. Closing in, his head ducked to capture her in another deep, lingering kiss.

The confused thoughts and questions that assailed her quickly dissipated. Instead, she turned into a puddle of lust as he drank her in, kissing her fiercely, greedy and passionate. He was so demanding—a powerful force of nature.

*I've never been kissed like this.*

The thought echoed through her mind as he drew back, turned, and walked away from her, just as the sky lit up with a dazzling explosion of fireworks. She put one hand up against the wall to steady herself.

A silent cry of denial leapt inside her. He was moving back

to the crowd in the plaza, with purpose, about to disappear into the night. He couldn't just walk away, not now, not without explaining himself. Her hand tightened on the satin eye mask she still held there, and she grabbed her bag from the ground, swaying as she darted after him.

He glanced over his shoulder, walked faster.

She broke into a jog, her heels doing their best to thwart her. Despite the fact that she knew this was wrong, and despite the fact that she had been warned about the black sheep of the family, she wanted him to stop. She called out to him. "Nicolas, please wait."

He paused, turned back. She'd caught up to him just before he reached the edge of the plaza and disappeared into the crowds of people there. Staring up at him, she wasn't sure whether she wanted to shout at him and curse him for tricking her, or beg him to kiss her again.

Mercifully, he spoke. "Señorita, I am sorry. *Por favor*, please, I would be grateful if you do not tell Sergio that you and I have met."

Unsure quite how to respond to his request, she shook her head. Something felt as if it was being wrung out inside her. "I ought to tell him, but I won't."

Her reply was barely a whisper, but it took away the frown that was marring his expression.

The logical part of her mind questioned why she was making such an unlikely promise to someone she shouldn't even be talking to. Her business was with the man's brother, and Sergio had made it quite clear that Nicolas was trouble.

"*Gracias,*" he said, bowing his head slightly at her.

Her body flared, yearning for more, the desire that had run rampant and unchecked refusing to disperse. She had to know. "Will I see you again?"

The *diablo* stared at her, one corner of his mouth lifting in a crooked but wickedly suggestive smile. "Perhaps."

Then he was gone into the crowd.

# 5

*Dawn was breaking, chasing the shadows across the city roof-*tops. Nicolas observed the landscape of roof tiles change color as the light spilled across them. He'd been sitting brooding in an armchair near the glass door to his tiny balcony for most of the night. His thoughts had been skewed in the dark hours, and the only thing he knew for sure was that he was a sorry fool. The scent of a lush, inviting woman had flicked some switch inside of him, making him behave irrationally. As a result, his opportunity to spoil Sergio's latest plans had been wasted.

It was almost full light when he heard a key in the door to the apartment. Kent entered and made an admirable effort at being quiet. He closed the door gently behind him and tiptoed across the living room.

Nico sat forward into the light. "No wonder you have to sleep all day, if this is what time you arrive home to your bed."

"Jesus Christ," Kent said, jerking back. "Nico! You scared the crap out of me. I had no idea you would be up." He faked a cartoon-style thudding heart and dropped into an armchair opposite Nico. "Hey, I can handle a few all-nighters along the way."

"You only get to study here once in this lifetime, right?"

"You know, Nico, my mom would really love you." Kent grinned. "What about you? What are you doing up?" He glanced from the empty wine bottle to Nico's cloak, which hung over the back of the chair. "Did you have a performance tonight?"

"I was at the festival," Nico nodded out of the window at the city. "And I sought out the English señorita."

Kent took a moment to register his meaning, and then his eyes lit. "The auctioneer, you spoke with her?"

"Briefly."

"So, come on, spill. How did it go?"

Nico didn't respond immediately, because that's what he'd been trying to figure out while brooding over his bottle of wine. Finding out who she was had been easy, and while he hadn't had a plan as such—beyond identifying her and making contact—he'd hoped to take her aside for a brief chat, put a few doubts in her mind before she reached Castagona.

The actual events of the evening had taken a very different direction, something that he was blaming on the mood of the festival. There was also the fact that she was a very responsive young woman. Unusual, too. Her beautiful green eyes were filled with curiosity about life, and there was a sense of rebellion about her that he found attractive. He had to face it; her combination of breathless eagerness and sensuality had affected him strangely. Then, her obvious confusion and disappointment when she realized who he was had made him feel guilty. He'd grown angry with himself about the way he'd handled it, and he'd had to walk away. Had he missed his chance to say his piece?

"Nico?"

"I introduced myself to the lady." He smiled. "She will remember me when we meet again."

"Meet again, huh?"

Nico nodded, and—on the spur of the moment—he firmed up a decision he'd been considering throughout the early hours, a decision that was guided by the señorita and her responsive nature. He could make use of that. Sergio was manipulating the woman. It was only fair that he bend her the other way. She was open to seduction, and he wasn't about to deny it as a means to influence her.

*Katrina was awoken by a rapid knock on the door of her hotel* room. Disorientated, she sat up and peered around. She'd had a restless night, confused by her attraction to Nicolas and worried about the fact that she had communicated with the disinherited son of the family she was working for. It was as if the danger had heightened her senses, though. The unusual events of the previous night, her heated and erotic encounter with Nicolas, had led her into strange dreams, sexual fantasies she'd never experienced before.

The knocking came again.

She climbed out of bed and pulled a long T-shirt over her head, covering her nudity as she went to the door. Glancing at the clock, she saw that it was too early for the driver who was collecting her that morning, so who was it? "It's your wake-up call and breakfast," she said to herself with more than a little self-mockery.

After the maid had set up her tray on a table by the window and left the room, Katrina realized she'd almost been hoping it was someone else at the door.

A man?

Which one? Sergio, or Nicolas?

She burned up with the rush of unfamiliar feelings that hit her as she considered that. Desire—lust even—for these two brothers she had encountered. That and a lingering dash of the old Katrina, the part that felt embarrassed at her own forthright attitude to them. On her first encounter with both these men, she'd acted like a wild woman, doing things she'd never normally do.

But, oh boy, had it ever felt good. Although now that she knew they were feuding brothers, she wasn't sure what to think. She had to reassure herself that she hadn't done anything detrimental to the job. At least, she didn't think so.

"It was just a bit of fun," she said to herself and turned on the television news channel for company. The breakfast of fresh fruit, coffee, and pastries looked enticing, but she couldn't eat very much. She drank the rich, strong coffee and enjoyed a few bites of one of the flaky pastries before heading for the bathroom.

Flicking on the faucet, she abandoned her T-shirt and stepped into the warm water. Under the powerful sluice of the shower she soaped herself and closed her eyes, turning around beneath the water. Her imagination immediately transported her back to the night before.

Would she ever see him again?

If she'd left the mask on, what would have happened? She wanted to turn back the clock. How far would it have gone? she wondered, and her body responded instantly. Her imagination was far too ready to fill in those details, to show her exactly what her body had wanted to happen. Her hands roamed over her breasts, feeling the weight of them, remembering how his hands had felt on her body, what his touch had done to her.

*If only I hadn't taken off the mask.*

She imagined him reaching down, pulling her skirt up around her hips, lifting her bodily against the wall. She would have wrapped her legs around his hips, welcoming him in between her thighs. Dying as she was for the hard, hot nudge of his cock, she imagined savoring the feeling of it when he thrust inside her. A moan of longing and frustration escaped her lips.

She cursed and snatched the showerhead out of its holder, drawing it closer to her body, moving the insistent zing of the pounding water over her skin, letting it sting her. It heightened the intensity of every picture in her mind with real, physical sensation. She could recall everything from the heady scent of white jasmine to the pressure of his mouth on hers. She could hear the sound of music and laughter in the distance, the rhythmic drumbeats, the whistles and chants capturing the heartbeat of every listener, pulling them into the experience.

He had murmured something in Spanish beneath his breath. What was it? How she longed to know. His voice had rippled through her, his accent rolling the words together like bodies rolling on a bed. Oh, how she wanted that. All night long she'd thought of it, restless with need, her pussy slick with wetness.

The soap had been abandoned. She wriggled and then braced herself against the wall, painfully aroused. There was no turning back; she had to reach climax, or she'd go mad. Moving the showerhead lower, she directed the spray over her belly and into the juncture between her thighs, where the water bounced off her tender, aroused flesh. Wedging her back against the wall, she put one foot on the opposite wall of the cubicle and pushed the showerhead lower, her free hand opening herself up to the jets of water right on her tender, swollen clit.

Oh, but it was good, harshly so, and she bit her lip, the pleasure/pain making her entire groin burn. Inside, her sex clenched rhythmically, responding to the images in her mind and the physical stimulation. With her back solid against the wall and her body locked in position by her raised leg, her hips began to move back and forth, undulating against her imaginary lover. Her free hand alternated between squeezing her breasts for relief, to opening herself up to the showerhead, running it back and forth until she almost cried with the pleasure/pain, her orgasm fast approaching.

*I wanted him. I wanted him inside me, over me. I wanted him to push me down on my hands and knees, to take me from*

*behind while he told me what I looked like, while he told me
how hot it was to see me like that.*

Admitting those thoughts to herself made her feel even hotter and wilder. "Take me, take me," she whispered to the imaginary man in the moonlight, wishing he'd been the stranger she
thought he was, just some guy cruising for the illicit encounter
that she wanted, too. But even as she thought that, she saw his
eyes and knew who it was: Nicolas, the black sheep of the Teodoro family, a forbidden lover.

"Oh, God, yes," she said, her eyes still closed to this bright
morning, her mind open to what might have been in the moonlight, the evening before. "Yes, yes."

It was as if he was right there with her, and she came, her
body trembling as her foot slipped down the tiled wall and back
to the floor of the cubicle.

Panting, she reached for the shower tap, hanging on it a moment to steady herself, then turning it off. The sound of water
gurgling down the drain and her rapid breathing seemed at
odds with the narration from the TV in the next room. The
showerhead dangled from her hand, and she laughed, grateful
for the sexual release. The tension that had built up inside her
had been almost unbearable.

Shakily, she returned the showerhead to its holder, opened the
glass door, and stepped out of the cubicle. She toweled herself
lightly, humming. The mirror in the bathroom was heavily
steamed, and she wiped her hand over it. As she did, she thought
she heard a sound. A knock at the door? Surely she hadn't been
the shower that long? It was too early for the driver to collect her.

Hurriedly securing her towel, she walked into the bedroom and over to the door. When she opened it, a tall, dark figure filled the doorway, one shoulder up against the frame, hands nonchalantly in his pockets.

"Sergio, I wasn't expecting you."

He leaned into her, looking at her state of undress, smiling. "I decided to spend the night in Barcelona after a meeting yesterday. I thought we could travel to Castagona together.

"How lovely," she replied, one hand gripping her towel in place over her boobs. He'd been in Barcelona the night before? Her mind flitted back to her unplanned rendezvous with his brother. Thank God it was a big city.

A slight five o'clock shadow was visible on his jaw, and his hair wasn't quite as well groomed as before. He wore a business suit, but the collar was open, and he had no tie, all of which only seemed to add to his appeal.

"I have to do some business," he added as he sauntered past her and into her room, "a few phone calls, but we can chat over lunch, I know a good place along the way."

He did look hungry, but it was her he was looking at with greedy eyes, as if delighted to find her half-naked. And now he was inside her space, and she wasn't quite sure what to do. Most men would have waited for her downstairs, but the Teodoro men weren't "most men," were they? Smiling to herself, she closed the door. Different cultures had different patterns of behavior, she reminded herself, and she wanted to experience that, not shy away. Or was that just an excuse?

"I'll be two minutes," she said as she lifted a few articles of clothing out of her open suitcase. She avoided eye contact, wondering if he was just going to stand there and watch her prance around in a towel.

"Take your time; there is no rush."

When she glanced back, she saw that he'd stepped out onto the balcony and was sitting in a cast-iron chair, observing the street scene. The position he had taken meant that he could glance back at her. Right at that moment he did just that, flashing her an admiring glance and a charming smile.

She took a deep breath, feeling slightly giddy because of his presence and his attention. It wasn't as if he was a complete stranger, she thought to herself, her face heating as she addressed the fact that she had now had sexual encounters with two brothers—Katrina Hammond, the respectable London valuation expert, the demure one.

But the Teodoro men had a peculiar knack of stepping into her life in the most intimate way. Last night one of them had half stripped her in the street, now the other was practically watching her dress. The irony struck her, but most of all, it was the secret thrill that she relished as she slipped into the bathroom to dress.

*Outside, the city was bustling with tourists and natives in the* bright Monday morning sunshine. People moved past carrying shopping bags or workbags, everyone filled with purpose. Katrina felt wistful for the more seductive air the city had after nightfall, the deeper sense of mystery that pervaded the streets then. It was an atmosphere that inspired her, one that seemed to make anything possible.

A gleaming black Mercedes C class stood outside the hotel on the cobbled street. The driver, a man in his fifties with sharp features and silver hair, was pacing up and down by the car, polishing it while he waited. When he loaded Katrina's bags into the car, Sergio introduced him. His name was Tomas. He nodded politely at Katrina and then shouted a warning at a teenage cyclist who ran his hand along the car roof as he passed.

Sergio was thoroughly charming, holding the car door open for her and apologizing that he had to deal with business calls during the journey. She observed the city streets through the tinted windows as she listened to him speak, wishing she could understand what was being said.

They were soon making their way out of the historic center of Barcelona, through the more modern districts and eventually onto a freeway north. As she watched the passing scenery, Katrina took surreptitious glances at Sergio from behind her shades, noticing the differences and similarities between him and his brother. Yes, now she could see it; Nicolas was younger. His face was leaner, his eyes more thoughtful, but his attitude more intense. Sergio had a sophisticated edge in comparison, that aura of being a wealthy businessman who always got his way in life.

Which brother did she find most alluring? Now, there was a question. She didn't want to decide. Not yet, at any rate. Her curiosity about Nicolas was not going to fade. And how could it? She hadn't even reached her destination, and the disinherited brother had preempted her arrival. She wanted to know why.

*I'm here to inventory the art collection,* she reminded herself and tried to focus her attention on the engaging scenery. She'd soon be busy doing just that. It wasn't her job to analyze the machinations of her host family, fascinating though they were. Most families had their tensions, their secrets, and their skeletons in the closet. Why should this one be any different?

6

*Farther away from the capital and the tourist-filled resorts that* ran along the coast in either direction, the towns and villages grew sparser and more rustic, the roads smaller. Katrina watched the unfolding scenery with interest. It struck her how the bright light and clear blue skies seemed to characterize this part of Spain, just as Salvador Dalí had depicted in his paintings.

Farther inland, the landscape on the horizon grew more rugged and mountainous. The palm trees that had marked out the city routes nearer the coast gave way to pines and eucalyptus. The landscape was patterned and made distinctive by its olive groves and almond and orange trees. Medieval villages dotted the countryside, places that were distinguished by whitewashed walls and terra-cotta tiles. Katrina soaked it all in, relishing this part of her time here.

Occasionally Sergio would break his call to point out one of his family's convenience stores. There seemed to be a branch in each of the towns and villages, outlets that looked as if they stocked everything.

They stopped for an early lunch in Caldes, a beautiful spa town where Tomas pulled up outside a small cantina on the outskirts. The customers were a mix of workers and business folk, chatting in clusters around rickety tables with checkered cloths.

"You will enjoy the paella," Sergio said as he pulled a chair out for her. "You know this Spanish dish?"

"A risotto, rice and fish, yes?"

"Yes, they make it very well here, with saffron rice, shellfish, and calamari. Lots of garlic." He grinned.

Everyone was eating the paella, and Katrina could see it being cooked in a huge, shallow pan some four feet wide in the kitchen beyond, so she took the recommendation. The food arrived quickly and was served in individual black metal skillets—which the customers ate directly from—accompanied by hunks of floury bread. The food was delicious, and the robust white wine they served in heavy tumblers made Katrina feel mellow and rather spoiled.

Over the meal, Sergio attempted to quiz her about London, but she only humored him until she got the opportunity to ask him more about his family.

"How long have your family lived in this area?"

"Many years now. My father was born in Barcelona, and we still have property there. He bought the Torre when my mother was pregnant with me. It was the home she preferred, so they settled here. I can travel to my office in around an hour, but I sometimes stay in the city."

Katrina nodded. "You mentioned you had a brother. Does he live at the house?"

She almost wished she hadn't asked.

Sergio stopped eating and put down his fork, reaching for his wine. "Not for a long time now." His eyes grew hooded, as if he didn't relish thinking about his brother. "I don't even know where he is or what he is doing." A sigh escaped him. "He was always a loner, and my father needed sons who would pull together and help to maintain all that he had built." He paused.

"He used to turn up on occasion, though, just to cause us trouble." He looked up at her quickly. A frown had developed on his forehead as if he was concerned Nicolas might turn up again, and he stared at her intently.

Katrina was frozen to the spot, waiting to hear what he'd say next, tension beading up her spine.

"He's a devious man, Katrina." There was a warning there in his eyes.

She forced herself to breathe. Well, she couldn't argue with what he'd said, Nicolas was a devious sort of a man. Look at the way he'd hunted her down, following her. Exciting though the episode had been, it definitely wasn't right.

Reaching out across the table, Sergio covered her hand with his. He smiled gently, which softened his expression. "Not a very nice person; I hope you don't have to meet him."

Part of her nervously cringed inside. "You think he might approach me?" Acting surprised, she hoped her response would cut it.

He lifted his wineglass and shook his head. "I don't think so. We haven't seen him for some time."

"I'm sorry I mentioned him," she said quietly, awkwardly, really wishing she hadn't brought the subject up.

"Please, forget it." He leaned back in his chair, breaking the mood with a gently dismissive gesture of his hands. "It is just trouble we could do without, yes."

He gave her a charming smile, veering the conversation onto neutral ground when he called the waiter and asked for more wine.

The journey onward from Caldes was relatively short, and Sergio talked to her, often draping his arm around her shoulder as they looked out of the window together. Nearer the border with France, the landscape was drier. While the vegetation was less, cattle grazed on the rough grass on the sandy hillsides that Sergio referred to as *garrigues*.

They passed through the village of Castagona itself, a pretty, rustic place, and then Sergio nodded at the higher ground above. "There, beyond the treetops, where you can see the tower, that's the house."

Katrina caught sight of the impressive stone edifice above the trees and nodded. "I wondered about the name of the house, so there is a tower."

"There are two," he explained, "one on each wing. From this viewpoint one stands behind the other, so only one tower is visible to the village. That's why the villagers call the house the Torre del Castagona. My father adopted the name. The art collection is housed in the tower you see now."

Katrina peered up at the impressive stone structure among the trees. It was almost Moorish in design, with its sand-colored stone and tall, solid shape. It looked as if there were two or three floors inside, with narrow leaded windows arranged around it, each underscored with a jutting stone ledge.

The Mercedes weaved its way along the winding road and through the eucalyptus trees that partially hid the large mansion from view. When Tomas turned the car onto a smaller road, she saw the house and gardens beyond the huge wrought-iron fence and pillars marking the driveway entrance.

The car pulled up to an electronic security system at the gates. The driver's window whirred down, and Tomas reached out and entered a number into the machine. A few moments later, the massive gates opened. The gates closed behind them, and Katrina noticed the automatic sensors as they passed.

Inside the fence, greenery was rife. Sprinklers watered the lush lawns. Leafy trees and tall hedges sectioned off the gardens, where borders were filled with low evergreen shrubs interspersed with rhododendrons. Geraniums grew along either side of the driveway, creating a weaving trail of color as they passed. But it was the house itself that captured both the attention and the imagination. The sand-colored stone frontage had perfect symmetry, and the placement of the windows suggested effortless grandeur. The staircase that ran up to the doorway was wide, and wrought-iron balconies swept around large windows along the front of the house on the upper floor.

Katrina counted ten balconies, five on either side of the entrance. Between the balconies were smaller windows. She noticed how high up the house was, beyond the trees the mountainous crags presented a starkly beautiful backdrop. She ducked and weaved in the backseat, managing to catch sight of the top of the two towers at either end of the building. They were set to the back of the house. "Do the gardens continue at the rear?"

"*Sí*, the grounds are extensive. The West Tower—where you'll be working—overlooks the gardens and the village."

When they climbed from the air-conditioned car, the heat was a sudden contrast. The lush gardens and water from the sprinklers added humidity to atmosphere, tempering the bright light and unrelenting heat. Katrina looked up at the house in awe. Jasmine grew along the walls by several of the windows, the slender stems as high as ten feet in some places. The stems were still dotted with yellow flowers, even though it was late in the season.

The sound of gravel crunching underfoot accompanied them as they made their way to the wide steps that swept up to the entrance, double doors flanked by glass panels. She could scarcely wait to get a look at the interior.

Behind them, the sound of another car approaching drew Sergio's attention, and he paused and frowned. A battered red Seat Ibiza pulled up on the driveway behind the Mercedes. At the same time, the door to the house opened, and a petite woman stepped out.

"Elaine, will you show Katrina to her room . . ." His voice trailed off, and he darted back down the steps.

The woman nodded and tossed back her hair, a glossy auburn bob that gave her a 1930s Hollywood look, marcel wave and all. She was pure style; slim, and elegant to a fault. Her fitted scarlet top, off the shoulder, and black hipsters were impeccably cut.

"You must be Katrina." She put out one slim hand in the offer of a handshake. "I'm Elaine, Señora Teodoro."

Katrina stared at her in disbelief.

*Señora Teodoro? Sergio is married?*

She'd read several biographies, and there was no mention of a wife or children. What with that, and his overtly flirtatious manner toward her, she'd assumed there wasn't a Señora Teodoro. She forced herself to return the handshake. "I'm afraid I hadn't realized that Sergio was married."

The woman stared at her with silent amusement for a moment, then gave a wry laugh. "He isn't. I'm Sergio's stepmother."

"Oh, right, I see." Katrina was relieved but only marginally less shocked by that information than she had been by her previous assumption. The woman couldn't have been much older than she was, and she was English. This was Jorge Teodoro's wife?

"Come on, I'll show you your room."

Katrina nodded and followed.

Inside, the reception hall was a large, airy space with polished parquet flooring that led to an awe-inspiring marble staircase. Tomas was on his way up there with her bags. At least fourteen feet wide, the steps turned left and right on a half landing. There on the landing was a full-size sculpture of a nude female clasping a jug. Her expert eye captured, Katrina glanced quickly in every direction.

As they walked down the hall, massive arched windows to left and right allowed a view into the reception rooms beyond. Katrina was entranced. Each consecutive room had one such arched window placed in line, so that the viewer could see into the rooms beyond and the light was shared. The windows were decorated with stained glass in beautiful Art Nouveau designs, each different, with minimal color strategically placed to affect the color of the natural light in the next room.

The adjoining room looked like it was an occasional dining room for a house this size. Long and narrow, it featured fine rosewood dining furniture; parquet floors, voile curtains, and port-colored drapes at the windows gave a decadent, sumptuous feel.

"It's beautiful, isn't it?" Elaine said, pausing alongside her to look through the interior window.

"Absolutely," Katrina responded. The inside of the mansion showed as much attention to detail as the outside, the rhythms of the seashore and nature reflected in the curtains, and Art Nouveau touches here and there in the furnishings. It was all done with a very light hand, giving a sense of symmetry and balance to the house.

"Ah, Raimunda, our housekeeper," Elaine said.

Katrina looked beyond Elaine, where a woman was now standing farther down the hallway. Still and watchful, it was as if she had just appeared on the spot, a brush with a massive polishing head in her hands. She was short and stocky, with iron gray hair pulled into a tight bun. Her black shift dress was tied with an apron that seemed to commence under her hefty bosom and ended at the hemline, which was just above her shoes.

"She doesn't speak a word of English," Elaine said dismissively. "Never even tries."

She made it sound like a crime, Katrina noticed, which she thought was rather unnecessary.

"I've tried to teach her the odd word or two, but she stubbornly resists. She brings in a couple of girls from the village to help with the cleaning, once a week, and even they make more of an effort than she does."

The housekeeper was staring fixedly at Katrina.

Katrina nodded at the woman and smiled. *"Buenas tardes,"* she offered.

The woman narrowed her eyes and looked at Katrina with even more suspicion. Her stare was so intensely disapproving that Katrina instantly felt uncomfortable. After a moment, the housekeeper resumed her polishing of the floor, moving quite rapidly in their direction. The head of the polishing brush was a good three feet wide, and Katrina had the impression that the woman wanted to use it to knock the pair of them down, like pins. She almost did, but paused just two inches away from their shoes and looked at them as if they were causing her a nuisance standing right there.

"Oh dear," Katrina said, giving a nervous laugh.

The housekeeper started muttering away in Spanish to herself.

"Ignore her," Elaine said, taking Katrina's arm and leading her around the obstacle that Raimunda had made of herself. "She's a grumpy so-and-so, talks to herself a lot. Mind you, that's preferable to her silences. That usually means she's in a *really* bad mood."

Elaine didn't seem in the least intimidated by the surly woman, but Katrina found herself wondering how on earth she'd manage to deal with her on a day-to-day basis. The housekeeper's stare was withering.

Elaine lowered her voice, ducking her head close to Katrina's as they mounted the stairs. "I think Raimunda has had a crush on Jorge for years. In fact, it was so obvious that when I moved in, I got Jorge to ask her to move out. She used to be a live-in, but with me here, he agreed that wasn't needed."

They turned the corner on the staircase, passing the life-size sculpted figurine—a pretty nymph holding a jug of water as if she was about to pour it—and Katrina found herself face-to-face with a Gustav Klimt painting on the turn of the stair.

"Oh, my, a Klimt." Work by Klimt, a master of late-nineteenth-century decadent art, was highly collectable. Sergio hadn't even mentioned it. Perhaps he didn't intend to sell the painting, a woman in profile against a richly detailed and stylized background.

Elaine paused. "One of a pair." She gestured at the opposite turn of the stairs, where a second Klimt was mounted, a similar but different female portrait. "I don't know much about art myself, but I do like these two a lot."

Katrina looked back and forth at the paintings. "I'm not surprised; they're exceptional. It must be quite something to have them to admire every day."

Elaine nodded and walked on, and Katrina vowed to come back for a better look later.

As they turned the stairs onto the next case, Elaine glanced down at Raimunda and continued talking about her. "I thought about getting a new housekeeper, but I was told that everyone in the locality respects her and that she didn't want to retire, so no one would have accepted the job."

Elaine shook her head. "That's the sort of thing I have to put up with out here in the countryside. So, we still have her, and she comes and goes as she pleases, but she does a good job keeping the place in order, so I put up with the attitude problem. The bedrooms are in the east wing."

Katrina listened while she took in her surroundings. Like everything else about the mansion, there was a pleasing symmetry to the upstairs corridors. Across a long landing she could see the west wing.

Elaine nodded over at that side of the house as she walked the other way. "The west wing is barely used on this floor, apart from access to the gallery in the tower. Jorge used to use the rooms along the corridor for offices, and there was quite a staff here then, but Sergio prefers to work at headquarters."

The east wing housed the bedrooms. The doors to the bedrooms were interspersed with windows, and Katrina glanced out one of the windows as she passed.

"The design of the house keeps it cool," Elaine said. "We only need air-conditioning in the kitchen." She led Katrina to the far side, where a window overlooked the back gardens. "You can see both towers from this vantage point."

She pointed at the farthest one. "The tower on the west wing is where the art collection is stored. There's a gallery space, an office where all the records are kept, and another three floors that are used as storage rooms."

Katrina looked again, doing a quick calculation. "I have a feeling the collection is larger than I anticipated."

"I told Sergio he should have taken the ledgers with him when he went to see you in London."

"Ledgers?"

"Yes, Jorge's first wife used to keep everything listed in these big old accountancy ledgers. Apparently she was an accountant, but Jorge wouldn't let her continue working once they got married, so she turned her skills to the art collection instead. I don't think anyone else has ever looked at them, but I suppose they might be useful to you."

"Absolutely. Anything like that is helpful. I have to make my own inventory, check that everything is present, and give each item an approximate valuation for the purposes of bidding in the auction rooms."

Elaine smiled but didn't respond and then nodded over at a doorway opposite, where Tomas was emerging, having deposited her bags. "We thought you'd like this room at the front; it has one of the best views."

The room that Katrina was allocated was another airy space, with parquet flooring and a curved wall to the front, just as she had expected. It had a massively high ceiling with an ornate plaster rose that sprang half across it, and a chandelier for light. Heavy, rich, red mahogany furniture anchored the space. She noticed her laptop bag and suitcase sitting on a stylish ottoman at the end of the bed. Then a massive painting on the wall facing the end of the bed caught her eye.

She turned to face it, stunned. It ran from floor to ceiling, an angle portrait of a bullfighter, some four or five times larger than life. His face was in shadow, but his eyes were highlighted, watchful, and focused intently. In the background the bull was painted in broad, heavy brushstrokes, a dark blur approaching on the horizon. The image was powerful and immediately raised numerous questions in her mind, as all good art should. Was he about to turn and face the bull? Was it a trick, or self-sacrifice on the fighter's part? She couldn't tell, and that fascinated her.

"I'm not keen on it myself," Elaine commented. "I hope you don't find it too disturbing." She moved her hand in a fluid gesture toward the painting as she strode past it to the window.

"Not at all." Katrina glanced at the eyes again. For some reason they made her feel very self-aware, the skin on her forearms and the back of her neck tingling. She was about to ask about the painting's origins when Elaine drew her attention to the window instead, beckoning her over.

Elaine unlocked the glass doors and opened them out onto the balcony. "You can't see the towers from this side of the house, but it's the best view."

"Oh, yes," Katrina responded and stepped outside with her, looking at the landscape while shielding her eyes from the sun. Beyond the gardens and the tall fences, the eucalyptus trees swayed in the early afternoon breeze.

"You can smell the eucalyptus when the wind is in the right direction."

"It's an amazing spot," Katrina commented as she took in the sight.

"It is, but it can get lonely."

"It must be difficult for you, especially with Señor Teodoro's ill health."

Elaine nodded. "You were shocked that I am so much younger than my husband, weren't you?"

Katrina was startled at the sudden, pointed remark.

"Most people are," she added. "That, and of course the fact that I'm British, surprises people."

Katrina couldn't read her expression, but Elaine seemed aloof and distant by nature.

"I was, yes. It was just because I didn't know." That was the truth. She got to meet a lot of women in Elaine's situation through her job. Younger, pampered wives, gym wives, wives who knew every designer fashion label but couldn't tell the difference between a Picasso and a Rembrandt. It wasn't that she thought there was anything wrong with that; she just couldn't get her head around it. Her enthusiasm for art and antiques drove her. She couldn't imagine her world without them. It also meant she remembered details about everything.

"Jorge was happily married for many years," Elaine continued, "to Sergio's mother."

Katrina noticed that she only mentioned Sergio, not Nicolas.

"He was understandably lonely when she died," Elaine continued. "He'd passed his business interests over to Sergio. When Jorge and I met, we got on well. Jorge likes to practice his English, but he was already quite frail and didn't want to travel so much; he needed a companion. We married because Jorge likes things to look respectable; he is a very traditional man."

Katrina nodded. She felt as if Elaine was issuing a statement, not opening the subject for discussion. Yet she couldn't help being curious about some of the things she said. "How did you meet?"

Elaine's lips tightened imperceptibly. She took a moment to reply. "Sergio introduced us." The answer was cautiously given, and then Elaine returned her attention to the view outside the window.

Katrina realized that she had been correct in her first assumption; the subject wasn't open for discussion. It was a strange setup, that was for sure. Perhaps Elaine wanted to head off those potentially awkward questions or comments that might embarrass anyone. Or maybe she didn't want to talk anymore about Jorge because he was so ill at the moment. It had to be hard for her, even if she was a companion and no more.

In the gardens directly below the window Katrina saw a man tending the plants. He wore sunglasses and a baseball cap on backward, ripped jeans, and a T-shirt that bore a slogan in Spanish. He was darkly tanned, the sleeves of his T-shirt rolled right up onto the shoulder, his muscular arms gleaming in the sunlight. Nearby, a large barrow on wheels was filled with garden tools.

As he moved between the plants he was tending, Katrina noticed he was wearing headphones. The wire led to his back pocket, and when he walked he was moving to the beat of the music, as if he'd rather be dancing. He made rather an incongruous gardener, and the image made her smile.

"That's Paco. You might see him around the grounds. He's here pretty much all day, comes up from the village. He's more of a handyman, but he does a good job of maintaining what's there." Even as she said it, Elaine was looking farther afield.

Katrina followed her gaze and saw that Sergio was talking to a man by the car that had arrived behind them. He was casually dressed, of medium height but heavily built, like a bodybuilder.

"That's Vincent, a friend of the family." Elaine gave one of her brisk smiles and drew Katrina away from the window.

"He's staying in the East Tower at the moment. That's where the guest rooms are. You might see him about."

It occurred to Katrina that either he or the gardener could be Elaine's lover. Hadn't she made a point of saying that Jorge only wanted companionship from her? Did that mean she was free to focus her physical desires elsewhere? She tried to banish the inappropriate thoughts, but even so, she mentally placed her bet on Vincent, the friend of the family. Paco was fit and attractive, but Vincent was older and had a more mysterious and brutish quality about him. For some reason she felt that might appeal to a woman like Elaine.

"Come on," Elaine said. "Sergio said he'd show you the collection, but it looks as if he's going to be held up talking to Vincent."

"I'd really like to get started as soon as possible."

"Why not? I'll take you up there now."

# 7

*Elaine showed her to the gallery and then left, clearly having* little interest in the art collection. Katrina, on the other hand, could hardly believe her luck. She couldn't keep the smile off her face as she wound her way through the glass cases at one end of the display gallery, eagerly checking the contents of each case. They were filled with small sculptures, while several free-standing larger works on pedestals stood in a circle at the other end of the gallery. Beyond them a long chaise longue covered in plum-colored velvet and an array of autumnal cushions invited the visitor to sit and observe the whole spectacle at length.

The surrounding walls were graced with the largest paintings in the collection, at least two mounted between each of the tall windows of the exterior walls. On the two floors above she found storage racks filled with paintings, drawings, and other work. There were several whole series of studies by well-known and popular artists. Many of the major works were ones she'd seen in large traveling exhibitions, and viewing them again after their return to their owner's home made her feel oddly connected to them.

*Start at the beginning and do it properly,* she urged herself, then headed back to the office area. It was adjacent to the main gallery on the first floor of the tower. As she passed one of the windows, she looked across at the opposite tower, admiring its design. The house was U-shaped at the rear, and that meant the two towers were deeply embedded in the sumptuous gardens at the back of the house. As she took in the view, the man called Vincent walked up to the window and looked out across the gardens as if he was looking for something, then moved on when he caught sight of her. He wouldn't be used to seeing someone in here, she thought, as she, too, walked on. He'd been able to enjoy the gardens without being easily observed before her arrival, she supposed. Not that he would see much of her at the window. She'd mostly be at the desk or working through the collection while she was here.

The office was the first room she'd come to when she entered the tower, and there, in a pleasant working space beneath the window stood a beautiful old wood desk with a roll top that glided easily up and down over a leather-covered work surface and pigeonholes. This was where the first Señora Teodoro had worked on documenting the collection, and her touch was everywhere. An array of ink pens stood in a pot in one of the slots, unused for many years, together with blotters and pretty jars of colored ink. An old ivory ruler, a real treasure of the Edwardian period, sat propped up at the back of the desktop.

Katrina wondered which son the first wife had favored, the curious thought entering her mind as she touched the woman's things. Had Nicolas strayed from the family after her death or before? What was it he had done that was so bad? She might never know the answers. It was rather like a mysterious object brought to the auction house with a history she could not easily fathom on her own. Every such case got her best shot, however, and this puzzle was no exception.

The ledgers that Elaine had mentioned were situated on a bookshelf close to the desk. Beneath it stood a polished oak table, conveniently placed so that the ledgers could be lifted down and opened there. A quick glance at the heavy, leather-bound books showed her that the navy blue covered books related to the acquisitions. Three were for sculptures; the rest related to the paintings and drawings. Inscribed on the first page of each book were the dates for the acquisition period they covered. The titles and artists were listed by the name they came into the collection with, mostly in French, followed by a translation in Spanish. Two separate ledgers bound in red recorded all the items that went in and out to be part of exhibitions all over the world.

Next to the shelves stood a fine set of old oak filing cabinets, the sort of thing that was collectable in itself nowadays, never mind the contents and those of the gallery and the rooms beyond. Although these items hadn't been used for several years, it was clear that someone came up here to dust and clean the place. The smell of beeswax polish was discernible in the atmosphere, and a vase of fresh flowers stood on the sill of the window that overlooked the gardens. Raimunda, for all her surly attitude, seemed to be an exceptionally good housekeeper.

Katrina picked up her briefcase and removed her laptop, setting it up on the desk. It looked oddly juxtaposed with the old-fashioned setting but fitted in the space nonetheless. Plugging in her mobile phone, she downloaded her mail and sent a quick message to Lucy to let her know she had arrived. She'd just pressed Send when she heard footsteps on the stairs beyond the office. She swung her chair around just in time to catch sight of Sergio entering the office. "Sergio, you startled me."

"You are working already." He glanced at the laptop screen and the open ledgers on the nearby table approvingly. "You're very conscientious."

"I'm excited to be dealing with the collection." She'd felt quite high just checking out all that wonderful art and hoped she didn't appear giddy over it. "I see from the ledgers that many of the items used to go in and out on a regular basis, when your mother was alive."

She paused a moment, wondering if she perhaps should not have mentioned that. He looked thoughtful, but he didn't look uncomfortable, so she continued. "In fact, I've seen several of the items in traveling exhibitions myself, when they were out on loan."

"After my mother died my father lost interest in the collection. It was something they did together. Perhaps he didn't like to be reminded . . . Who can say?" He gave her shoulder a quick squeeze and smiled. "The important thing is that he is happy for the collection to be sold."

Katrina was relieved when he said that. She hated to see

people selling collections that they were truly loath to part with. That was the real downside of her job. Knowing that Jorge Teodoro had lost interest in the collection and that selling it may help him to be comfortable made her job that much more pleasant. When she'd first entered the office and the gallery space, the place had a well-loved feeling. Neglected now, yes, but there was an immense amount of work, care, and love here. If that was part of the past, it made things easier.

"I'm glad to hear that. I hate to see our clients needy or unhappy."

He didn't respond to that. It couldn't be easy, not while his father was so ill. He hadn't mentioned the fact his father was in a hospice since their initial meeting in London. It had to be preying on his mind, but he'd obviously rather not to talk about it, which she respected.

"I'm very impressed with the professional storage," she said, trying to change the subject. "I noticed that each section is removable. Would you be happy for the collection to travel in its current housing? It would simplify matters, but if you prefer to keep the storage units, that's not a problem. I just need to know in advance."

He shook his head. "Please, use it." He glanced at the doorway and into the gallery beyond. "I think we will . . . redecorate."

She jotted a quick note. "I also need to ask you, is it just the items here, or are there other items you wish to be included in the sale that are located around the house?" She didn't want to specifically ask about the two Klimt paintings, but they would be the jewels in the crown of the collection.

"We'll see," he replied.

"Perhaps if I do a rough estimate on the stored items first, that would help?"

He nodded. "You're making this easier for me, Katrina, as I knew you would."

He was so self-assured, and the way he watched her made her self-conscious, reminding her of what had happened in London. Right now he was looking at her with that same assessing stare—the one that had made her act differently in London—and yet he was almost nonchalant in his attitude, as if moving from business to pleasure was something he did frequently and with ease.

He gestured at her laptop. "You can send and receive e-mail from here?"

"Yes, my phone has GPRS. It means I can communicate with my boss about the collection while working through it."

"I hadn't thought of that." He smiled suddenly, and glanced directly at her hands. She realized she was clutching the hem of her skirt as if it was about to peel back from her thighs of its own accord.

"Do I make you nervous?"

She gave a breathy laugh, releasing some of the tension she felt. "A little. Our last meeting . . . It was somewhat unusual."

Honesty seemed the best policy under the circumstances. She felt as if she needed to refer to what had happened between them to get it out into the open, or she would self-combust.

"Unusual? A woman like you does not attract that kind of attention all the time? I am surprised." The look in his eyes was teasing.

"No, not very often." She couldn't help smiling. He was easily the most polished, overtly charming man she'd ever met. Those were qualities she admired and responded to. Henry could have learned a lot from this man.

"Women need to be appreciated, to be savored." He gestured with his fingers to his lips as if tasting a fine wine.

The way he said *savored* seemed to ratchet up her internal thermometer. The skin on the back of her neck prickled.

He raised one eyebrow. "I like to see a woman taking pleasure in her sexuality." He paused very deliberately to emphasize his words. "I liked you because you did not act like a stuffy businessperson, but a full-blooded woman with physical needs and desires."

Expectation assailed her. It felt exceptionally naughty, almost deviant, but she wanted him to kiss her again. She wanted to compare his kiss to the kisses she'd had in Barcelona the night before. It was odd, because she'd always been slightly shocked that a girlfriend at university had a ménage affair, a fling with twins, but she supposed it had left her curious. It wasn't something similar that Katrina craved, but there was a certain thrill to trying both men. The old Katrina would never have done that, she mused, and the thought made her want it all the more.

Sergio moved behind her, glancing over her at the laptop where it was set up on the desk. He paused, and she felt the heat of his body against her skin and the weight of his stare on the back of her shoulders. He lifted her hair against the back of her head, holding it there while he ran one finger down the side of her neck.

"It is right that you work with art; you are a work of art yourself, Katrina."

"That's very flattering," Katrina said, delighted by his attention. *Business first,* she reminded herself. Glancing back at him with a smile, she swung her chair, trying to look nonchalant as she reached over and fished in her briefcase, bringing out the paperwork, passing it to him.

"Before I forget, I must give you this. It's the ownership release papers." She held out the envelope. "We'll need your father's signature in order to begin preparing the brochures. Perhaps you'd like to give the documents to your solicitor to review first."

Sergio stared down at the envelope, and his expression changed in a flash. His mouth tightened, the expression in his eyes growing distant and shuttered. "Won't my signature suffice? My father is very ill."

It was as if a curtain had been dropped, and she saw another side of him. What was it, the tough businessman? The guy who kept a huge chain of stores running smoothly?

"I do understand that. I can deal with your solicitor myself, if you'd prefer? I know you're very busy."

"No." Sergio pulled his phone out of his pocket and flipped it open, looking at it distractedly. "Leave the documents with me, I'll bring them to London when we ship the collection over."

"Sooner would be better," she said, standing her ground, awkward though it felt. Going ahead with the inventory without the appropriate documentation wouldn't impress Mr. Pocklington.

He gave her a cool, assessing stare. The atmosphere in the small room had shifted dramatically. Tension emanated from him, and Katrina drew back in her chair, suddenly wishing she had asked Elaine for the solicitor's name and handled it that way.

He reached over and snatched the envelope out of her hand. "I'll organize it."

"Thank you." She was relieved, but there was something odd about it, too. The mention of documents had altered his mood, vastly so. Was it the reference to his father? "Sergio, I'm sure you have a lot on your mind with your father's illness. I hope I didn't seem inconsiderate, raising the issue of his signature."

"No, we must do it properly."

Relief washed over her. For a moment there, she'd started to worry about his attitude.

"You are right. I'm preoccupied about my father. Thank you for your understanding." He gave her a slight smile.

She was about to say something else when he stepped away. "I admire your dedication. That suits me well." He gestured with his phone. "I have a call I have to attend to; excuse me."

Whoa, that was some turnaround. Had she said something wrong? "Yes, of course."

"We'll see you at dinner," he added, "yes?"

Suddenly wary, she resisted. "Perhaps a sandwich up here, so I can work into the evening? Make up for the late start."

He nodded. "As you wish."

She watched him walk away. That was really weird. For a moment there, she wished she were far away from this place, this opportunity. Something about his mood change made her uneasy, and even as she began her work, she found it difficult to cast that feeling off.

*Sergio threw the envelope down on a chair as he joined Elaine* in the drawing room. He hadn't wanted to accept the legal documents, but he was sure that Katrina had been about to ask for the name of his father's solicitor, and that had to be avoided at all costs.

"What's that?" Elaine said and picked up her wineglass.

"Business." Papers. He hadn't been prepared for that, and he'd reacted badly. He would catch Katrina later, apologize properly, and make it up to her.

Elaine glanced at the envelope again and then gave him a concerned look. "What do you think of her? Do you think she will get the job done adequately?"

"Absolutely." He gestured toward the hallway. "She's working on it now. She's keen." He smiled. "Everyone wants their cut, after all."

Elaine gave a harsh laugh, and then she took a sip of her wine.

He needed everyone on board, including Elaine, and she could cause him grief all too easily. He crossed to the sideboard where he poured himself a large brandy. Strolling back, he sat down near her. "Do you remember the night we met?"

Her eyes glittered. She lifted her chin, resting it on one elegant hand. "Of course."

Across a poker table he had asked her to trust him, and

together they had played the game to win, splitting the rewards. It had been exhilarating and hugely successful.

Sergio reached over to chink his glass with hers. "This is no different. We are in this together, and when we work together, we are invincible. No one can stop us."

*Nico's phone rang as he stepped into the dark street outside the* community theater where he'd been working that evening. "*Sí, Raimunda.*"

She'd left the Torre for the evening and had rung to tell him that the Englishwoman had arrived at the house. Even though he knew that, the message sharpened his mood. He pictured the attractive Englishwoman in the house he knew so well, and he smiled to himself.

As he mounted his motorcycle and revved the engine, he glanced at his watch. He'd be in Castagona before midnight.

*Katrina worked late into the night. The procedure of adding* each item listed in the ledgers to her own spreadsheets helped to blot out the tension from Sergio's earlier visit to the gallery. The place had returned to its previous calm and inviting atmosphere, and she rather wished she could stay up there until the job was done.

She concentrated on the sculpture. Every five entries she transferred over, she would go into the gallery and storeroom with her notebook and check that the items were present in the collection, note their condition, and go back to the laptop to enter that data. All went well. There were a couple of items she couldn't immediately locate. She marked them up, assuming they had been misfiled in the storage system or were on display elsewhere in the house. The job was methodical and straightforward, and it cleared her head.

It was with reluctance that she finally switched off the lamp over the desk and packed her laptop away in its case. When she stood up, she rolled the top down on the desk, admiring it as she did so. It was a beautiful piece and bore the evidence of use by a loving owner, wear in the appropriate places, the lingering smell of beeswax polish making it feel familiar.

She thought again about the first Señora Teodoro working here, cataloging the items that her husband collected as they came in, documenting each exhibition they went to, storing the associated documents in a meticulous way. What would she think of the collection being sold? She glanced around, wondering about the memories that might have soaked into the walls.

She turned off the lights and exited the tower. All was quiet, and the corridor of disused offices gave her the creeps as she walked along it. Closed doors, silent rooms, what history did they hold? It was a question she often asked herself when she examined a particularly interesting item for auction. This house seemed riddled with such questions, and it was as if the questions multiplied in the night hours, as if they seeped out from the walls to lure her into the house's history.

Instead of walking straight across the landing to the bedrooms, she went down to the half landing and looked at the two Klimt paintings mounted on the walls there. She'd seen the pair before though, at an exhibition, maybe eight years ago. Jorge

Teodoro was a collector who shared willingly, which set him in high esteem in her mind. Art was meant to be enjoyed, and she didn't understand collectors who selfishly wanted to keep the items to themselves, although in her job she came across many such types, buying items up to keep them closeted away.

Small and lavishly colored, the paintings each depicted an unashamed, hedonistic beauty set against a symbolically rich background of color. One of the women was red haired; the other had an ebony mane. They were first-rate examples of Klimt's work, beautifully done, exquisitely rendered pieces of decadent art. They suited the setting so well, from the design of the building to the attitude of its inhabitants.

She glanced down into the hallway, where the shadows were far too mobile for her liking, as if the ghosts of the house were about to emerge from the walls. Stepping quickly across the half landing, she went upstairs to the wing where the bedrooms were located. Pausing at the end of the corridor, she noticed that the wall lights had been switched off. Only the occasional ceiling lights every ten feet or so illuminated the corridor, which gave it even more of an air of mystery than the office area.

Except for the sound of crickets outside, all was quiet, but the scent of the night was heavy in the air. The moist plants outside the windows omitted a heady smell, made stronger after the gardener had watered the foliage beneath the windows at sundown. She breathed it in, noticing the aromas of earth and the eucalyptus trees from farther away mingling with the scent of the garden. As she watched, the night breeze shifted the curtains at the open windows between the doorways. The long swaths of sheer fabric lifted eerily in time, one after the other, like the tide along the shore. It was a ghostly image, and it reminded her of any number of scary movies. This corridor felt even spookier than the rest of the place, as if an unknown presence lurked nearby.

The curtains lifted again. The skin on the back of her neck prickled, and Katrina felt herself becoming aware of all the lives that had been lived here, the people who had walked these corridors in years gone by. It was a beautiful house, but a strange one, too—a house full of secrets and ghosts.

She clutched her laptop bag against her chest and tiptoed quietly along the corridor. As she did, she heard a sound. She paused, but other than the movement of the curtains, all was still. She walked on.

A door to her left, at the rear of the house, was ajar. She kept walking, eager to get to her room. As she passed the open door, her footsteps slowed. She could see a large bed and beyond it a desk. Sergio was sitting at the desk, working, but with the door open. Was he waiting to catch her as she walked by? If so, she wasn't ready for that, not now. Could she creep past unseen? Cautiously, and as stealthily as she could, she moved on. When she reached her door and had her hand on the handle, she glanced back down the corridor to see if Sergio had emerged.

Her breath caught in her throat. There was someone standing there in the half-light, but it wasn't Sergio.

At the end of the landing where she'd been just moments before, Nicolas Teodoro stood watching her. At first glance she thought she was imagining it, that she had conjured forth an image from the shadows to satisfy her desire for him. But no, he really was there.

Dressed entirely in black and still as a statue, he looked like a cat burglar. Is that what he was, a forbidden intruder here? He was looking at her intently, his eyes black in the dim light, his unruly hair falling forward over his face. She sensed that he was ready to act. Would he take flight if she raised the alarm? Confusion riddled through her, and that wasn't all that she was feeling. He looked so darkly sexy, and she'd been held in those arms, felt those lips on hers—a forbidden liqueur that she had tasted in a dark street during the festival.

Why was he here?

He put his fingers to his lips, and at first she thought it was a signal to be quiet, but then he turned those fingers toward her and mouthed a kiss, winking at her. Katrina's legs felt shaky under her, and she gripped the door handle tighter. As if she hadn't been aroused enough the night before, here he was making a secret connection with her, reminding her of what had happened between them.

Glancing from Nicolas back to the open door halfway between them on the other side of the corridor, she could scarcely breathe. If Sergio emerged now, he'd see them both; he might even guess she'd had contact with his disinherited brother, the brother she had been warned about.

Nicolas followed her glance and then gestured at her, nodding and indicating that she should go into her room. Then he tapped his chest and pointed at her door. Katrina stared at him. He couldn't be serious? He was going to just walk down there to her room, past the open door, past his estranged brother?

No. He stepped quickly to the nearest window on the front side of the house. Signaling again, a master of mime, he indicated to her that he meant to come to her room from the outside of the building.

Her concern ratcheted. The balconies were too far apart, surely? That would be even more dangerous than walking past Sergio's open doorway. But before she could even react, he was climbing out the window, and as she watched his fit rear end disappear through it, she couldn't decide what unsettled her more: that he was risking the climb, or that he would appear in her room at the end of it.

Her legs swayed; she felt suddenly weak. He wasn't supposed to be there at all, not in the middle of the night, and especially not in her room. And yet he was scaling the outside of a building, aiming for her window.

*Go in and refuse him; lock the windows to the balcony.* Even as she thought it, she knew she had no intention of doing so. She had to know what he was going to say. The way he'd held her in Barcelona and the way he'd touched her, all of it echoed through her senses, and she staggered against the wall as she went inside and closed the door, pressing it closed and holding it that way, as if that would ground her.

The curtains wafted in the breeze, and she stared at them, not daring to blink as she watched the moonlight filtering into the room—until she saw a shadow move at the edge of the balcony.

What if her clients found her talking to him, in here, in their home? There was still time to run over there and bar the window before he got inside. But Katrina didn't want to lock him out, and as she watched the shadow climbing onto her balcony in the moonlight, her heart raced, her body suffused with anticipation.

8

*Nico hadn't traversed the balcony framework at the Torre for* several years, but he was eager to do it now. Undertaking the act was a deeply ingrained ritual, a crucial part of his childhood and adolescence. Deep inside he recognized that, and it made the climb so much more appealing than darting down the corridor to reach his goal. He took the first jump from the window ledge across to the adjacent balcony as if he had done it the night before. That was the most dangerous part, and he relished the familiar sense of accomplishment he got from undertaking it.

Once connected with the wrought-iron structure, he moved around it easily, his hands reaching for the familiar iron struts that formed the seaweedlike net across the front of the house. When he was a teenager, he liked to think that he was outside the net—that he had mastered it—and those left inside the house were trapped.

He'd first traversed the framework when he was nine years old, on a dare from Sergio. Sergio later told him he wanted him to fall, to show him how stupid he was. But Nico never fell. In fact, the dare had shown him what he might achieve physically—from acts that required strength and agility, to those requiring subtlety and illusion—and within weeks he could stand on the rail with perfect balance and then somersault off it, landing safely on the ground below.

Sergio had sneered at his efforts, jealousy and scorn pouring out of him. He was often that way. Whatever Sergio had in this life—from their father's respect to his business and money—he always wanted more. But Sergio wanted to get it the easy way, and some things had to be worked for.

Wrapping his hands around a familiar joist where the balcony was riveted deep into the wall, he swung loosely for a moment, savoring the tension in his upper body and the fluidity in the lower. Adrenaline pumped through him. Transferring his weight to one arm, he reached out for the next strut. He curled his legs under him and hoisted himself up, his back muscles at full stretch and his legs tight, winding his body around the frame and inside it.

Sergio had been jealous of that, too, the rush that Nico got from physical challenges. When had the jealousy started? he wondered. It was difficult to pinpoint. In his earliest memories, Sergio had been away at boarding school in England. Their mother had refused to let Nicolas do the same, claiming that she had missed Sergio and that she would be lonely without Nico nearby. Perhaps that was it. Sergio came home from school angry at their family's closeness without him. He used his foreign schooling as a weapon, but Nico was happy as he was, attending school in the village. Or at least he had been, until his father had grown increasingly dissatisfied with him and his adult goals in life. His mother spoke up for him, but they were an old-fashioned couple, and if Jorge was angry, she would grow silent in his company and whisper her encouragement to Nico in private.

He hurried on, taking the next part of the framework between the balconies, cursing under his breath when one of the fixtures moved in the wall. The jolt of it loosening threw his rhythm. He grabbed the next handhold and tried to remember where the loose fixture was located.

When he reached the third balcony, his mother and father's room, he jumped lithely onto it, the solid stone beneath his feet dispersing the energy through his body. The room was in darkness, shutters closed. He'd only ever seen this room shuttered in darkness once before, when his father was away on business and their mother had gone with him because it was their anniversary, many years ago. Normally, she had stayed at home.

He glanced across at the next balcony, his target. The doors were open, and the curtains drifted in and out of the room on the moving currents of air. That room was also in darkness. Maybe the *inglesa* hadn't gone into the room after all? Maybe she had gone to alert Sergio instead. It was a possibility. He didn't know the woman, but her reactions had given him the impression that she would not do that.

He hurried on, crossing the final space quickly. Climbing onto the balcony, he paused and listened for a moment. All was quiet. Even if Sergio had been alerted, Nico was ready for that. He walked into the room, pushing the curtains aside.

Moonlight lit an area of the floor, and beside the bed, a single lamp glowed bright enough for him to make out her figure, standing in the darkness by the door. Her perfume was in the air—a musky fragrance, sensual, just as she was—and he saw her things lying about this room that he knew so well. It made him want to touch them, to know her through them. The night before, in Barcelona, she'd tempted him with her feminine allure, and now there was a strong sense of intimacy between them. It was almost tangible, like strands wavering on the atmosphere between them, connecting them as they stood there on opposite sides of the room.

He stayed where he was; he didn't want to alarm her by moving too quickly.

"You shouldn't be here," she said.

"Are you so very sure of that?"

She considered his words silently for a moment. "I'm sure that you shouldn't be in this room with me right now. I was about to go to bed."

He liked her responses, they showed spirit, and to think he'd been expecting some stuffy *inglesa*. She definitely wasn't that. "Actually, you are in my room."

She looked startled at his comment and then broke into a soft smile. "That explains the painting."

She was intelligent; that was good. He hoped that she would be clever enough to see through Sergio.

"Did you do it?"

"Many years ago, yes. I don't paint anymore. I left it here as a warning for anyone who saw it."

She looked at him with curiosity, and for the first time she moved away from the door and walked toward him, her head slightly on one side as she contemplated both him and the painting.

He admired her as she slowly, cautiously, began to close the space between them. There was an openness about her expression that appealed to him. That's what it was last night. There had been an instant sense of communication between them and an obvious mutual attraction, yes. But it was her attitude—vital and alive, yet straightforward and honest—that had harnessed his attention above all.

She studied the painting, and then her glance flickered back to him. "A warning? The danger approaches from behind?"

"Perhaps. But we do not only rely on our eyes to sense danger, do we?"

"No." She stared at him and then ran one hand around the back of her neck. He hoped it was because she was sensitive to the hidden meaning in his words.

Her eyes were bright, her pupils dilated. She was aroused. Without meaning to, he recalled the feeling of her lips softly opening beneath his, her body yielding and warm beneath his hands. He wanted to feel that again. What was it that he came here for? Ah, yes, to bend her in his direction. Gently, he decided.

Coaxing her would be a pleasure. As the thought crossed his mind, he smiled, his body responding to the idea of coaxing her in physical terms as well as intellectual. He took a step closer, moving slowly around her, the pair of them circling each other like curious but wary cats with overlapping territory.

"How did you get into the grounds?"

"There is a way, a loophole in the security fence."

She nodded.

Did she trust him? He thought she was willing. Perhaps she was curious by nature, or maybe intuitive. He noticed her trinkets as he passed the dresser and thought of a way to make his point. Palming her watch, subtly, he moved on, stepping closer to her.

"Why are you here?" she asked.

There was a touch of shyness in her expression as she asked that, as if she'd had to push the statement out. What did she want to hear? He had his goal—to influence her—but he had to tread cautiously. There was more than one reason why he was here, anyway.

"I'm not sure anymore," he responded and smiled. "You seem to distract me whenever we meet." It was the truth. He would rather ask her to leave and take her out to a bar where they could get to know each other a little better. The nagging sense of duty and his lingering concern for his father's whereabouts stopped him from doing just that.

She lowered her eyes for a moment but not before he caught sight of her smile. He noticed then how perfectly her dress outlined her figure and remembered the pleasure of holding and touching her. She was shapely, and he had the urge to lift her in his arms, to feel those curves as he took her to bed and claimed her.

Pushing her hair back, she met his stare. Her eyes were sparkling. "Last night, you said you wanted to see who Sergio had brought here. And now? What is it you want from me?"

Her lips remained slightly parted as if she was anxious about his reply. Her lower lip was lush, and he imagined how it might feel to grasp it softly between his teeth and hear her moan with pleasure as he made love to her.

*Bend her. You need to make her ask questions, to doubt Sergio's word.*

He opened one hand, empty palm upward. "To sell something at auction, you must be the rightful owner, yes?"

She nodded, staring at his palm. He could see her mind was racing ahead.

"Sometimes we might appear to own what we do not." With a sleight of hand he moved his other hand across his palm and deposited her watch there. He waited for her reaction, wondering if she would be shocked. It was a risk; she might be offended or, worse still, think him a thief.

She gasped softly, entranced, and quickly glanced at her wrist. "But I wasn't wearing it; I took it off earlier this evening." She looked over at the dresser, where he had picked it up. "Oh, you're very good. I didn't see you take it." She smiled with delight.

"Thank you. But I am no thief." He lifted her hand in his and placed the watch around her wrist. "I only wish to make the mental suggestion, you understand?"

Her hand felt warm and soft against his, and he sensed it would tremble if it were free. He held onto it even after he had put the watch on, stroking the soft inside of her wrist.

"Yes, I do understand what you are saying," she replied breathlessly. "I can guess what you are getting at, but I must reassure you. As auctioneers, we do check these things properly."

"That pleases me." He lifted her hand to his mouth and kissed her forearm in the spot he had been stroking before releasing it. "I only want the right thing to be done. Justice, you would call it, yes?"

Again she nodded, and then studied him intently, the hand he had been holding clutched against her chest as if to capture the memory of his touch there. She'd liked that, he noted. He'd enjoyed it, too.

"Do you believe in justice?" he asked, resisting the urge to take her in his arms again.

"Of course, but it's not my place to judge," she whispered, her voice low, her eyes on him as she said the words. "I haven't judged you . . . even though I've been warned against you."

"You have?" That pleased him, too. It meant that Sergio feared he could disrupt his plans.

"Yes . . . and yet I find myself allowing *this* to happen." She lifted her chin, her silky hair falling back over her shoulders.

He knew that she meant the discussion between them and the fact that she had let him in here, but her body language betrayed her deeper meaning. The pulse at the base of her throat beat fast, and her breasts rose and fell with the speed of her breathing.

His back tensed, and he grew hard in response to her. He could no longer resist. "Allowing what to happen?" He reached out and took her hand once again. "This?"

He lifted her fingers to his mouth, kissed her palm, and then the inside of her forearm. "This?"

She didn't have to respond in words. He could see it in her expression each time he glanced up: desire, pleasure, and breathless anticipation. He was rock hard for her now, and he moved quickly. Sliding his arm around her waist, he pulled her in against him so that she was locked in his arms.

"Or this?" He bent his head and kissed the side of her neck.

She moaned aloud, her head dropping back, her body undulating against his, showing him very clearly that she wanted this, too.

He stroked her from the place where he had kissed her neck to her shoulder and then on to her fingertips. His other hand moved down the outline of her hip, holding her close against him so that she could feel his erection.

Reacting, she moved quite suddenly, grasping him with both hands, kissing him full on the mouth, her fingers locking together at the back of his neck. She felt so alive, so eager in his arms. His hands roved her back, measuring her outline, soaking up every glorious ounce of her. As he stroked her bottom, she pulled her head away from his and gasped loudly.

Her pupils were dilated and her face flushed. Her hand moved toward his belt. "You feel so hard," she whispered.

That made him even harder.

"It is because you're so inviting."

"So are you," she breathed, laughing softly.

Admiration shone in her eyes as she ran her hands over his chest. Through the fabric of his T-shirt, her inquisitive touch maddened him. His blood pumped faster, his need for her pressing. He walked her backward toward the bed, and she locked eyes with him as she sank down on it, pulling him after her.

She looked like the subject for a painting, and he watched as her hair spread out against the bedcover, like light spilling in a dark sky.

When he climbed over her, she drew one knee up alongside

his flank, which made his cock ache. Flexing his back, he blurted his need for her in his native tongue.

"I don't understand," she replied.

"No Spanish?"

She looked embarrassed as she shook her head.

"I said you are so sensual, you make me ache to be inside you."

She moaned with pleasure, clutching at him, smiling and kissing him all at once.

Hungrily, he tasted her mouth, his hands moving around the outline of her breasts, overcome with the need to explore every part of her.

She pushed her hand between them, plucked at his belt, and then reached to feel the shape of his cock through his jeans. He growled, pulling back, his eyes closing. He had to lift up on his hands and pause; the feeling of her reaching for him that way threatened to make him go too fast.

Focusing on her, he moved onto his side and stroked her inner thigh, roving into the hot spot he found between her legs. She pressed back against the bed, her eyes almost closed, a pleasured smile on her lips. Through the fabric of her underwear, her mound showed itself plump, a soft cushion he wanted to sink his cock into. Her underwear was damp, and he stroked it, his balls aching in response to the sweet, physical signal of her desire.

"Oh, please, I want you," she whispered, her hands reaching for him.

Those words on her lips sounded so good to him.

"*Sí*," he replied, rolling back over her, no longer wanting to hold back the urge to drive himself, pistonlike, into her lush body. Her hips rolled from side to side beneath him, making him long for the clutch of her on his rigid shaft.

Somewhere outside the room, a door slammed.

She tensed beneath him.

He swore under his breath and automatically looked at the door as well.

Her hands went to his upper arms, and she gripped him tightly. "Hurry; you must leave."

Concern flickered in her eyes, and she moved against him. That didn't encourage him to leave; in fact, it made him want to stay and to ease inside her where she felt so hot and damp.

"I don't want to go; I like it right here." He grinned and rocked his hips between her thighs, letting her feel how ready he was to be inside her. "What makes you think I care if I'm found here?"

She moved her hips against his and flashed her eyes, tantalizingly matching his threat. "You care. I saw you look at the open door, and you avoided it. You didn't want Sergio to know you're here, and I don't blame you. He thinks you're trouble, and I think so, too!"

He gave a quiet laugh, enjoying her spirited response. "You're very observant and so very, very beautiful, especially so when you are aroused."

She was watching the door as much as she was watching him. "I'm trained to be observant. It's your fault I'm aroused."

He liked that.

"Now go," she whispered, frowning. "Hurry."

Raised voices issued from the corridor. He recognized Sergio's voice. Perhaps it would be bad to be found here right now, for her. That wasn't his aim, after all. He would just have to think of something very grim indeed, to get rid of this erection. His hand went to her cheek, and he stroked it gently, drawing her attention back to him.

"Thank you for caring whether I get caught."

"Just go, before I change my mind."

"About what?"

"About judging your behavior." An amused, challenging look flashed in her eyes.

"Don't judge me just yet, Katrina Hammond, not until I've given you something worth judging." He bent to kiss her mouth, his blood roaring when she moaned with longing against him.

She lifted from the bed as he stood up, one hand on his arm as he got up. "Nicolas?"

"Yes, you can count on it."

She frowned. "Count on what?"

"Last time we met, you asked if you would see me again. You can count on it."

Warmth glowed in her eyes, but she didn't say anything in response.

The shouting grew louder, the noise getting closer to the door. He waved and turned to go.

*"Never a dull moment,"* Katrina muttered ruefully to herself as she watched Nicolas slip through the curtains and out onto the balcony, a figure dressed in black like a shadow.

He hadn't felt like a shadow between her thighs, far from it, and her body was on fire. When she stood up, she felt dizzy from arousal and need.

She started stripping off her clothes. There was no way anyone could have slept through that noise. Houseguests would be out in the corridor by now, looking as if they had been in bed asleep when it kicked off, not secretly canoodling with the bad-boy black sheep of the family in the middle of the night. Too reckless? Maybe. But she was weak, and she hadn't been able to stop it.

She didn't want to face Sergio, whose voice she could hear, or Elaine, for numerous reasons, but she'd either have to say she was wearing earplugs and had taken a knockout sleeping tablet, or she had to make an appearance out there, and soon.

She'd never got undressed so quickly. The irony was she wished she'd been doing it when her moonlight visitor was still in the bloody room. Typically, she had to do it now, when he was gone. Where would a few minutes more have taken them?

Kicking off her shoes, she shoved them under the bed. Throwing her dress and undies over a nearby dressing chair, she darted to the bed and grabbed her dressing gown from the ottoman that stood at the footboard and pulled it on, fiddling with the belt hurriedly as she stepped over to the door. Taking a deep breath, she opened it.

She saw Elaine immediately, also in a dressing gown, her arms folded defensively as she looked farther down the corridor.

"Are you okay?" Katrina whispered when Elaine looked her way. Elaine nodded but seemed uncomfortable about Katrina's sudden presence in the corridor.

Katrina stuck her head out the door and looked at where the noise was coming from. Sergio and Vincent were arguing at the end of the corridor, near where the entrance to the guest apartments in the tower stood. Vincent was fully dressed, as if he'd just come back from somewhere. Sergio only wore boxer shorts.

Vincent was a houseguest in a bad mood. She knew she shouldn't be nosy, but she couldn't help wishing she could speak Spanish. She felt excluded from all sorts of juicy gossip here, not to mention whatever Nicolas had said, those fevered words he'd breathed in her ear earlier. She'd badly wanted to understand him without having to ask.

"Sergio," Elaine called, and gestured at Katrina. "It's the middle of the night, you're waking everyone in the house, deal with it in the morning." With that she joined Katrina in her doorway, blocking her view.

"I'm sorry, Katrina. Sergio is a very hotheaded man at times, and they had a disagreement about something or other." She gave a dismissive gesture in their direction. "Rent, I think."

Katrina noticed she didn't look too sure on that last point. A door down the corridor slammed. Sergio stomped past the pair of them and disappeared into his room without a backward glance.

Elaine sighed. "There, we can get back to our beauty sleep." She gave a brisk smile and a wink and urged Katrina back into her room.

Katrina was happy to oblige.

Back inside her room—or Nicolas's room as she now thought of it—she darted over to the glass doors and stepped out onto the balcony. Leaning over the rails, she peered down into the gloom below. It struck her then how high up it was, and she wondered how on earth anyone would get down from there without breaking every bone in their body.

Moving to the far side, she noticed that the room next door to hers was in darkness. She supposed Nicolas was limber enough to jump from here to there, but would he be able to get into that room? And where would he go from there? He couldn't walk out into the corridor, not yet. It was then that she saw him, much farther along the building.

Her eyes nearly popped out when she saw that he was traversing the outside of the rail along the adjoining balconies before leaping across to a nearby ledge located somewhere in the area of the entrance to the house. Her mind flicked back through the stored images in her memory, and she recalled that there was a frieze there, over the front door.

He walked along as if it was a footpath on the ground, not the top of a narrow panel high up on a building. Then he dropped into a crouch as if preparing to jump to the ground below.

Katrina gripped the rail, leaning forward. Surely he couldn't intend to jump down from there? She saw the black shape move in the moonlight and put her hand to her throat. He did a double somersault and some sort of backflip and then landed on his feet in a squat on the ground, fingertips splayed for balance. A moment later he stood up and set off at a slow jog across the grounds. She saw a flash of his face in the moonlight and his hand raised in her direction.

He could see her.

Her heartbeat regulated as she returned the wave. He was safely gone, undiscovered.

Back in the room, she looked across at the bed, unconvinced that she would be able to use it for the purpose of sleep. It was his bed, and moments before, he'd been about to make love to her in it. That kind of prelude didn't put her in the mood for sleeping.

It was past one o'clock in the morning, and she was wired. What a day. What a strange two days, in fact.

Meandering back to the bed, she looked down at the cover where the impression of two bodies had made an obvious dent. She smiled and lay down in the same spot, wishing she'd hidden him here in the room instead of outside of it. What did it all mean? The arguments in the night, the peculiar tension surrounding Sergio, the midnight visitor who made her do crazy things.

Above all, she wondered why she wanted Nicolas at all, and she wanted him a lot. Was it because he was the black sheep, the bad-boy disinherited son of the family? Maybe. It had a certain dangerous appeal. But no, she didn't think so. She hadn't known that the first night he'd come to her. The attraction was tied in with the way he'd approached her; she recognized that. She'd been hooked from that moment on. Even though he was what her grandma would have called "a wrong 'un" she could scarcely resist him.

Maybe she should have said no to him this evening, though, and ended the liaison. It would make her job here simpler, but she didn't want to say no. He had his motives, too, and she wasn't blind to that. He was pursuing her because he wanted his say about the collection.

It was an inheritance issue. They cropped up from time to time in the business. She'd never experienced it directly, but she'd heard enough tales. Great-Aunt Matilda phoning Pocklington's to point out that she was promised the Venetian glass when she was eight years old, that kind of thing. Nicolas Teodoro was no Great-Aunt Matilda, but he had a similar sort of issue. It didn't stop her wanting him, though.

In the dim light, she could make out the painting on the wall. The eyes of the man—they were Nicolas's eyes. It was a self-portrait; she could see that now. And he seemed to be staring right down at her. She sighed.

She could still smell his cologne, and when she closed her eyes she could hear the murmur of his voice against her throat, feel him moving between her thighs. She'd wanted him then, and she wanted him now.

"Oh bloody hell," she whispered into the night, incredulous laughter escaping her lips. "I'm never going to get a wink of sleep."

# 9

*Katrina stood on her balcony and blinked into the sunshine. It* was another gloriously hot day, with clear blue skies overhead. She felt inspired by it, radiantly excited by everything that had gone on the night before. The secret of her midnight lover was something she savored and nurtured inside her. She approached the day ahead with zeal as a result.

When she opened her bedroom door, she heard footsteps and paused. Raimunda passed along the corridor with a tray in her hands. The housekeeper threw Katrina a disapproving glance as she passed, heading right down the corridor where the entrance to the East Tower stood within an arched door-way. Raimunda rapped on the door and waited expectantly, her face set in a steady look of disapproval.

The tray had to be for Vincent, the houseguest.

Sure enough, the door opened, and Vincent appeared. Katrina

took her time, hovering to see what would happen, curiosity getting the better of her. Vincent said nothing to Raimunda as he took the tray of food from her, didn't even thank or acknowledge her. Raimunda rubbed her hands on the front of her apron as if she had touched something dirty and said a few words that sounded very disapproving. To Katrina's amazement, Vincent responded by hissing at her, loudly, his eyes wide open as if to scare her off.

Raimunda jerked away from him, muttering and shaking her head, crossing herself and rolling her eyes to heaven as she tottered off.

Katrina was astonished and only managed to shift herself when she realized that Raimunda was just about to return down the corridor. She stepped back into her room, determined to avoid another withering glance from the housekeeper. As she did, she heard Vincent's door slam. A houseguest with a temper. How unusual, Katrina thought.

After a few moments, she headed out again, but the sound that greeted her was raised voices shouting in Spanish.

"Again," she murmured, curiosity instantly gripping her. What was it about this house that was making her so nosy, the secrets she sensed, or the subterfuge?

She paused in the corridor outside her door, listening to the argument that echoed up the stairs from the hallway—two men, by the sounds of it. Something thudded and shattered, and she heard another voice. Was it Raimunda? Then she heard heels running up the stairs. Elaine turned the corner and headed directly toward her, quickly, and with a bright, artificial smile on her face.

"Ah, Katrina, you're awake, but then I'm sure you couldn't help it with all this noise."

"I didn't hear anything until I came out into the corridor." Katrina straightened her sleeveless shirt, aware that Elaine once again looked as if she was in a fashion display, whereas she had dressed for manual as well as desk work in the gallery.

"It's like last night all over again." Elaine chuckled.

"I'd forgotten about that . . ." she lied. Her voice trailed off as she thought about last night.

Elaine put her arm around Katrina's waist and led her along the landing in the direction of the stairs. "Sergio has an uninvited guest: his brother."

"His brother?" she repeated, disconcerted. Nicolas was here?

"They always fight," Elaine added, with a strange half smile as if she were either bemused or pleased, Katrina couldn't decide which. "With that going on, I've decided to take you out for breakfast. We can avoid them while they sort out their little problem."

*Little problem?* Katrina couldn't help wondering if everything Elaine said was sugarcoated. Whatever was between the brothers was no "little problem," and the shouting issuing from downstairs testified to that.

"We'll take Sergio's Porsche."

"Thank you, Elaine, but I really should get on with the job I've been brought here to do." Even she could hear the wobble of uncertainty in her own voice. What with everything that had gone on the night before, valuing the collection seemed to be the last thing on her mind.

"A couple of hours out of the house will do us good. You can catch up later." Elaine was clearly intent on getting Katrina away from the argument that raged on downstairs. "Come on; if we head out straightaway, we'll be back before you know it." She hugged Katrina around the waist as if they were old pals and ushered her along the corridor.

"But I dressed for work." She'd put on a short-sleeved, buttoned-up shirt, jeans, and practical shoes for comfort while she worked in the storerooms, where she needed to check the deep-storage items off against the spreadsheets.

"Don't worry about it." Elaine's smile became rather fixed as they reached the top of the half landing and could see the hallway below.

Both women peered down. Katrina felt animosity rising like a tidal wave up the stairs, soaking into her bones. The arguing voices were louder, the vehemence obvious in the tones used. Even though Katrina couldn't understand the words, she picked up the odd one or two phrases; but they were speaking so fast and heatedly it was virtually impossible to get the gist of it. Once again she felt thwarted by her lack of Spanish. It was infuriating.

The sun was pouring in along the reception hallway, and two shadows fell across the parquet floor, showing the furious gestures one of them was using.

Getting out of the house seemed a good option. Even so, they would have to walk through the hallway in order to leave the building. Both brothers had their hands on her the previous day, and it seemed as if Katrina was going to have to walk past them while they were at each other's throats. The prospect made her blood run hot and cold, and she shivered involuntarily. The palms of her hands grew damp.

"Come on," Elaine said with purpose. "Let's go."

The raised voices dissipated as the two women descended the stairs. That only seemed to make it worse. Dread crept over Katrina. The hallway slowly came into view. Silence descended as they approached. She didn't want to do this. *It's their problem, not yours.* Yes, it was their fault she felt this way, she thought. She shouldn't feel bad because of their feud. Even so, the stairs seemed to go on interminably. Then she felt the weight of their stares. It was as if there were a million eyes looking up at her, not just Sergio and Nicolas.

It was the first time she'd seen the two men together, in the same room at the same time. Her heart was thudding, and she was aware of Elaine making some inconsequential remark about them going out for breakfast, but she couldn't focus on the words.

She was too busy watching the men. Sergio's tie was half-undone, his jacket flung on the floor nearby, his hair awry. His expression was furious. Nicolas was far from calm, but the mood he exuded was much more controlled. He looked eminently fit, his posture proud and sure. Maybe it was what he was wearing, Katrina thought with no small sense of irony. Dressed entirely from head to toe in black leather—leather pants and a biker's jacket—he looked sturdy and invincible . . . and devilishly sexy.

Even though there was anger in his eyes, he was proud and somehow more grounded than his older brother. It really struck her, because when she had first seen him two nights before, she'd initially thought he was more of a wild type than Sergio. Perhaps it was his more bohemian nature that she had seen then.

Nearby, where Sergio's jacket had been flung, Raimunda was slowly clearing up an overturned potted plant with a dustpan and brush, cautiously observing the four of them as she did so.

Katrina could hear Elaine speaking, and her words were directed at Sergio. She said something about the car. Sergio nodded, watchful of Nicolas, his glance darting at the women and then back.

*Don't acknowledge Nicolas,* Katrina reminded herself. *I don't know who he is. I've never met him before.* Try as she might, her attention seemed magnetized to him. She longed to greet him; it seemed cruel not to be able to do so. Even if he were a stranger, she would look his way, smile, and nod, wouldn't she? She wasn't quite sure what to do. This was hard; she had to force herself to be distant.

His eyes glinted at her, and then he said something to Sergio. She recognized the word *introduzca* in there, something about an introduction, and he nodded at her. He was asking to be introduced.

What would Sergio do? Her mind ticked over quickly. In London, Sergio had told her he wanted to be discreet, that he didn't want Nicolas to draw the newspapers to them. If Sergio introduced her, he would be revealing something he thought his brother didn't know: that an auctioneer was in the house. What would he do? Glancing at Nicolas, she could see the tension in him and knew that he wondered the very same thing.

Sergio muttered something under his breath that sounded like a curse and involved the words *al infierno*, a reference to hell, then snatched up his jacket from the floor. As he pulled it on, he laughed and then hauled Katrina into his arms as he passed her by.

His action came out of nowhere. Winded by his sudden approach and the tightness of his grip, she struggled to maintain her footing. What the hell was he doing?

"Sergio, Mr. Teodoro, please."

Ignoring her, he held her so that she faced Nicolas and spoke in Spanish over his shoulder. Again, she picked up one or two words. Sergio was taunting his brother, saying he would never have any of this. Was she included in that remark? Did he think she was a woman to be brought here and controlled by the master of the house?

The idea shocked and annoyed her.

His arms locked around her, and she jerked her shoulders away from him angrily. His grip on her waist tightened in response.

"Sergio, leave Katrina alone." It was Elaine, and it was clearly an instruction, the annoyance in her tone obvious.

But Sergio had no intention of letting her go, because his other hand went to the base of her throat. Stroking it, he breathed the smell of her hair as if she were an object he was examining.

When she shifted in his arms, making ready to break free, his hands splayed on her throat like a warning to be still. His actions seemed crazy, even taking into account his foul mood. Exactly how megalomaniac was her host?

"Our beautiful guest Katrina likes to be admired and appreciated, don't you?" Sergio said in English.

Katrina wanted the ground to open up and swallow her. Anything she might choose to say could implicate her.

"Let me go," she demanded angrily, prizing Sergio's hands away from her. She pulled free, quickly stepping away from him across the hallway.

"Bravo," Elaine declared and clapped her hands. "A woman of substance. I like you even more each passing moment."

A barb meant for Sergio, Katrina felt. Sergio ignored Elaine and gave Katrina a little bow. She saw a nasty look in his eyes that she hadn't noticed before. He was annoyed at her for breaking free.

"Forgive me, Katrina, I was being playful in order to rid myself of my bad humor." When he said, "rid myself," he practically spat the words in Nicolas's direction.

The look Nicolas threw his brother held a mixture of disgust and pity. "You are more of a fool than I thought you were, if you truly believe a woman enjoys being treated like that."

"Why don't you just fuck off once and for all!"

*Sergio really has misplaced his charm today,* Katrina thought.

Nicolas ignored that remark. Instead, he smiled directly at Katrina. Pride and desire flamed into life in his eyes. Her body responded as if he'd touched her. He was flirting with danger as much as his brother was, she knew that, and it made her skin prickle with delight that he'd taken a risk to connect with her.

She nodded politely in his direction, as if they had just been introduced, and then rejoined Elaine, but the look he'd given her made her burn up inside with a different heat, a secret thrill. The memory of a passion shared in the dark hours. Dangerous? *Hell, yes.* But somehow that made it all the more exciting.

Elaine took her chance, grabbing Katrina's hand. She pulled her in the direction of the door, false laughter on her lips as if it was all a game and she'd claimed the prize.

Blinking in the bright sunlight outside, Katrina couldn't help wondering if that's what it was: a game. Elaine seemed to treat it as such. Maybe it was a game to her, but for the brothers something much more serious was at stake. Deep down, she felt it. Not just the obvious stuff, the money and the power, but something she couldn't quite put her finger on. Yes, she was curious. With each passing moment she seemed to become more deeply entrenched. Nicolas had impressed her in there. He had a personal ax to grind, that was for sure, but he seemed so measured, so rational, compared to his brother.

Had she become part of their battle now? Even though she didn't understand the whole picture, it fascinated her. The Teodoro family was a puzzle that she wanted to solve. Beyond that, the fire she'd seen in Nicolas's eyes had rekindled the physical memory of their passionate encounter the night before.

"You okay?" Elaine asked as soon as they got outside.

Katrina nodded. "What's the problem between Sergio and the other guy?" she asked as they walked down the steps. A certain mysterious brother had raised questions in her mind, questions that wouldn't go away. "His brother you said, yes?"

She figured that most people would want to know. It might seem odd if she didn't ask.

"Some old family feud." Her comment was dismissive. "We'll put the top down on the Porsche, blow the cobwebs away," she added as they approached the car.

"Sounds like a great idea," Katrina managed to reply as she climbed into the low-slung seat, her body still burning from that proud glance Nicolas had sent her way. Whether it was right or wrong, there was no denying that Nicolas was a delicious secret to have.

Elaine glanced across at her as she maneuvered the car down the driveway, her auburn hair blowing around her head in the breeze like a flame. "Sergio gets hotheaded, you know." She added, "He's one of those passionate types."

Katrina nodded, deep in thought. *Passionate* wasn't a description she would associate with Sergio. Not now, at any rate. He had a blatant lothario-like sexuality about him, yes, but it was all about power and control; it was neither subtle nor responsive. That wasn't what passion was about to her.

It wasn't something she had thought about in any great depth before, but now that she did, she saw that passion was all about sensuality for her, that, and a strong sense of mutual attraction, one that had such a powerful draw that it was undeniable. The night before she'd been in the grip of true passion in Nicolas's arms. She'd wanted to turn him away, known that the reasons for him being there were all wrong, and yet something had happened between them that was above and beyond the reasons for him being there.

Musing on it as the car sped through the countryside in the radiant sunlight, she recognized that she was drawn to Nicolas in every way. She couldn't deny that, even if it was totally wrong, and she knew it was. Her commission was what was important, not some . . . crush . . . on a mystery man whose motives for seducing her were probably suspect.

She had to see the job through properly, and that meant putting her personal attraction to Nicolas aside, keeping her interactions with Sergio professional, and getting on with the job. Thank goodness she hadn't got any more involved with Sergio. Something had made her mistrust him, and she was glad of that now. He had seemed so polished, but she'd seen another side of him and knew that he was power hungry, moody, and childish. Yes, she needed to distance herself from Sergio's unpredictable mood swings.

She had a job to do. It didn't mean she had to like the man she was working for, right? *Right.* That decided, she felt more levelheaded and strong than she had since she'd arrived.

All she had to do now was stop thinking about Nicolas.

That might prove to be the most difficult.

*Sergio was seething. Rage had him firmly in its grip, and he'd* barely been able to keep a hold of it when the women passed. He was furious with Nicolas for turning up here now, while they had the auctioneer in the house. He barely waited until the shadows disappeared from outside the doorway before he turned on him, reverting to their native tongue as he continued their earlier, more bitter, row.

Nicolas was frowning at the doorway.

Sergio took his chance. "How dare you try to disrupt our lives!" he shouted as he launched himself at his brother.

Nicolas didn't move fast enough, and Sergio landed a right hook on his cheekbone, drawing blood with the ring he wore.

His heart pumped wildly as he watched the startled look on his brother's face. Grinning, Sergio reveled in it. In the background Raimunda dropped the dustpan and brush she was holding, her arms lifting in the air in horror. She crossed herself and started mumbling away to the heavens. It was something she'd seen before, and she returned to her task while letting Sergio know of her deep disapproval.

Nicolas placed his hand to his cheek, saw the blood on his palm, and shook his head. "Why wait until the women have gone, if you think they enjoy witnessing your bully tactics so much?"

Sarcasm rang in his remark.

"They enjoy the sight of power; they are hungry for it, too. You can see it in their eyes." He expected Nicolas to react, to fight back, but instead his little brother smiled.

"Your understanding of power over women is very different than mine."

Sergio's blood boiled. He went in for another punch. Nicolas saw it coming this time and sidestepped it. Sergio's forward momentum took him toward the wall. Nicolas pushed him up against it, holding him fixed there with one arm bent behind his back.

"Let me go, you little shit," Sergio demanded.

"No way." Nicolas laughed softly, and he sounded irritatingly sure of himself.

He tried to break free, but Nicolas was strong and had the upper hand in this position, holding solid when he struggled. He was like a creature in a trap; the more he forced back on

Nicolas, the more pain shot up his arm. But he couldn't stop himself fighting Nicolas, never could. Pain seared into his shoulder; his vision blurred. Finally, his body crumpled. He slid down the wall, blurting out his relief incoherently and unwillingly when his arm was freed.

Nicolas grabbed him and dragged him away from the wall by his jacket, flipping him over onto his back. Standing astride him, he dropped into a squat, his knees pinning Sergio's shoulders to the ground.

Sergio tried, but couldn't move his arms enough to push him off. He thrust his body up, but couldn't force Nicolas away. He writhed and bucked, furious at being held down this way.

With one hand Nicolas grabbed his face and forced Sergio to meet his eyes. "You need to get in shape, big brother, if you're going to try to take me on."

He laughed and mock-hit Sergio on the chin.

"Go on, hit me; you know you want to." Sergio willed him to do it. It would give him just the excuse to get the police involved and make sure Nicolas would never set foot inside the house again.

"You'd like that, wouldn't you?" Nicolas grew serious and pushed Sergio's head back, forcing his neck to full stretch.

The floor was hard against the back of his skull, and pain shot down his spine.

Nicolas stared into his eyes, and for several long moments, Sergio thought he was going to keep him that way until he asked to be let free.

"I'm not that stupid, and you're not worth it." Nico let go his grip and sprang easily to his feet.

Sergio hated him for his limber strength. He clicked his neck back into shape, sitting up and watching as Nicolas said good-bye to Raimunda, touching her affectionately on her shoulder as he passed.

He paused and looked back. "If you won't tell me where my father is, I'll find him for myself."

"Now you want to talk to him," Sergio spat back, while he struggled to his feet. "Now that he is dying, and you want a share of the spoils."

"Don't judge me by your own standards." Nicolas shook his head at his brother and then went to leave. "Think what you like; I don't care. I only want to know that he is okay," he added.

"You will *never* find him." Sergio enjoyed a sense of smug pleasure in telling him that.

"Oh yes I will." Nicolas smiled wryly and walked to the door. "And I have a gut feeling you'll regret you ever tried to stop me."

"Fuck you," Sergio shouted after him.

He ground his teeth, angry and unnerved as he pulled himself together. Nicolas's best efforts were wasted, he assured himself. He would never, ever find Jorge. Straightening his tie, he waved his arms at Raimunda, who was still fussing over the broken pot.

She scurried away.

Just as well; he wasn't in the mood for her black looks and insubordination. He glanced at his watch. He was going to be late for a meeting with a major shareholder, and because he'd been too angry to think about it earlier, he'd let Elaine take his

Porsche. Now he would have to find Tomas and the Mercedes, a further annoyance and a further delay.

"Today must get better than this," he said, cursing Nicolas as he left the house.

## 10

When Katrina finally got to the desk in the tower that day, she decided to give Lucy a call. Her intention was to check in, but deep down she also felt the need to touch base with someone familiar. Since she'd arrived in Spain, some pretty unusual things had happened, and she was a bit weirded-out by it all.

Lucy sounded pleased to hear from her, which was a comfort. "How are you doing? What's the collection like, as good as you'd hoped?"

"Oh, Lucy, it's truly unbelievable. On one hand, it seems a shame to split the collection up, but on the other . . . it's buried here. As far as I can tell, no one even comes in to look at it these days. The husband and wife who put the collection together aren't around anymore, alas. I'd love to have met them. The wife passed on, and the husband is in a hospice. It's very sad."

"That is a shame. It's hard when an item or a collection comes to us with that kind of history."

"Yes. I feel privileged to work with these things, you know."

"Is the house nice?"

"Nice like you wouldn't believe." She chuckled. "Nice would be the understatement of the century."

"In that case I'm even more glad you got this job and Henry didn't get a look in. He's dragging his feet around like a real misery-guts here, he's so jealous."

Katrina smiled and picked up a pencil as they chatted on, turning it between the fingers of one hand.

"So, anything I can do for you?" Lucy asked.

"Yes, actually. I wondered if you could do me a favor. No rush, just when you have a moment. Could you ask around, see what people know about the Teodoro family and their collection?"

"Of course I can . . . Any particular reason why?"

Lucy was pretty astute, and Katrina was unsure how to verbalize the disconcerted feeling that she'd got from being alone up here with Sergio the afternoon before and all the other tensions in the place. She also couldn't trust her own reactions, because she was so attracted to his brother. "It's going to sound a bit odd, but I want to be entirely sure that I can trust the client, my host. Does that make sense?"

"Ah, I see. Leave it with me. I'll see what I can find out for you."

"Thanks. I did some research on the family before I came over, but mostly I was looking at the origins of the collection, for the valuation, not . . . anything else."

"Are you okay?" Lucy said, concern in her voice.

*Am I okay?* Oddly, yes. Sergio was a loose cannon, something she'd like to feel more secure about from a business standpoint, at the very least. Other than that, she hadn't ever felt so alive before. She was wildly attracted to the mystery man who kept approaching her, and she was feasting her eyes on a wonderful private collection. Regardless of all that, somewhere deep inside, a small part of her was being sensible, or trying to. "I'm okay, really. Look, it's probably nothing. Don't worry about it."

"I'll do what I can. Speak to you soon. Call me anytime, okay?"

"Will do." Katrina put the phone down and shook her head, laughing at herself. She was bound to feel uneasy; she'd had two secret encounters with the disinherited black sheep of the family. Yes, she had to face up to it, that was not going to make her feel relaxed around her host.

*When he got back from his office, Sergio poured himself a* large drink. Try as he might, all day long he couldn't quell his annoyance about Nico's arrival at the house that morning. The potential for things going wrong unnerved him. Knocking back a mouthful of the potent Jerez brandy, he watched Elaine wander into the drawing room. She was becoming more of a thorn in his side every day.

Elaine frowned at him. "That girl you brought in, Katrina, started asking questions this morning after that scene with Nicolas. The sooner we get her out of here with the collection, the better. Less chance to get suspicious."

"All she has to do is make a list of what's up there, for Christ's sake, Elaine. What can possibly make her suspicious?"

She gave a noncommittal shrug and plucked at the necklace she wore. "I just don't want to take any risks. She says she should be done and ready to e-mail the inventory to London by the day after tomorrow. I arranged to have her food sent up there again today. She seemed happy with that. I told her I would be visiting with Jorge this afternoon."

Sergio nodded reluctantly, even though he thought the reference to visiting Jorge was a nice touch. "*Sí*, we do want this done quickly, and I am in no mood for pleasantries over dinner."

"Bad day at the office?"

She was attempting to be sympathetic, but she barely needed to ask. The days would not be good until he had more free cash, lots of it.

"Nicolas has been on my mind since this morning. My day went from bad to worse when I got to the office. We're closing several of the stores as an immediate precaution. We selected the places where renewals on the leases are due."

Elaine reached out and rested one hand on his shoulder, but he did not want her comfort. He was nurturing his discontent. Right now, he wanted to tackle his mood by playing with someone, or something, to help reaffirm his sense of power. He'd been anticipating a tryst with Katrina since yesterday. He'd missed her going back to her room the night before, and Vincent had turned up with a grievance. Then, when he'd held her in his arms again that morning, his lust had been stirred again. He'd sensed his brother's envy, and that alone had made him want to put his mark firmly on the pretty Englishwoman.

He took another swallow of brandy, savoring it in his mouth. He would visit her later tonight, after she had finished in the gallery. He would gloat at the memory of his brother's face while he experienced some more of her eagerness firsthand. He would possess her completely.

"Let's eat," he said to Elaine.

She looked relieved. "Yes, let's."

Would she be as content if she knew what he had in mind for later? No, she was jealous when anyone else got attention; he could tell that when he'd handled the Englishwoman in front of her. He smiled to himself as they walked to the dining room. Here in this house he was omnipotent, and he needed that in order to deal with the problems he had elsewhere.

*By ten o'clock that night, Katrina was deeply puzzled, and her* mind was working overtime on the mysteries that had presented themselves over the course of the day.

On a personal level, she was wondering whether she'd see Nicolas again, and if so, when. After his comments the previous night and the subsequent connection he'd made with her that morning during his row with Sergio, she felt sure he would appear again, no matter what trouble it caused. Even though she had doubts about her sanity, her body responded, anticipation growing inside her. The risk element both excited and unnerved her. Waves of self-doubt washed over her occasionally, doubt about what she was doing. Was that what made her feel slightly giddy, slightly crazy?

That personal mystery was a stimulating one. On a much

more worrying level, she'd been puzzling over the collection inventory for the best part of the day. She'd had to start a separate spreadsheet just to list the items that weren't in the place they were supposed to be. There were now eight missing pieces, none of which she'd seen elsewhere in the house—and she'd looked—and all of them were valuable. The collection boasted five works by Degas: a small painting and four sketches. The painting and two of the sketches were missing, along with a work by Edvard Munch, three Egon Schieles, and an unfinished Klimt. It was as if someone had rifled through the collection and taken the most valuable pieces before she had even got there.

At first she'd just made a note on her main spreadsheet, but when the number of notes kept growing and none of them turned up as she went through the storage areas, it became obvious she was going to have to take the list to Sergio.

Potentially, he might not even know the pieces were missing. She wouldn't have, if she weren't working with the ledgers. It was the late Señorita Teodoro's ledgers that had highlighted the discrepancy; otherwise Katrina would have just listed what was there and been none the wiser. They'd all come back from their latest exhibition appearance and then . . . vanished.

Sergio hadn't mentioned any thefts to her, nor had Elaine. One of the staff may have stolen the items, or a visitor to the house, or even a thief who'd targeted the place and escaped without discovery. The security system was far from invincible, as proved by Nicolas. Had he taken the art? If he had taken it, why come back? To take more? That didn't seem to be what he was doing when he was here though, did it? she thought with a secret smile.

If the house had been in a more populated metropolitan area, it would need a whole lot more security than what was in place here. Whoever had taken these items—and she'd already considered that might include Sergio himself or Elaine, as well as Nicolas—she had to broach it with Sergio, however awkward and potentially flammable the subject might be.

She was also concerned that Sergio hadn't got back to her about the ownership release documents. Were they with his solicitor, or had Elaine taken them with her on her visit to her husband that afternoon? That was likely the case, but Katrina had to chase it down, and soon. Pocklington was waiting for her to say she had the signed papers in hand so that he could announce the forthcoming sale in the press.

Not only that, but the missing items weren't the only things puzzling her about the collection. There was a group of paintings stored in a cupboard that she had located by chance, when searching for the missing paintings listed in the ledgers. These paintings were not originals. She counted eleven, all of them copies of items from the collection, and reasonably good ones at that. They wouldn't fool an expert, but most people would be proud to have them in their homes.

Pushing back her chair, she thought it through. She estimated that she had a full day's work left to do, at least, and that would be spent on the supporting documentation, letters, and provenance. Most of the documents originated in France. The rest would have to be tagged for inspection on arrival at the auction house. Meanwhile, she'd been through every item in the collection. She was doing well with the job. However, she had a number of missing valuable items and several copies of items from the collection. It suggested criminal behavior, whichever way you looked at it.

She didn't have access to a printer, so she scribbled a list of the missing items onto her notepad with the intention of drawing it to Sergio's attention the following day. She'd successfully avoided him since this morning—which was a relief—but tomorrow she'd have to steel herself to talk to him again.

What if the missing paintings were hidden in the same place that the copies were? The question nagged at her. She went back to the cupboard. Examining them closely, she looked for signs that there was something older under the new paintwork, of which there were none. She also checked the cupboard out for a secret panel, because she'd heard that collectors sometimes hid their most valuable pieces behind copies.

All of these tales were things that she'd heard about but not experienced herself. Shaking her head, she realized she was checking for obvious signs of deception. Here in this house full of secrets and ghosts, it seemed that another level of mystery prevailed. It was here in the gallery that she felt most relaxed. There was a bathroom up here, and Raimunda brought her trays of tempting food: tortillas for lunch, and a delicious risotto in the evening accompanied by a half carafe of wine.

It was when she was considering any other possible hidey-holes she should investigate, that she heard a sound, like a small ping. Tensing, she listened. It sounded like tapping on glass. Her first reaction was that she must have imagined it. It was far too high up for someone to be tapping at the window.

*Nicolas?*

A moment later the sound repeated. Yes, after his performance the night before, she wouldn't put it past him to try to scale the tower. Her heart beat a little faster, and she held her breath, alert in every sense. When the sound happened a third time, she leapt to her feet and darted across the room. In the tower opposite, a couple of lights were on, showing through closed blinds. The moon barely struggled through the clouds and the grounds below were so dense with foliage that when she looked, all she could make out at first was inky darkness.

Tentatively, she opened the window and glanced down. She struggled to see anything, but as her eyes became accustomed to the gloom, she saw a figure moving below. Moonlight brushed the side his body, making him seem ethereal and ghostlike. A hand lifted. Anticipation rippled through her, and she returned the wave. When she did, the figure moved quickly to the wall beneath her. For a moment he disappeared from view, and she realized he was climbing onto the ground-level window ledge below, where a storage room below this floor housed cleaning equipment.

Leaning out of the window, she felt like Juliet looking for her Romeo. That tale had ended badly, and the mental connection made her shiver. She knew this was wrong. She was supposed to be working for her hosts, her clients, the people who had commissioned her on behalf of Pocklington's to undertake this job. Instead she was colluding with the disinherited son, a man she had been warned about, a man who was lurking around the building like a thief in the night.

*What the hell am I thinking of?*

Then she remembered the way Nicolas had looked that

morning when he had connected with her, and she felt torn. He had his motives. She was attracted to the man, but was he just using her? It *did* matter to her. Over the course of the day while she'd been anticipating seeing him again, she'd thought it didn't matter, but deep down it did. When you are attracted to someone, you want them to be attracted to you for the right reasons, the same reasons. Either way, he was on his way up here, scaling the wall by moving up the jutting plinths and ledges, and he was about to climb into the gallery.

*I'll confront him before he touches me. Yes, find out what he really wants from me.*

Stepping back, she watched as he came through the window, awed at the easy way he moved, every limber flex suggesting fitness and vitality. He grinned at her as he landed on the floor and then straightened up.

Oh, but he was gorgeous.

"You can't use the door like a normal person?" she said, a soft laugh escaping her.

"I have the security code, but every time it's used, it is logged by the system. I don't want to use it at night unless absolutely necessary."

She recalled Elaine hitting a panel to one side of the front door as they left the house that morning. Presumably the doors could only be opened from the outside if you had the code.

He closed the window behind him and glanced around.

She noticed there a fondness in his eyes as he looked across at the collection on display. That struck her oddly. Did he want it? Was that what this was all about and, if so, had he taken the missing pieces?

"The dining room window was open last night," he added.

For the first time, she noticed that he spoke simply, as if he was still learning English and sometimes had to reach to find the appropriate word. Sergio was fluent. Then she noticed something new, a scar, a thin red line on his cheekbone. "What happened to your face?"

"The argument continued after you had gone." He shrugged it off. "It is nothing."

Nothing? They were fighting verbally and physically. God, she was fool to let him in. "You shouldn't have risked coming here again."

"I had to come." He eyed her up and down, slowly and deliberately.

The weight of his stare made her feel weak. How was it that he affected her so easily? Did he represent desire, or rebellion? *Or do I understand just enough about psychology to cripple myself with it?*

She backed away.

His smile faded.

"What is it that you want from me?" she demanded.

His eyelids dropped, and he stepped away from her, moving between the cabinets, looking in at the contents. "Please don't be afraid; that is not my intention."

Slowly, she turned on the spot, keeping her eyes on him, watching him as he moved through the gallery space.

He paused, ran one finger along the top of a glass display case, and then glanced back at her. "Last night, you said you wanted me."

Swallowing, she forced herself to lift her chin, to face him.

"I did . . . But I'm working for Sergio. I shouldn't even be talking to you."

A slow smile passed over his face, and he returned his attention to the cabinet.

Was this leading her into big trouble? "I hardly know you," she whispered, "and I don't understand what is happening here."

"You don't understand the desire?" He flashed her a teasing glance as he continued his circuit of the gallery.

Oh, God, the look in his eyes right then made her melt. "That part I understand completely." She folded her arms, attempting to give herself a backbone. Apparently one look at him had made it melt away into nothing. "I mean . . . I'm not sure about everything else."

"I understand that." He leaned his head to one side to observe a set of small plaster figurines, early models of the larger ones that stood on pedestals, before he continued.

"Katrina, when I originally made contact with you, it was to talk about all of this, not risk my neck for the sake of another kiss." He gestured around the gallery with one hand. His mouth lifted on one side. Then he moved on, strolling in and out of the cabinets. "I needed to know what my brother was doing with the family collection, and I . . ." He glanced around the gallery. "I wanted to see the collection one last time."

He looked back at her. "But now that I am here, I find it is you that I want to see, more than any of it."

Her pulse raced, anticipation crackling in the air between them.

"I think perhaps it was the lure of *un amante* that has

brought me here, as much as the art." Brooding, hungry eyes fixed her on the spot.

"*Amante?*"

"Lover."

A delicious shiver ran up her spine. Oh, how that made her want him, and how hard it made it do anything other than respond in kind, her body craving his.

He was closer now, having circuited the display cases, a mere four paces away. Her pulse raced, her body hot and alert with anticipation. Her resistance was melting, but unease still wrestled with the desire increasing inside her. "I'm concerned. Sergio was acting crazy this morning. You've been injured. This doesn't feel right. It's dangerous. Wrong."

"I had to come, to see you." His voice, deep and suggestive, claimed her. "I've been thinking about you all day. This morning . . . I wanted to take you out of here myself."

*Take me away, away from the job, so that Sergio can't sell the art?*

And then his hands on her body took away every last shred of rational thought, any ability to question his motives.

He cupped her cheek in one warm hand and kissed her, brushing his lips over hers and barely making contact. The gentle caress was powerfully seductive, nonetheless. "I want you," he whispered against her mouth.

The possessive edge to his words brought about a rush of heat, a liquid density inside her that had responded to his secret and forbidden presence.

Her head dropped back, and she stared into his eyes. Their

bodies were touching, and she swayed under his spell. Her lips parted, yearning for more; her legs felt weak.

His hand was grasping her around the waist, squeezing her closer, so that she could feel how hard he was. "This desire between us, you want to know more of it, don't you, just as I do?"

There was still time to end this, to do the right thing, the professional thing. This was her telling moment.

*Yes, or no?*

She ached for him, an undeniable sense of wanting that he had stirred in her, a nagging need that had to be fulfilled. Her heart raced, her blood on fire for him. There was no turning back, not now. At her core, her body silently throbbed its response.

*Yes, oh yes!*

Swallowing, she managed to get the words out. "Yes, I want to know more of it."

His eyes glittered with certainty, with a rich, seductive power that took her breath away.

His fingers twisted around one of the buttons on her shirt. "This thing between us is all that matters right now, *sí*?"

He drew her chin to face him with firm fingers, waiting for her answer.

Her lips opened, a gentle pant escaping her. He was so close, so real and strong and so very determined. "*Sí*," she responded as his mouth descended to hers, capturing the word between them.

His tongue probed deep into her mouth, and it was a hungry, possessive kiss, one that suggested the sex act in its very thrust, claiming her. The pulse in her core pounded out a relentless rhythm. She responded with longing that equaled his, her hands moving over his shoulders, sliding around his neck and into his thick hair. Whimpering inside, she welcomed his thrust, running her tongue along the underside of his.

Lifting her easily into his arms, he carried her across the gallery, through the statues and the glass display cases, toward the chaise longue.

He stood her by the side of it and undid the buttons on her shirt while he kissed her, hard and long. When he drew back, he pushed her shirt off, stroking his hands over her shoulders and breasts when they were exposed to him. Wild threads of sensation flew out from where he touched her. He unlatched her bra, dropping it to the floor. She stared at him as he caressed her nipples, and he watched her as her lips parted with pleasure.

"I had to come back. I realized that last night." He paused. "For more of you, for another taste."

Her body trembled, a flush rising to her face and the roots of her hair.

He began to stroke his hands around her waist, taking charge, undoing her fly and easing her jeans down over her hips. She stepped out of them and her panties and sat down on the chaise longue. He knelt at her feet, leaning into her. His tongue went to her nipples. Needles of sensation coursed through her. The pulse in her clit pounded, her head falling back as she gave a low moan.

"Dear God, Nicolas, what are you doing to me?"

He gave her a dark smile. "Everything that I wanted to do last night and all of today."

He put his hands beneath her knees and moved her legs onto the chaise, handling her gently but firmly. The velvet felt delicious against her naked skin, and she reclined against it and watched as he pulled off his T-shirt, dropping it onto the floor. His chest, bared to her eyes for the first time, was perfectly formed. Strong but leanly muscled, his body rippling like that of a dancer.

Dark hair covered his chest and ran down to his waist and beyond in a thin, dark line. His hand went to his belt, and she watched longingly as he popped each button on his fly, the sound of each one opening making her hotter, wetter, and more needy. His cock bounced free, hard and long.

Squeezing her thighs together and rolling her hips, her body anticipated the feeling of it thrusting inside, and she moaned aloud, the back of her hands against her mouth as she did so.

He stroked his erection with one hand and with the other reached into his pocket and pulled out a condom. All the while, he looked at her with lust-filled eyes.

She was mesmerized by the look of him, so proudly sexual and determined. Again, her sex contracted with need when he rolled the condom onto his thick, long erection. Climbing over her, he gently stroked her open, teasing her clit until she moaned before venturing down and moving his fingers into the slippery heat of her entrance.

Gripping his shoulders, her sex clenched onto the hard intrusion of his fingers inside her. "Oh please, Nicolas, I want you."

His eyes flashed darkly, his smile a promise of what was to come, and then he climbed over her, and his long, hard thighs were pressed against the insides of hers. Hot juices spilled onto him when he eased the crown of his cock inside her. She was more than ready for this and gasped as he entered her fully, panting with need.

He lifted her legs higher against his hips, angling their bodies, and thrust deeper, giving her his full length. When he lifted up onto his arms and pulled out slowly, so slowly, her hips arched. Her sex contracted wildly, embracing the length of him when he moved back in. He nodded at her, each thrust he made slow and deliberate, so maddeningly slow, but so filled with purpose. All the time his gaze never left hers; he captured her attention in every way.

"It feels so . . . intense," she cried.

"*Sí*, you feel so good, I want to come badly; the way your body holds me is making it hard not to."

Oh, how those words made her melt, and yet so easily it seemed he controlled the speed of those thrusts, his hips moving, grinding as he drove into her again. Each thrust bordered on too much, and yet each thrust unleashed a secret part of her. She turned into a creature: a creature made only of carnal responses, a creature captured by him in every way. He groaned in response when her body clutched his.

She gasped for breath, pleasure suffusing her entire body. Her neck arched. She trembled, and her first wave of release rolled over her.

"Oh, Nicolas . . ." Clinging to him, she ground her hips against his as her body spilt, her emotions soaring when hot liquid pleasure poured through her, her entire skin tingling and hot.

He flashed her a look of admiration, stroking her cheek, still moving inside her, faster now. She turned her face into his hand, kissing his palm. She saw his eyes flicker shut for a moment before he focused on her again, gazing into her eyes as his body grew tense with imminent climax, the muscles in his neck cording, those in his biceps gleaming in the gallery lights.

The connection she felt in that moment was almost too much to stand. He thrust hard, and then his thumb made contact with her clit. Wedged deep, his cock throbbing, the touch of his thumb flicked her into overdrive as easily as hitting a switch.

"Oh, oh, oh," she panted.

Her groin was on fire, and she half sat, her hands moving to his upper arms as she ground her hips against him, her second orgasm building fast. She rocked forward when it hit, melting into him in every way.

He blurted something in Spanish, his hands holding her hips in place and his cock rock-hard and jerking as he came.

## 11

*Nico was holding Katrina in his arms, still in the throes of* climax and wanting to make it last longer, when a heavy sense of guilt stole over him. It was as if a black cloud had been hovering nearby, threatening to ruin the moment, and now it was rolling in. He had come here for this, with the sole purpose of seducing her, and he had succeeded. The opportunity to pick up where they had left off the night before was the perfect way to reach her, and despite her resistance, she had wanted this, too. But his intention had also been to sweet-talk her, afterward. Now, however, his conscience was forcing a restless, uneasy sense of guilt onto him, a burden it would be hard to shrug off.

"You feel so good," he said, closing his eyes and nuzzling her neck beneath her ear, closing out what had to come next for as long as possible.

Stroking his head, she let out a soft and bubbly chuckle,

one that was filled with pleasure. As she did, her body tightened on his cock once again, and he shuddered, sensitive from release.

"Be careful; I'm a vulnerable man." Even though he grinned, he sensed an ironic truth in this statement. The look of her when they had made love filled him with pride. From the feeling of her clutching at him to the scratch of her nails on his shoulders when she came, it made him want to bring that expression to her face over again. That was not good.

This woman worked for his brother, and that meant she was the enemy by association. He did this only to cause trouble for Sergio and to get the truth. And yet he stayed between her thighs, lingering there in her exquisite, slippery hot spot, his body unwilling to disconnect from hers, even while he grew limp inside her.

"I'll try to be more gentle, but you seem to bring out the fierce side of me." Teasing, she drew her nails over his shoulders, causing him to tense and growl.

She gave a throaty laugh.

"You look even more beautiful now, now that I have made you come."

Pressing back into the cushions, she gave him a mock assessing stare. Her fine, pale hair spilled across the velvet like moonlight. A pleasure-filled smile teased at her mouth as she looked up at him. "Taking all the credit, huh?"

"But of course." Unable to resist, he ran his fingers over her breasts again, so proudly peaked and lolling. The flush that was high on her cheekbones was echoed at the base of her neck, as if her orgasm had brushed over her skin, leaving a subtle painted kiss here and there. Touching her, stroking her, he became mesmerized by her sweet softness and the warmth in her eyes.

This felt too good, too comfortable.

*Disengage, idiot. Remember what you're here to talk about.*

"What did you say," she whispered, her eyelids lowering, "at the moment you came? You said something in Spanish."

He'd said too much in the heat of the moment, something about not wanting it to end. Drawing away from her, he forced a laugh, trying to keep the mood level. "Did I say something?"

He got to his feet and reached for his clothes, removing the evidence of their lovemaking. He did up his fly, pushed his feet into his shoes, then grabbed his T-shirt and pulled it over his head. She took his cue and sat up, running her hands through her hair. He passed her her clothes.

She looked slightly adrift as she accepted them from his hand, and that unsettled him. "I guess I make a lot of noise when the sex is so good," he added, and then ducked down to give her upturned face a kiss on the nose.

Smiling, she nodded and began to dress, but she seemed slightly withdrawn. He resisted taking her into his arms, which is what he wanted to do, but he couldn't help watching, noticing her fluid, graceful movements. She looked as if she were one of the statues come to life to dance in the night, the moonlight captured in her hair.

Once she was dressed, she plumped the cushions and straightened the tassles on the old gallery sofa. So like a woman.

Then her head snapped around, and she stared at the office

doorway, her eyes widening. Her glance darted back to him. "Did you hear that?"

He shook his head but sharpened his attention.

She reached for his arm and clutched it with both hands. "Someone's coming up the stairs. You must hide."

Before he could answer, he heard someone call out, "Katrina," in the distance, in a singsong voice. Sergio.

"You must hide, quickly, behind the base units of the display cases, I'll head him off."

Her reaction interested Nico. Was it her honor or her professional status that she wished to protect?

She leaned into him, whispering. "It's Sergio; if he finds you here, he'll kill you." Her eyes grew wide, her gaze darting from the door back to him. "I avoided him all day; he must want to ask me about my progress."

Nico hated to see that frown on her face, and she seemed so concerned about him. "I'll speak to him."

Her eyes rounded. "You'll do *what*?"

"I'll speak to him. I'll say I came to talk to you about the collection. It is the truth."

"No, don't do this," she begged, looking at him with horror.

"I don't want to hide from him. I want this over." A gnawing longing to break this situation apart had him in its grip. He was ready for it. Now Sergio would know he meant business. He flashed her a reassuring grin. "Katrina, my father said I could come back here anytime I wanted."

"He did?" She looked amazed.

What had Sergio told her that made her look that way?

"Katrina, are you still in here?" Sergio's voice called out again, and this time he was closer, maybe even in the office.

Katrina shook her head. "Don't do it; he'll use it against you."

"Maybe; he's threatened a police injunction before."

"Please, please, Nicolas. Stay out of it. Do it for me." She was pulling him in the direction of the glass display cabinets.

He could see her apprehension. She was truly afraid, and that made him feel torn. He wanted to derail Sergio's plans, but he didn't want to hurt Katrina, and that would surely happen. Inwardly cursing himself, he knew he'd got himself into this difficult situation by using her as a means to thwart Sergio.

"Okay, I will stay out of his way, for now. Your honor will be safe." Reluctantly, he moved behind the cabinets, dropping to a squat so that he was hidden behind the solid bases.

She rolled her eyes at him and then faced the door, squaring her shoulders, pushing back her hair.

He liked the way she looked in that moment; there was fire in her, another side of the powerful female magic he had seen made real just minutes before. At the same time he could see this boldness was new to her; she was feeling her way in this situation.

The sound of her footsteps moving quickly across the gallery floor made him instantly tense, and he turned so that he could look out across the space between the cabinets. She'd made it almost to the door when Sergio appeared there, blocking her way.

"Ah, here you are." Sergio nonchalantly leaned against the doorframe. He had a bottle of wine in one hand, two glasses in the other. Apparently Sergio wanted to party.

He'd already been drinking; Nico recognized the signs. His shirt was hanging loose, and his hair was messy. He lost his cool so easily, Nico thought with a certain satisfaction.

"Sergio. You surprised me. I was just checking a detail on something." She gestured vaguely behind her and then moved to block Sergio's view into the gallery. "Let's go into the office. I can show you the spreadsheet, and you can see how far I've got with the job."

Sergio didn't budge.

She was doing her best to get him out of there, and Nico craned his neck, peering around the corner of the cabinet so he could watch for Sergio's reaction. Sergio shifted, but instead of turning away and going back into the office as Katrina had suggested, he backed her into the gallery.

Something about his attitude riled Nico. The two wine-glasses, the look in his eyes, the late hour. Nico cursed under his breath, looking possessively at the woman he had just made love to.

Sergio put the bottle and glasses down on a table inside the gallery and reached for Katrina, clumsily pulling her against him. "Katrina, you're working too late. I think you should go to bed now."

"I have so much to do," Katrina responded, trying to move out of his grip.

Anger flared in Nico. There was no way he could stay there, not now.

"I am your client," Sergio declared. "You are working for me, and I insist. No more work tonight. Play now." His hands went to her bottom, which he grasped.

Nico leapt up, rounded the cabinet, and crossed the gallery at a pace. "Leave her alone."

"What the fuck are you doing here?" His smug expression disappeared, quickly replaced by disbelief and anger.

"Visiting the gallery." Nico gave a slow grin, knowing how much that would annoy his older brother.

Katrina had taken the opportunity to move away, but she shot him a look that told him how much she disapproved of his action.

"Visiting the gallery," Sergio repeated with a sarcastic tone, grimacing.

"No, really," Katrina said. "He said he wanted to look at the collection one last time."

"And you believed him, this . . . loser?"

Folding her arms across her chest, she glanced between the two of them, looking as if she was judging them against one another.

"My brother has no right to be here!" Sergio bellowed. Displeasure and barely restrained violence echoed in his posture. His eyes flashed with malevolence, and the attempt at a smile he gave Katrina was painfully forced.

Nico was about to respond, but Katrina beat him to it. "Look, Sergio, your brother indicated he had concerns about the way the collection is being dealt with. It is often the way with families, and the sale of goods. I have assured him everything is being done properly."

Her response sounded professional and distant, but Nico wasn't sure he liked what she said. Granted, she was trying to make this situation simple, but he also had to wonder whether he would have any impact on her professional desire for the sale, despite the level of intimacy they had enjoyed.

Sergio gave a tight smile, but Nico could see he was grinding his teeth, a habit that always revealed he was close to cracking. "Step outside," he said, narrowing his eyes at Nico. "We have private matters to discuss."

Although he was speaking in English for Katrina's benefit, he obviously wanted to discuss the matter away from her.

Nico lifted his eyebrows, eager to bait him some more. "Are you afraid Señorita Hammond will hear something she is not supposed to?"

"Not at all."

Katrina looked tense.

"I bet it was Raimunda who told you about our guest," Sergio said. "I really must fire her now that Father is no longer here."

"Leave Raimunda out of this."

"Ha! If you came here expecting to charm my guest into believing your bullshit," Sergio continued, "you have a lot to learn, brother of mine. Katrina responds to a much more sophisticated approach than you could ever manage."

"Sophisticated?" Nico gave a dry laugh. He knew how Sergio treated women. His brand of sophistication was a veneer, at best. "She'll see you for what you are soon enough. Let her make up her own mind what sort of man you are."

"Katrina already has, haven't you?" Sergio smiled at her and put his arm around her possessively, his eyes filled with self-assured power.

Nico couldn't think straight. Was Sergio suggesting intimacy between him and Katrina, something that had led to him arriving here with the wine and two glasses? The idea of it made something twist inside of him. Nico looked at her, assessing the troubled expression he found in her eyes. Yes, there was something there, a reaction to what Sergio had said. A reaction that wasn't denial. It made him experience an unfamiliar emotion: jealousy.

He'd been on the receiving end of that from Sergio, as a child. He thought he'd left it all behind when his mother had died and he left his father and Sergio to each other. But now a woman had resurrected it between them. This time he was the one who was experiencing it, and he didn't like the way it made him feel.

Was Sergio bluffing about the two of them? Nico hoped so, but he feared otherwise.

Katrina shifted uncomfortably. "Sergio, I was brought here as a professional auctioneer. I do not wish to be dragged into this feud between you and your brother. It is between you to decide if this auction goes ahead or not. In the meantime, I have to assume it will. I have a job to do, and I would appreciate it if both of you just left me alone to get on with it."

She was drawing a line; she was strong. He noticed that his brother's reaction to her statement was not positive. He wouldn't like being told what to do by an employee.

Sergio ignored her and gestured at the door. "If you ever set foot inside this house again, I'll make sure you get a police record, and where would that leave you with your precious career?"

Nico resisted the urge to punch him. "That is low, but coming from you I am not surprised."

Katrina's frown deepened as she looked at Sergio. Had the threat disturbed her? Whatever it was, she looked suspicious. Maybe there was hope for him after all. When she looked back at him, he saw that she was unsure.

"You've seen the collection; maybe it would be best if you left." She didn't make eye contact with him as she spoke.

She didn't know who to trust. And who could blame her? Even so, it made him want to snatch her into his arms and carry her out of there, flattening Sergio as he did so. She was falling victim to Sergio's manipulation. Nico barely knew the woman, but in his soul he believed that she didn't deserve it.

As her eyes lifted to meet his, there was a wounded look there. Regret, too. He didn't regret it, what had happened between them, and he was angry that she did.

"There's nothing here for you," she said, her stare deliberate.

Sergio bared his teeth. "See, she knows."

Nico glared at him and then looked at Katrina. "This is not over yet."

*Katrina was smarting. Thoroughly dazed by what had happened,* she felt Nico's departure like a deep emotional tug, even so. He hadn't wanted to hide after all; he wanted to annoy Sergio. That's why he was doing this. How was it that she let herself get so entangled in this?

The sound of his footsteps had barely faded away down the stairs when Sergio turned back to her, his expression dark and uncontrolled. "What the hell did he say to you?"

"He didn't say much of anything. I already told you he came to see the art."

Sergio's eyes narrowed. Not good enough; she had to feed him more info before he would believe her. "He hadn't been here long. He told me he wanted to take one last look at the collection, and he was having a wander around. He mentioned he was concerned about the sale, but I assured him it was being handled properly."

"Why didn't you say he was here when I came in?"

"Because you warned me that he was trouble, and I realized that I shouldn't have let him look at the collection." She prayed that he would believe that. In part it was true, although that wasn't her entire motivation.

Sergio stepped over to where he'd left the wine on the table and snatched up the bottle, pouring out a glass. The wine sloshed across the table, pooling on the polished wood. He gulped the wine quickly, wiping his mouth with the back of his hand as he put the glass down. He looked as if he'd had way too much already, and she had a bad feeling.

"How the hell did he get in here? Did you let him in?"

Her stomach rolled. "He climbed in an open window." Please let him believe it, she prayed silently, discomfort ratcheting up inside her as Sergio stepped closer, eyeballing her in the most disconcerting way.

"I'm glad that you remembered I warned you he was trouble. I insist you take that more seriously from now on. We are both aware that this collection will give you a nice juicy commission. You wouldn't want me to take that business elsewhere, would you?"

"Of course not," she replied, trying to keep her voice level and friendly.

"I had faith in you, Katrina. This has been disappointing for me. I hope I don't have to go to your boss."

Another threat. What a nice guy. He had threatened his brother just a couple of minutes earlier, but somehow he looked even meaner now. With Nicolas it had been vindictive. This was all about control. Just a big, selfish kid not wanting to share the toys.

But she didn't want to lose the job, no way. She could just imagine Henry gloating at her if she did. "I made a big mistake tonight; I see that now. Sergio, please forgive me. I won't let it happen again."

*Swallow it,* she prayed silently.

He stared at her, making her restless.

"I'm a professional," she added, "I want to do the job quickly and well, distribute the art, get a good commission, and shake hands with a satisfied client." She meant it. Steeling herself inside, she knew she had to get tough because she couldn't afford to mess this job up.

Sergio's expression relaxed a tad, and he reached again for the wine bottle, only this time he poured it out into both glasses.

A feeling of dread rose inside her. Earlier, it was obvious he'd come up here for some late-night entertainment. Surely he wasn't going to pursue that now. He passed her a glass, and she clutched it tightly, forcing a smile as she thanked him.

He raised his glass to his lips, looking at her lasciviously over the edge of it as he did so.

She was just wondering if she should down the wine or make a break for the door, when a high-pitched wailing sound filled the tower.

"Fuckin' bastard," Sergio declared, angrily. "He's set the alarm off on the way out. He's done this on purpose." He slammed the glass down on the table, glancing back at her regretfully. "I have to go, the police will be on their way up here."

"Saved by the bell," Katrina whispered under her breath with a huge sigh of relief as he disappeared out of view. She put her glass down and managed to count to ten before she hurried around the gallery and office, turning out the lights.

If he had to deal with the police, she was going to take this opportunity to close up shop and go to bed, door locked and all. She'd messed up big time, but she believed she'd hung on to the commission by the skin of her teeth.

# 12

*Katrina's mood the following morning was grim, and wistful,* too, no matter how determined she was. She'd slept badly, and when she eventually did fall asleep, it was with the vow not to be distracted from the job she was there to do. If she focused on that, it might mean the other things didn't come rushing in on her, causing her grief. In the more rational morning light, that seemed like a ludicrously far-fetched goal, given the people that she was dealing with, although she was going to do her best to get the job done properly, despite their interference.

Nicolas's statement that it was not over yet echoed through her mind. What did he mean? Was his comment only aimed at Sergio? Or was he referring to their relationship as well? Nicolas had made her feel so alive and so pleasured. She craved more of that, not less. But she couldn't even begin to entertain the possibility that she would see him again. If he had just been using her to get at Sergio, what use would he have for her now? She'd made it clear she meant to complete the job.

It closed him out, and he'd been annoyed about that; it was written all over his face as he'd left. And Sergio's attitude made a shudder run down her spine. It wasn't over yet between the two brothers; Nicolas was right. They had to sort it out between themselves. What she had to do was get her job done and get out.

She showered, dressed, and went down to breakfast. As she descended the stairs, she sensed a brooding, tense atmosphere in the house. Thankfully all was quiet, so she went to the dining room and helped herself to cereal from the selection on the sideboard.

Raimunda appeared and, surprisingly enough, graciously offered Katrina fresh-brewed coffee. A few minutes later, she returned with an omelet that made Katrina's mouth water just looking at it and freshly toasted bread. Katrina wasn't sure what to make of Raimunda's less surly, almost courteous behavior.

"*Gracias, Raimunda.*" She smiled and nodded. Raimunda nodded back and headed off with purpose. Was she going to report to Nicolas, like Sergio had suggested? *Maybe.*

That thought made her smile, even though she knew it probably shouldn't. She ate the delicious omelet, drank her coffee quickly, and prayed that Elaine wouldn't appear. The last thing she wanted to do was make polite chitchat with her. When no one came to join her, she left, stopping briefly at her room to pick up her phone, then made her way across the landing to the west wing and into the tower.

The office and gallery felt much more tranquil, and she breathed easy. Something about the place made her feel at home: its order; its solid, cared-for feeling. Perhaps it was because here she followed her usual routine, and from that came familiarity, or perhaps it was because she felt closer to the first Señora Teodoro, who Katrina sensed might have been the most normal member of the family.

She rolled the top up on the desk, reaching in to lift out some of the old ink pens as she did. They were lovely items, but the bottle of ink that stood there had all but evaporated. As she put the pens back, she noticed something behind the pen pot that caught her attention. Moving it aside, she reached in and pulled out the old photograph that was stashed there.

It showed a family, a mother and father and two little boys. She recognized the boys immediately, even though they were grown men now. Her attention went straight to the youngest, Nicolas. She stared at him for a long time, smiling wistfully as she recognized the features of the man there in the face of the gangly boy. Looking from one to the other of the four, she was eager to familiarize herself with the parents who were so much in this house in spirit, and yet who she would never meet.

Jorge looked as if he was already in his early forties in the photo, his hair thinning, and laughter lines on his face as he smiled for the camera. She saw a reflection of Sergio and Nicolas there in their father's face. He had one arm around the shoulders of the woman who stood beside him. She looked pretty and unassuming, a happy young woman. She had one hand on the shoulders of each of the young boys who stood in front of them. There was pride in her pose. Presumably Señora Teodoro had this photo on display on the desk when she worked here, and someone else had put it away. Katrina felt as if she were finally getting to know this unusual family. She was being given odd glimpses into their history as well as their current situation.

Sergio was groomed and wore a smart school uniform. Nicolas, on the other hand, was wearing a T-shirt and shorts, his hair longer and uncombed. He was younger, though, perhaps aged about seven or eight in the photograph. He looked like a gypsy boy in comparison to Sergio. Even then, there was a devil-may-care charm about his smile. *El diablo*, the roving gypsy who scaled the building and seduced her in the night. The thought gave her an inner rush, and she propped the photo up at the back of the desk where she could see it, before she opened up her laptop and booted it up.

Raimunda had put fresh flowers in the vase on the windowsill, and she inhaled the late summer scent while she connected up her phone to download her e-mail. She was grateful to see Lucy had sent through a reply from Pocklington. She'd been beginning to wonder if being out of sight meant she was out of mind as well. He would have been busy on the floor in the auction house the day before, but even so, the communication was a relief. She barely felt attached to the office in England, with all that had gone on in the short time she'd been here. The message was brief, but it helped ground her, nonetheless.

*Give the collection the time it deserves to catalog it properly. Yes, go ahead and use the owner's ledgers, but cross-reference everything to make sure nothing is*

*missing or has been added. Gather each item's*
*provenance on a separate spreadsheet and e-mail that to*
*me as soon as you can. Contact Lucy with a proposed*
*shipping date, and she can provisionally book that.*
*Don't forget the ownership release. Any questions, don't*
*hesitate to e-mail Lucy, and she'll pass it on.*
*Pocklington*

Nothing she hadn't already done, or aimed to do, which set her mind at rest. Today she intended to work on the provenance, the historic documentation stored in the filing cabinet. She sent him a quick reply, updating him on her progress, and attached the inventory to give him an overview of the collection so far, making sure she hadn't mentioned the missing items on that spreadsheet. She still needed to bring that subject up with Sergio, but it was irrelevant to the auction house unless the items actually turned up.

To close, she mentioned that she hoped to return to London by the end of the week. This was hard for her to do, because she didn't want to think about leaving, because leaving might mean never seeing Nicolas again. Not only did that possibility make her ache, it made her resent the collection for being the battleground between the two brothers, drawing her into the feud. If only . . . if only Nicolas had been a stranger who she had met in Barcelona at the festival. Resting her head in her hands, she sighed.

The sense of longing deep inside her was very specific. Yes, even though the quickie orgasm Sergio had given her in London had been a highly pleasurable experience, she wanted to be held, to be cherished by a lover. Nicolas Teodoro—now, that had been a seduction. She gave a wry smile. *Silly, foolish woman.*

Before she closed down her e-mail, she sent a quick message to Lucy suggesting a packing and shipping date be factored in two weeks from now. As soon as she had pressed Send, her phone rang. It was Lucy.

"Katrina, I got your mail. I was just about to call you."

"You were?"

"Yes, I just wanted to let you know the only dirt I managed to dig for you was about Elaine Teodoro, the second wife. She has quite the checkered history. Nothing overly dramatic, but her name sprang up in quite a few places, not all of them the socialite column, if you know what I mean. Oh, and she's been arrested twice. The first time it was to do with an unpaid hotel bill; the other was related to an item of jewelry she borrowed from an acquaintance but failed to return. Charges were dropped on both counts, but it makes you wonder, doesn't it?"

Katrina wasn't overly surprised. Elaine left her cold. There was something about the woman she really didn't like. But it wasn't her that she was concerned about. "That doesn't surprise me; I haven't taken to her. Was there anything about Sergio Teodoro?"

"Nothing unusual. He took over his father's company around ten years ago. That's all I could find out about him asking around and on the Net. It's as if he kept his head down."

Katrina didn't know what she'd been hoping for, but there was no real reason for her to mistrust Sergio, other than that he was a control freak. Her misgivings had to be because of her secret assignations with Nicolas. The fact that Sergio had come on to her the night before was pretty inevitable, after what had happened between them in London. But she'd drawn back since then, mostly because of Nicolas.

She was attracted to Nicolas, that was the truth of it, and she felt guilty when she was around Sergio. That's all it was. Had to be. As a result, she couldn't trust her own reactions. *And I can't trust Nicolas's motives for pursuing me. Great. Just great.*

It was then that it occurred to her that she could be trying to find out information about the wrong brother. "Hang on a moment, did you find out anything about another son along the way, a Nicolas Teodoro?"

"Yes, actually. There was mention of another son attending the mother's funeral. I didn't chase that one down . . . Would you like me to?"

What else was there to learn? That he wanted his father's art collection for himself? That was increasingly obvious. Morbid curiosity had her firmly in its grip, though. It was kind of inevitable, seeing as she'd been inexorably drawn to this mysterious man.

"Yes, just out of curiosity." It was a good job Lucy couldn't see her as she said her good-byes because Katrina was blushing. Disconnecting the phone, she put it on the window ledge, out of her way. She was about to turn back to the desk when something outside caught her eye.

Vincent, the houseguest, was walking determinedly across the lawns at the back of the house. Paco, the gardener, was standing by expectantly. What were they up to? She watched as they exchanged a few words, Vincent glancing around furtively as if he didn't want to be seen in discussion with the other man.

Her eyes opened even wider when Vincent turned back to his

companion and grabbed him around the back of the head, kissing him passionately. Transfixed, she watched as Paco ran his hands down Vincent's back, stroking his large palms over the man's buff upper musculature and down to his tapered waist.

The houseguest and the gardener were secret lovers. Had she inadvertently discovered another layer of secrets at the Torre Del Castagona?

A moment later Paco grasped Vincent's buttocks firmly and squeezed. Vincent staggered, and Paco moved against him, his body rubbing against the other man's. The pair of them looked so horny, Katrina could scarcely believe what she was seeing. She'd never seen two men kissing that way before, and it fascinated her. It was arousing, too. They were groping each other frantically while they talked, and then they moved out of her view.

Craning her neck, she leaned right across the window, her heel sliding from under her as she tried to see where they'd gone. Couldn't have been too far, judging by the urgency. Pulling her sandal back on, she realized she might get a better view from the gallery room next door. Biting her lip, she gave a nervous laugh.

She looked back at the laptop, then at the door to the gallery room. She couldn't resist. Darting through the other room, she hurried through the glass cases over to the window at the far end of the room. She approached cautiously and peeped out. Any notion of doing the honorable thing and not looking was gone when she caught sight of them again. They had gone a bit deeper into the trees, away from the entrance to the house and into a more concealed spot. Paco had his back against a tree, his zipper open, and his belt hanging down one leg. Vincent was on his knees in front of him, his mouth riding up and down on the gardener's erection. Vincent's hands were on Paco's buttocks, controlling them, lifting him away from the tree, pulling and pushing as he sucked the cock into his mouth. Paco's head was thrown back against the tree in ecstasy, his mouth open, and one hand clutching the tree for support, the other holding the base of his cock as if offering it to Vincent.

Katrina ran a hand under her hair and down the back of her neck. Her hairline felt damp. Right at that moment, the sprinklers came on, dousing the two men. Katrina's hand went to her mouth. What would they do? Vincent jerked back as if startled, but Paco laughed aloud, unperturbed. Playfully, he dropped to his knees and rolled Vincent across the ground directly into the sprinkler's path. She could actually see them better now, and glimpsed a smile on Vincent's face, the first she'd seen him give. They were both well built and attractive in their own way, and there was a joyous quality about the way they handled each other that entranced her.

Paco clambered over Vincent, squatting over Vincent's thighs, resting his knees either side of the older man. Paco looked like a sexy calendar pinup; his hair was stuck to his head, his T-shirt transparent on one side with the fallout from the sprinkler. An X-rated calendar—his pants were still open. Katrina couldn't help wishing she was closer and could get a better look.

Vincent went for it, grasping Paco's cock with one hand, while the other fumbled with his own belt. Paco assisted. His position straddling Vincent's thighs gave them perfect access to each other, and they were soon locked into each other, completely, a mutual hand job in full flow. The sight of them massaging each other's erections made Katrina squeeze her thighs together; her body was tingling with arousal. They were closing fast on orgasm; she could see it in Paco's face. Her hand went to her pussy, and she applied pressure through her skirt, her lower body pressed up against the wall beneath the window.

Paco's jaw went slack as he came. Vincent came moments after. He then dropped back onto the lawn for a minute, sprawling with his arms splayed as if catching his breath. Katrina stepped aside quickly, looking into the gallery.

Her gaze drifted through the sculptures to where the velvet chaise longue stood at the far end. Wandering toward it, she thought about the secret affair of the two men she'd seen in the garden and her own secret affair with Nicolas. A house of secrets, she had thought it, when she got here. How right she'd been.

Staring down at the velvet seat and its array of cushions, she pictured Nicolas making love to her there. Already heated from what she'd witnessed in the garden, she couldn't resist lying down, closing her eyes as she sank into the cushions and relived the memory.

Breathing in deeply, she could picture him standing over her, about to climb between her thighs. Had she ever known such a passionate, persuasive lover? No. She laughed ruefully, a sound that floated through the empty gallery as wistful as a wish that he was there with her now.

Her hands rested on her thighs, and she moved them higher, to her breasts. They were aching for contact, aching for his solid, naked chest against them. When he'd thrust inside her, he'd claimed her to the core. She couldn't imagine another lover living up to the effect he'd had on her. It would take her a long time to get over it, and she'd never forget.

Unable to resist, she slipped her hand beneath the waistband on her skirt and cupped her mons through her underwear, rocking her hips and clasping the aroused flesh tightly, squeezing her clit within it. *If only it were his hand on me.*

Pushing the lace fabric into the crease of her pussy, she rubbed it over her swollen clit, her breasts rising and falling fast as she remembered the pressure of his hard body there and his erection inside her. Rolling her head from side to side against the velvet cushion, she moved her hand under her panties, pursuing those forbidden moments of pleasure with Nicolas that were outside of her physical reach now. The memory of him was so vivid though; so fierce and inescapable, it brought the climax closer. As she silently celebrated the fact that she'd willingly stripped and mated with him in a gallery, surrounded by expensive, beautiful art objects, she trembled on the verge.

Now she was reliving it, bringing herself to orgasm in the very same place, a blatant sexual creature pursuing her fantasy. Reveling in it, she stroked herself faster, chasing it. The concept of doing such a thing would have been so alien to the old, demure Katrina, and as that thought echoed through her mind, it sent her over the edge, and she came in a sweet sudden rush, a precious echo of the night before.

"Nicolas," she whispered as her body shuddered in the aftermath of release. She breathed hard, coming back to reality unwillingly.

Could just a few days make such a difference to a person? she wondered as she opened her eyes to the bright gallery once more. It could, if you came into contact with someone who made you want to push back your boundaries and live a whole lot more. The moment Nicolas had stepped into her life, he'd altered her. Gone was the demure Katrina. She'd been on her way out, but Nicolas had chased her away forever.

*Even if he is someone you are not sure whether to trust or not?* She sighed. Pulling herself together, she walked around the gallery, engaging with each and every painting on the walls, each of the small works in the display boxes, and the statues on their pedestals. She knew them well now, knew their history and the papers that went with them. She was their agent for their new destinations, and that was why she was here—to make sure they went to the best places—places where they would be loved and admired by many people.

When she eventually went back to the office, her lunch tray had been left on a table by the door. A domed cover protected a colorful salad dotted with big fat olives and finely cut cold meat. Fresh bread, fruit, and a pot of coffee had been included. Katrina glanced at her watch. It was past eleven o'clock. She had to make up for lost time.

Sitting down at the desk, she noticed that the photo had moved from its previous position by a couple of inches. Raimunda had noticed it. For some reason, that made her smile. She lifted the first stack of letters she had to go through and began to work.

*Nico was standing on the side of the freeway, topping up his* fuel when the message he had been hoping for arrived. Earlier that morning, Raimunda had reported that Katrina looked a little sad but was otherwise well. He hated to think of her unhappy and was still concerned that she was okay after Sergio's mood the night before. The second message told him exactly what he was waiting to hear, and for the first time that day, he smiled.

*Sergio was staring at spreadsheet printouts, in denial, when his* intercom blipped on and his secretary announced that Señora Teodoro was here to see him.

What the hell did she want? He was about to instruct his secretary to let her in, when the door sprang open, and Elaine entered. He waited until she shut the door behind her, then he dropped the papers in his hands onto the stacks on his desk. "What are you doing here? You should be at the house, making sure that nothing goes wrong."

She gave him a tight smile. "You refused to speak to me at home, so here I am. I figured you wouldn't want to make a scene in front of your staff, seeing as they are watching your every move right now . . . so you can't walk out on me this time."

He gritted his teeth.

Drawing off her sunglasses, she assessed him coolly. "I'll help myself to a seat, shall I?"

He watched her as she sat down, straightening her smart suit as she did so, never a hair out of place. Normally, he admired that in her, but for some reason, right at that moment he resented it. He felt so much less together than she looked, and that was not good. "Elaine, I'm busy here."

She cast her eyes over the piles of paper on the desk. "I can see that. You are letting things slide, Sergio."

Annoyance bit into him. He didn't want to explain himself to her. He sighed. "If you're talking about Nicolas—"

"I'm not talking about Nicolas," she interrupted. "I'm talking about your behavior in general. You were in a state when you were talking to the police last night. You've got to keep yourself together, whatever happens."

He wanted to snap back, but deep inside he knew she was right. He'd been furious with Nico for setting off the alarms. He pressed his lips tightly together, glaring at her.

She scrutinized him. "There's something I need to know, Sergio." She gestured at the mess of papers on his desk. "The sale of the collection, will the money be enough to sort this out?"

He slammed his fist down on the papers. "How the fuck do I know?" he snapped back. "I know nothing about art. That's why I got her in. As soon as she's completed the list, we'll have an estimated figure."

Elaine shook her head, eyes glacial. He didn't like the way she looked. It was as if she was pulling away from him.

"It better be enough, Sergio. It's taken three years to get to this point. When we met, you said I could be a rich widow inside eighteen months. Your inheritance would be assured, and my life turned around. A big gamble, but I loved that, and so did you."

She gave him an intimate smile, tapping in to the thing that had drawn them together. "But now it's been going on too long. I want this sorted and over with, and soon."

"You know it took longer because he wouldn't budge on the collection. I had to play this hand differently. But we're winning now. You said Katrina was nearly finished. It's nearly over."

"But how long will it take to ship and sell the art? Will it be soon enough to shift the money and stop the share price dropping even further?"

These were things he was worrying about, too, constantly, but he needed her on his side, and he needed her at the house. "Don't worry about that. I will hurry her along. Once we know what we've got, we can breathe easy. I'm sure it will be enough, I asked around."

He stood up, walked around her side, and squatted down beside her chair. "Elaine," he breathed, and smiled at her, running his fingers down her cheek and then into her hair. "Trust me."

"Trust you?" She raised her delicately arched eyebrows, a pout of disapproval shaping her lips. "What were you doing up there with her in the first place last night?"

"I wanted to see how it was going, and I wanted to be sure Nico hadn't got to her." Again, he was annoyed at having to explain himself to her, but he also didn't want to be alone in this situation, and he wasn't really sure whether he could trust her with what she knew about him and his father, if she split from him.

She dropped her head back and gave a mock laugh. "I'm not that stupid. Besides, what on earth made you think he would talk to her?"

"He saw her at the house yesterday morning, remember. All he would have to do is ask Raimunda, and then he would know exactly why she was there. Elaine, I've got this under control; I'm watching all the time, because one idiotic move by my brother could destroy this for us. Ever since yesterday morning, I have expected him to return."

She stared at him for an age, and then she rested her hand on his arm. "You should have told me that."

"You have enough to worry about. It will be over soon, and then you can concentrate on enjoying life again."

Her eyes lit up.

"All you have to think about is whether you want to go to Las Vegas to celebrate, or Monte Carlo."

The starry look in her eyes confirmed he'd done it; he had her back on board.

# 13

Midafternoon, Raimunda arrived in the office with another tray, this time carrying a coffeepot, a small cup, and a delicious looking pastry on a plate.

"*Hola, Raimunda,*" Katrina said, standing up and mustering a smile when the housekeeper entered. "*Muchas gracias.*"

Raimunda nodded. She set the tray down on the oak table by the filing cabinets and tapped it with one finger, before taking her leave. Curious, Katrina waited until she'd gone and then went to pour herself a coffee. Glancing down, she saw a piece of paper folded neatly on the tray.

A note. She almost didn't want to pick it up. But how could she resist? When she opened it, she recognized the handwriting immediately. It was written by the same hand as the note that was waiting for her at the reception desk in the hotel in Barcelona. It was from Nicolas.

*Both Sergio and Elaine are out.*
*Go to the window at the far end of the gallery.*

That was all it said, but the short message made her nervous. Nicolas obviously wasn't going away. And she still didn't know whether or not to trust him. Obviously, Sergio's remark about Raimunda the previous night was true. She was indeed willing to help Nicolas. Raimunda was probably the one who'd told him the name of the hotel Katrina'd been staying at in Barcelona. She felt as if she'd been given one of many missing pieces to the puzzle. For whatever reason, Raimunda hadn't excluded Nicolas from her life the way everybody else had, which was interesting.

Holding the note in her hand, heart racing, she paced up and down the small office wrestling with her indecision. She desperately wanted to see Nicolas again, but after what happened last night and Sergio's threat, she had to wonder if she was completely mad even contemplating any sort of communication.

*Yes, I'm mad.* Pushing the note into her briefcase, she walked to the gallery. She tried to keep her breathing even, glancing behind her, alert for any other presence. The note said Sergio and Elaine were out. There were others around, though: the gardener and Vincent.

What if they saw her colluding with him again and reported to Sergio? But she had to know, had to see him. She took a deep breath and opened the window, peering down. At first she couldn't see anything; then she caught sight of him standing among the trees, looking up at her. He was dressed in khaki clothing, and his arms were folded across his chest. His expression was brooding and thoughtful as he stared up.

Mercifully, he stayed where he was. He wasn't intending to climb up here again. That was a relief. However, a second later, when he gestured at her, beckoning her to go down to him, she swore under her breath. If she did and she was seen, she'd be on the first plane back to England with her career in tatters. He had picked a good place, though, somewhere where they wouldn't be seen from the other tower or from the majority of the house. Could she risk it?

It was as if his presence had a magnetic pull on her body, something she couldn't deny. He was luring her out of the house, had been all along. First, he'd come to her in her bedroom, which should have been her stronghold. Then in the gallery, keying into her professional zone, and now—now he was pulling her out of that zone and into his world. Or trying to.

*Surely, surely I am stronger than this,* she reasoned, as she fought back the desire to go to him. But, no. He lured her to him just by standing there, looking so bloody gorgeous, beckoning to her with those dark, sexy eyes. She was doomed. She shut the window, her feet carrying her back through the gallery and toward the staircase, even while she was still turning her doubts over in her mind. *This is madness.*

Even so, she ran quickly along the corridor in the main house, glancing around her all the while. All was quiet, and when she looked down the main staircase into the hall, there was no movement. When she got down there, she found that Raimunda was waiting to one side of the staircase. She gestured beyond it to a narrow corridor that led toward the back of the house. Raimunda was doing more than passing a note; she was acting as a full-on go-between.

*"Gracias, Raimunda,"* she said as she walked by, wishing she could speak Spanish and could say more to the woman. That might be an enlightening conversation.

Raimunda nodded. There was a hint of a smile on her face, not something Katrina had seen before. If Raimunda's allegiances were with Nicolas, no wonder she was so rude and surly to Elaine and Sergio.

Beyond the door at the end of the corridor, a utility room housed various items including a range of cupboards, a set of golf clubs, and two coat racks. There was a security panel to one side of the exterior door, and when she touched it, the door buzzed. Opening it quickly, she stepped outside, taking a quick glance around. There was no one in sight, so she darted quickly across the lawn to the spot where she'd seen Nicolas from the tower.

He'd moved farther into the trees but reached out for her as she passed his hiding place, drawing her into his arms.

"Are you okay? He didn't hurt you, did he?"

His sudden close proximity and the concern in his eyes made her stumble, and she put her hands on his chest, leveling herself against him.

"I'm okay." *Be wary,* she reminded herself. He wanted to mess up Sergio's plans for the sale, and that meant messing things up for her as well. *Get yourself a backbone, girl.* It wasn't too late to stand up to him and show him what she was really made of. She drew away from him.

"Sergio is an unconventional client." She avoided eye contact at that point, in case he could read too much. "But he is trying to get a job done; just as I am." Looking back at him, she tried to give weight to that statement.

He laughed softly, reaching out to cup her cheek. "Sweet, Katrina," he murmured. "You are so trusting."

She gave a dismissive laugh. "You don't know me."

His expression grew serious. "Maybe not, but I know you are trying to do the right thing, but you're getting it wrong."

*Wrong?* She glared at him. "Nicolas, why the hell have you dragged me out here? What do you want?"

"I want you to leave this house."

Narrowing her eyes, she steeled herself for battle. "Yes, of course you do; you want me to leave so that I don't complete the job."

He looked skyward and gave a deep sigh. "More than that, I'm concerned about you."

*There it was.* He didn't want her to complete the job, that was the bottom line, and he would try anything to stop her doing so. She shook her head at him, her emotions too scrambled to respond.

When he looked back at her, there was an exasperated expression on his face. "Please consider it. You will see things easier if you get away from here."

She looked away. She wasn't going to give in to his demands. Lord knows, she wanted to leave this bloody house. She'd even considered getting a room somewhere, but the nearest hotel was in Caldes, and traveling back and forth would drag the whole job out. If she worked into the night again tonight, she'd be on her way home soon. Moving out would add another day, and she couldn't face that. The atmosphere in the house was not good.

Looking back at him, she longed to trust him. Her lips

parted as she remembered what it had been like that first night in Barcelona, before she knew who he was. The look in his eyes grew hotter and more demanding, desire flaring in them as if he, too, was thinking of more pleasant moments.

She began to turn away, but he stopped her, backing her against a tree, pinning her there.

"Let me go."

"You don't mean that; I can see what you really want in your eyes."

"Don't tell me what I mean." She squirmed in his grasp, shifting against the tree. The rough bark against her back felt oddly exhilarating, as if she needed the rough handling to ground her unsteady emotions.

He inserted one strong thigh between both of hers, making her gasp when he applied the pressure of his hip at the juncture of hers. She turned her face away, but he forced it back with one hand, kissing her demandingly.

The anger she felt at his demands only seemed to fuel her response. Thumping him with her fisted hands, she wriggled and twisted in his grasp and attempted to kick his shins. Her pussy was throbbing with arousal from the pressure he exerted on her so easily, making her fume. How could her body do this to her, give in, while she tried to stay sane? But even while she squirmed, her mouth opened to him, taking his tongue, and before she knew it, she was returning the kiss just as demandingly. Her hands opened and roved over his torso as if to absorb every ounce of him into her physical memory.

*I'm going to walk away, but let me have this moment.*

Murmuring fierce-sounding words in Spanish, he led a trail of hungry kisses across her cheek and down her neck, sucking on her skin, moving her top out of his way to reach her breastbone to kiss her there as well.

Leaning forward, she clutched at him frantically and breathed the scent of his hair, savoring the touch of it on her face as it moved in the afternoon breeze. Then her hands were around his head, and he was kissing her mouth again, hard, bruising her lips, riding her body up against the tree, his hands working their way down her hips. She lifted her knee against his thigh, her body inviting him in. He clasped and held it there in one large palm, their bodies riding each other furiously in the angry, desperate embrace.

When he drew back, his eyes were wild. "Tell me you don't want this as much as I do."

Furious, she locked eyes with him. "I do want it as much as you do; you know that. But we are doing it for all the wrong reasons."

Denial was there in his eyes as he shook his head. "No, that is not the case."

He was never going to let it go; all he cared about was getting his way. Hurt and angry, she pulled free, breaking away from him. "Leave me alone, Nicolas."

He looked amazed by what she had said, one hand up against the tree, his chest rising and falling. "Katrina, you are messing with my head!"

*What?* Her head snapped round. She couldn't believe he'd had the cheek to say that. "*I'm* messing with *your* head? You pursued me in order to get at Sergio. That's messing with some-one's head!"

Oh, but he looked guilty. He couldn't deny it, and that certain knowledge cut her to the quick.

*Walk away, now.*

"Good-bye, Nicolas."

Turning away from him, she headed back to the house, her legs trembling beneath her as she broke into a run. But he didn't come after her, and the angry, hurt knot in her chest burned. With her hand hard against it to quell the ache, she ran back inside the house, never once looking back.

*Nico's hand curled into a fist, and he pressed it hard against* the tree in frustration. What was worse? Knowing that he couldn't have handled that any worse if he had tried, or finding out that Katrina thought so badly of him? But she was right. Everything she had said about him was true, and he hated himself for that. Somewhere along the way, Katrina had become important to him. He was no longer just looking out for his family; now he wanted to protect Katrina as well.

As he watched her disappear into the house, he took a deep breath and quelled his anger and disappointment. He needed a clear head, and he needed space to think. If only he could make contact with his father. That had to be done more than ever now.

Raimunda said Katrina wasn't done with the inventory; there was still time for her to realize the truth about the collection, to call a stop to the sale. Would she ever believe the truth? But even as he thought it, he realized that raising her opinion of him had become every bit as important as educating her about Sergio, if not more so.

*Once again, Katrina worked late into the night, desperate now* to be on her way. It was nearly midnight when she finally gave in to her body's need to stretch out and rest.

On exiting the tower, she crept quickly along the office corridor, listening to see if anyone else was still up. When she reached the landing, she glanced down the staircase. The lights were all off downstairs. She stared across the landing and down the corridor where the bedrooms were located. The curtains were already lifting on the evening breeze, ghostly and suggestive. It sent a shiver through her, just as it always did. She'd been well and truly sucked into this, lured in by this house with all its secrets.

*Soon I'll be gone.*

Hurriedly making her way along the landing to her room, she'd actually gone past the half-open doorway when she realized what she had glimpsed, only drawing to a halt when she'd overshot the door. Glancing back, her blood racing, she wondered if she were imagining what she saw. Elaine was in there on Sergio's bed, naked except for a bra, which she was busy pulling down in order to bare her breasts to the man between her legs: Sergio.

Sergio and Elaine? Katrina was shocked, shocked to the core. Sergio and his young stepmother? Was this an ongoing relationship? Did Jorge know that his wife was sleeping with his son? Did Nico? But as she turned it over in her mind, their relationship made sense of various things.

She darted toward her own doorway across the corridor and hurried inside. Closing the door, she locked it firmly behind her, relieved to be alone, and yet . . . astonished and curious by what she had just seen. More than ever, she was relieved that she hadn't got any more involved with Sergio. He'd been toying with her, but it had been fun for a while. What she'd done with Nicolas was more than fun—it was deeply passionate, intense, and intimate lovemaking—but it had happened for all the wrong reasons. As she accepted that fact, disappointment washed over her, because she was drawn to him in ways beyond her own comprehension.

Did he know how much he'd affected her? She hadn't guessed her own feelings, not until they were right there under her nose and undeniable. Two days earlier she'd been debating whether it was Paco or Vincent that Elaine was keeping for her lover. How wrong could she be? Elaine was sleeping with her own stepson, and the two men were shagging each other senseless in the garden.

Shaking her head, she walked toward the bed, kicking off her shoes as she went. She wondered how many other things she hadn't quite figured out yet. She knew there were more secrets; she could sense them at every turn. The various mysteries in the gallery had raised her level of awareness about what was going on here, in every way. Apparently she was completely unable to do her job and keep her nose out.

Sitting down on the edge of the bed, she stared up at the painting that harnessed her attention whenever she was in the room. Only the area around the bullfighter's eyes was visible in the low lamplight, the area that was most intense in color and meaning. The image of those eyes would be ingrained in her memory forever.

"Why the hell did I have to go and fall for you?" she whispered into the night with a deep, regretful sigh.

Lying back on the bed, alone in his space, she ruefully nursed the aching need at her center. She had to face it; she'd had a taste of heaven in her secret moments with Nicolas, but it wasn't meant to be.

# 14

Doubt had chipped away at Sergio's equilibrium. Ever since he discovered Nico in the house talking to Katrina, he'd been agitated. Elaine gave him bulletins on Katrina's progress, asking him to keep out of her way so that she could get on with the job. He wasn't satisfied with such a hands-off approach, though. He wanted to ensure that Katrina was moving forward with the collection, and that Nico truly hadn't said anything to make her suspicious.

After breakfast on Thursday morning, he went up to the gallery himself. Katrina was working at a table next to the filing cabinets in the office with stacks of what looked like letters tied with ribbons surrounding her. Her head snapped up when he reached the top of the staircase, and she looked uneasy but quickly covered it with a smile.

"Sergio, good morning. How are you today?"

Sergio glanced around the room, but he was pretty sure Nico wouldn't risk setting foot inside again, after he'd threatened him with a police record. He nodded and smiled. "Good, thank you. How is the valuation going?"

"I'm on the last lap now: paperwork. If all goes well today, I intend to book my flight home for tomorrow. Will your driver be able to take me to the airport?"

"I'll arrange it. Just let Elaine know the time of your flight."

She had turned to face him and was leaning up against the table she was working at, her fingers clutching the edge. Even though she was attempting to look casual, she was nervous around him, he could tell. Had been since just after her arrival. Was it because she was not on her own territory, or was it something else?

"I will need the ownership release papers," she said. "I wondered if Elaine had taken them to your father when she visited."

Silently, he cursed the damn papers. No worry, there was still time. He could check through them later that day and forge the signatures himself. "*Sí*, I will have them for you this evening."

He gave her one of his most gracious smiles, and she looked relieved. He was, too. They were nearly in the clear. "Okay, I have to go. I'll see you tonight. We must have a drink to celebrate a job well done."

"That would be lovely."

"Good. I'll tell Elaine to expect you at dinner."

Katrina looked pleased.

He nodded and left, making his way quickly down the staircase, somewhat more sure of things now that he'd spoken to her himself. She'd be gone tomorrow, and shortly afterward, the collection would be gone, too. They would have the money from the sale before the end of the year. That moment couldn't come quickly enough, as far as he was concerned.

*It took the rest of the morning for Katrina to relax. The gallery* was her safe haven, but every time Sergio turned up she lost that feeling for a good couple of hours. She could see the light at the end of the tunnel with her work, though. She had mixed emotions about that, but she'd got her head around the fact that this was a job, and the job had to be done as quickly and smoothly as possible in order for it to be a success. Personal emotions shouldn't come into it.

Her phone rang, and she saw that it was Lucy. "Hello, you put a smile on my face."

"Katrina, you sound a bit tense."

"I'm just finding the job a bit of a slog; there was so much to inventory." It was a lie; the collection was a joy to work with, but she could hear the tension in her own voice, and she didn't want Lucy to worry about her. After the run-in between the brothers and Nico's subsequent attempts to get her to leave, her emotions were more mixed than ever. Part of her wanted to get the job done and get the hell out of here. The other part wanted to linger, hoping to see Nicolas, despite her better judgment and all the warning signals that were going off around her.

Lucy gave a sympathetic sigh. "It does sound like a big job

for one person, just looking at the inventory you're sending through each day is quite amazing. You should have seen Mr. Pocklington's eyes light up."

Katrina chuckled at the familiar image, and it made part of her relax. "I can just picture him."

"He's looking into a shipping date today."

"Great. Let me know when you get it. The client will be pleased."

"Oh, this guy Nicolas, he's quite an interesting character."

*You can say that again.* Katrina tried not to sound too eager when she responded. "Is that so?"

"Yes, over the last few years he's been responsible for an enormous amount of positive press about street art and performance artists in Catalonia. Oh, you might have seen some of those artists in Barcelona."

Unbidden, an image of Nicolas dressed as *el diablo* stalking her through Las Ramblas entered her mind, and her body shivered with arousal, as real as if he had lifted his cloak and drawn her beneath it, holding her against him for a forbidden kiss.

"Yes, I know what you mean," she managed to reply, and then jolted in her seat when she heard a noise behind her. Raimunda was standing in the doorway to the office with a tray. She really did have an uncanny knack of appearing suddenly and silently.

Katrina raised her hand and nodded at the housekeeper.

"Lucy, I'm sorry I'm going to have to go. Thanks for the info." *Had there been more?* She hesitated. "Look, I'll call you back at the end of the afternoon."

There had been more; she was sure of it.

*Nico sat at the simple kitchen table in Raimunda's home in the* village, staring at his phone, deep in thought. At first he wouldn't even begin to entertain Raimunda's suggestion about what to do next. Then she phoned from the Torre and pointed out that it was the perfect time. Sergio was at work, and Elaine was out of the house for a couple of hours, shopping.

Perhaps it would work, but how would Katrina react? He had to get her out of there, get her somewhere they could talk properly. At the house, there was always a reminder of her professional role there. He could see that in her responses, and he didn't blame her. However, he wasn't sure about Raimunda's remedy for that. It verged on criminal behavior, and he'd much rather leave that to his brother.

He had to make a decision, though, and quickly. He checked his phone again for messages. He was clinging to the hope that Kent would locate his father, and then he could leave Katrina out of this. At the same time, he found himself angry. He wanted to claim Katrina, to remove her from Sergio's poisonous influence. The situation was *insano*. How could he have got emotionally involved with the auctioneer?

He'd only meant to bend her, not become entranced with her. Their deep mutual attraction had caught him off guard, caught him on unfamiliar ground. He found himself possessive and ludicrously territorial about a woman he barely knew. It felt loco. He didn't like his emotions controlling him that way.

He was spending too much time away from his job, too; he needed to be back in Barcelona the following evening at the latest. The group of older kids he worked with had a crucial dress rehearsal for their first public performance, and a makeup artist from the national theater was coming by to help them prepare. If he didn't turn up, he couldn't guarantee some of the less involved teenagers would stick with the program, and he didn't want to see that happen.

Perhaps Kent had news. He flicked open the phone, scrolled to Kent's number, and pressed Call.

"Hey, Nico," Kent said. From the background noise it sounded as if he was walking.

"Kent. How's it going? Anything to report on the list I gave you?"

"Nothing yet. I've just got a few more numbers to phone. I'm going into a seminar, and then I'll be able to finish up the list. I'll call you back later. Sorry not to have any news."

Nico rested his forehead in his hand, disappointed. "Okay, I understand. Thank you."

"No worries. Talk to you later."

Nico ended the call but kept the phone in his hand. He *did* have a choice, he told himself. He just felt as if he didn't. Did it really matter where his father was? He could just walk away and forget the whole thing. It would be the easiest thing to do, and he could get back to his real commitments. Could he abandon his father, though?

One thing was certain—walking away at this point wouldn't satisfy his need to find out about Katrina. And for some reason he had to know what she felt about him and if what Sergio had indicated about himself and Katrina was true. Had she been involved with his brother, too?

If he went with Raimunda's suggestion, that question would be answered, if nothing else. He didn't have any option; he wasn't allowed in the house. Sergio really meant to carry out his threat this time, and he couldn't afford risking his career as a teacher by gaining a police record. If he wanted Katrina on his side and talking to him, the only thing to do was to get her out of there by whatever means necessary.

Even though he wondered about his sanity, he scrolled to the number of the kitchen extension up at the Torre, where Raimunda would be working, and pressed Call.

*It was near three o'clock when Katrina heard a sound, and* Raimunda's ample frame once again filled the doorway. She nodded at Katrina and then glanced at the family photo propped on the desk. Katrina noticed and smiled. It was as if they shared an unspoken understanding about displaying it more prominently.

Katrina stood up, lifting her empty lunch tray from the table to pass it over. *"Hola, Raimunda. Muchas gracias."*

The housekeeper took the tray but continued to stand in the doorway with a determined, thoughtful expression on her face. She seemed to have something else on her mind. Katrina tensed, wondering if she was going to pass her another note. She was so close to finishing that she didn't want any interruptions. And yet . . . curiosity and longing flared inside her. She couldn't help it.

After a moment Raimunda issued an unintelligible sentence, then frowned and rolled her eyes skyward, as if annoyed with herself. She opened her mouth and delivered the sentence again, very slowly, and loudly. "Cup of tea?"

She said the words and then pressed her lips together again, awaiting Katrina's response.

Katrina couldn't withhold her surprise. The stoic housekeeper had tried to speak to her in her own language, a learned phrase. She hadn't noticed her make any such concession for Elaine. In fact, Elaine had commented on how little effort Raimunda made to speak English. Raimunda really didn't like Elaine, but Katrina couldn't blame her. Elaine wasn't the easiest woman to warm to, and Raimunda's allegiance to Nicolas couldn't have eased the situation. Were Nicolas's feelings behind this peace offering, too? Had he taught Raimunda the sentence?

Katrina was touched by the effort the housekeeper had made. She nodded. *"Gracias, Raimunda."* Tea would be good. *"Sí,* cup of tea."

Raimunda's tightly compressed lips widened into a big smile, then she lifted one hand and beckoned to Katrina, turning and beckoning again as if she wanted her to follow.

That wasn't quite what Katrina had in mind; she still had a lot to get through before she could relax and confirm her flight, but since the housekeeper had made such an effort, she could hardly refuse the kindness. She switched her laptop to standby and followed, taking her phone with her in case Lucy called with the shipping date. She wanted to be ready to give it to Sergio.

Without saying another word, Raimunda led her out of the tower. As they walked along the corridor, Katrina glanced down into the hallway where Nicolas had stood a couple of days before, and a dart of anticipation moved inside her. She shook it off. This was a peace gesture from the housekeeper. Nicolas wouldn't come back again, not after the threats, and not after what had happened between them yesterday.

She followed Raimunda down the main staircase, through the dining room and beyond, into a vast kitchen. Katrina looked around with interest. Plants filled the windowsill over the deep sinks. A massive range nested between cupboards, over which a wood rack was chock-full of pans of varying sizes. A well-worn wood table ran down the center of the room. At one end of the table two fine bone china teacups were set up, together with a dainty milk jug and a sugar bowl. A plate of pretty, tempting sponge cakes sat nearby. Raimunda gestured Katrina toward the chair and then turned to her cooking range, shifting a large, old-fashioned kettle over the flame as it lit.

Katrina sat down, setting her phone down on the table. The kettle soon hummed into a simmer. When it did, Raimunda went to the back door and rapped on the frame with one knuckle. A moment later the gardener, Paco, appeared at the window. He peered directly at Katrina sitting at the table and then he nodded and waved at Raimunda before he headed toward the door, taking off his hat as he did so.

Was he coming in for a tea break as well? Would the three of them sit at the table together? For some reason, Katrina was reminded of the Mad Hatter's tea party. As if being here wasn't strange enough. She already felt as if she'd moved in with the Addams family, with Elaine playing Morticia, and Sergio doing a particularly lecherous Gomez. Now she was going to take tea with Paco, the gay gardener, and Raimunda, the housekeeper with a grudge . . . or ten.

The door opened. Paco stepped back and ushered someone else in before closing the door quickly behind him and returning to the garden.

The smile died on Katrina's lips.

*Nicolas.*

Her heartbeat grew erratic as she looked at him, taking in his apologetic expression as he made eye contact with her. The now-familiar response to his appearance was in full throttle: her pulse racing, her body anticipating his touch, her mind a mess of confusion. But he looked guarded, serious even, as if he had the weight of the world on his shoulders.

Katrina stood up.

Raimunda moved, standing between the table and the door to the hall, so that her exit that way was blocked.

The true reason for her "cup of tea" invitation was now all too apparent. Sergio had banned his brother from the house, threatened his reputation, too. But Raimunda had got her down here into the kitchen to facilitate an audience between them, despite Sergio's threats.

"Nicolas, you shouldn't be here. You are making trouble for us both, and you know that."

"I want to resolve this."

Resolve it? Did he mean what had happened between them, or something else? *Silly fool.* He was here to discuss the collection, not to see her, because . . . because of what had happened between them. Even though she knew that, the fledgling hope kept rearing inside her.

"I asked you to leave me alone."

"I know, and I know I've gone about this whole thing the wrong way. But I'm willing to admit that I made a mistake."

Making love to her was a mistake? Of course it was; she knew that. So why did his words hurt so badly?

"I need your understanding. Katrina, I ask only for a few minutes of your time."

Unable to deny him, she chose not to respond.

"I want you to reconsider the job you are doing here. Sergio does not have the power to sell the collection, and—if you'll give me some time to speak with my father—I will prove it to you."

Her chest felt hollow. She had to guard her emotions, or she would be badly hurt by this. Nicolas didn't really care about her. The brothers were competing with each other. It was about the art collection, and she was merely a pawn in the game. "I will not be pulled into the feud between you and your brother. I'm here to do a job for a client. That's it."

He lifted his eyebrows.

Her face heated in response to his accusing glance. No, that wasn't quite true, was it? She hadn't behaved entirely professionally at all, and that put her on dodgy ground when it came to being indignant and righteous about her relationship with him and his family.

She went to leave.

Nicolas stopped her, his hand on her arm. "Please, I understand how difficult this is for you, believe me. I know you're trying to do the right thing. I just want to make sure you know what the right thing is."

"You mean you want me to think your case against this sale is valid," she snapped, her voice rising.

"Yes, I do." His reply was simply stated.

"I'm not working for you." Childish, yes, but for some reason she felt like being childish.

Raimunda began shuffling about, muttering in Spanish under her breath. Nicolas spoke to her, and she went about her business quietly.

"It is not Sergio's to sell. You cannot sell anything without my father's permission."

"I'm well aware of that. I know how to do my job." She was annoyed now. "I have papers for your father to sign. I have a reputation to maintain."

Why hadn't he discussed this in the first place, before they made love in the gallery? It was what she had wanted to do. *Because we probably wouldn't have made love.* Yes, he was cleverer than her on that point, she mused.

*Men!*

Not that she regretted their relationship, not one bit. Looking at him, even in her pain, she couldn't, never would be able to regret it.

Nicolas seemed irritated. "And I bet you've given these papers to Sergio."

What was he getting at? "What if I did?"

He stepped away and opened his hands in a dismissive gesture as if he didn't even need to comment.

Raimunda muttered something under her breath to him, the kettle in her hand raised over a teapot. Nicolas paused, frowned. Eventually, he nodded and responded quickly, talking to her in a low voice. Katrina didn't have a hope of catching what they said. Presumably he had to translate their conversation for Raimunda.

"I would like to tell you everything," he said in English, returning his attention to her, his tone somewhat more measured. "There are things I want to ask you . . . but it is too difficult here in this house, with the threats that hang over us both."

"I can't just up and leave, if that's what you're getting at again. I have a job to do." She clung to her professional role, her life raft in a tide of emotional confusion. There were no seductive overtones in his approach today. To her eyes, he looked like a man on a mission of a very different kind. She felt put out, because it cast an odd light over their previous encounters. It left her smarting.

"Katrina, I am offering you a choice, I'd like you to walk out of here with me, now."

"A choice? How ludicrous. I choose to do my job, thank you very much. I'll be done in just a few hours, and then I'm out of here."

He stared at her incredulously.

That was the last straw. She looked away, staring pointedly at the door, avoiding eye contact. She was pretty annoyed herself.

Raimunda poured her out a cup of tea, glaring at Nicolas as she did so. Feeling sorry for the old woman, Katrina thanked her, then dropped two sugar cubes into the cup, stirring the tea rapidly to distract herself from Nicolas and the way his presence affected her. She lifted the cup and went to walk away with it.

"Sit down; drink your tea," he said.

"What?"

"Raimunda has gone to some effort; please don't hurt her feelings."

"Jesus, you really can lay it on thick, can't you."

"She'll be upset."

Katrina looked at Raimunda, who craned her neck with an expectant look on her face.

She glared at him. "One minute, then I'm back to the job."

Sitting down, she faced away from the pair of them and sipped her tea. What was this crazy effect he had on her? Taking a surreptitious glance his way, she knew.

*I'm wildly attracted to him. I actually like him. Damn. I'm doomed.*

She let her hair fall forward to hide her face from him while she sipped the tea. It wasn't like the black China tea or Earl Grey that she drank at home, more like an herbal brew. It was light and refreshing though, with a delicate scent of flowers. Raimunda and Nicolas were talking in low voices in Spanish, and she ignored them as she sipped it, noticing as she did that her limbs began to relax almost immediately; the tension in her was dissolving. Yes, it was an herbal brew, no caffeine there.

Maybe she should get out of here for an hour or so, she mused. Being in Barcelona was very different from being here with him, but she hadn't known who he was then, had she? It was tempting, all the same. Just a drink in a bar somewhere, something normal. That might level her head and give her time to think about what was really going on here with these two brothers and their father.

She felt tired. Maybe she'd been working too hard up there in the gallery, she needed this break. Shame to spend the time arguing, though. There were better things to do with Nicolas than argue, she thought languidly, eyeing him up across the kitchen as she sat back in her chair.

He was so fit and attractive. Had she really made love with that gorgeous man? She felt the urge to laugh at that thought. Fighting it back, she suddenly yawned loudly instead.

She saw Nicolas whispering in Raimunda's direction, but they were both watching her carefully. She blinked, fighting back another yawn. She lifted her hand, attempting to push her hair back from her face. Her fingers loomed large in her vision as she moved her hands.

"It's very warm in here," she murmured, feeling incredibly sleepy all of a sudden. Her head drooped, and she stared into the teacup. *The tea.* That unusual taste, what was it? She lifted her head with effort to look at them both.

Nicolas was moving toward her, concern on his face.

"This bloody tea is putting me to sleep," she blurted, the urge to giggle welling uncontrollably. She sounded like an irate British tourist complaining about the tea. How embarrassing. She laughed aloud, her hands covering her face as she did so, her body swaying.

Nicolas's voice reached her; he was saying her name.

"I feel weird, innee . . . ineee . . . briated. You did this to me," she said, pointing at him, her head swaying over the table even she did so. She snatched up her phone, holding it to her chest. "I'm expecting an important call, and I can barely keep my eyes open."

He looked at her with a rather panic-stricken expression.

"I'm so sorry," he said, as he knelt down beside her and held her safe. "I didn't want to do this, but it seemed like the only way to get you out of here. I want to talk to you, alone, properly alone."

What he said didn't quite make sense, but he was close by her side, and that felt nice. His arms went around her, and she felt herself lifted from her seat.

"Ooh, the earth just moved." She gave a lazy laugh as her head lolled against his shoulder. He smelled good; he smelled of soap and cologne and of Nicolas. *This is so lovely.*

"You feel ever so good. I like it here." She nestled closer, where it felt safe and solid and warm. Looking up at him as he walked, she poked him in the chest with one wobbly finger. "You could have just asked me for a date," she said and snickered away to herself, her eyes closing even while she did so.

He gave an incredulous laugh, muttering to himself in Spanish. That was the last thing she heard before she dozed off in his arms.

# 15

*Katrina opened her eyes and then shut them tightly. She'd been* in a deep sleep, dreaming lovely, erotic dreams, and her bedroom was far too bright after her pleasant sleep.

Her eyes flashed open almost immediately, and she squinted. She wasn't in her bedroom. She was flat on her back on a soft, plump bed. Nicolas stood at the end of the bed, watching her, his hands locked over an iron footboard. He looked darkly handsome as he loomed over her, his eyebrows drawn down while he studied her intently. Behind his head on a plain white wall hung a large wood crucifix. It was so oddly juxtaposed with his devilish good looks and black clothing that it shocked her out of her slumber.

"Bloody hell, what's going on?" Her head swung around, feeling too heavy for her to balance, as she sought out the door.

"Don't even think about it; it's locked. It won't be opened until you hear me out."

It all came flooding back: the kitchen, the tea, the sleepiness. He'd carried her off somewhere. "Nicolas!"

Smiling, he stood up straight. "Call me Nico, please. My friends do."

She stared at him, openmouthed. He'd knocked her out and brought her here without permission—wherever here was—and expected her to use nicknames? The room was small, almost filled by the soft, overstuffed bed and its frame. There was a bedside table, and a small, plain dresser stood in one corner, dotted with a few ornaments. Sitting up, she made for the edge of the bed but swayed to a halt.

"Don't get up yet, please; you are still sleepy. You might hurt yourself."

"You bastard," she said as she slumped back on the bed. "You can't keep me here like this."

"It's only for a little while; I promise." He looked down at her thoughtfully, his gaze moving along the length of her body in a decidedly sexual appraisal.

The weight of his glance made her body respond, which annoyed her to the max. "How dare you? You expect me to listen to you after you knocked me out?"

"It was a risk, I agree. But I had to get you out of the house." He paused. "I did give you a choice."

"Oh right." Sarcasm rang in her voice. "I get it now. My choice was walking out or being carried out in a stupor. Silly me." She put her hand to her head as she looked around again. "Where the hell are we?"

"At Raimunda's home, in Castagona."

"You can't keep me here against my will. This is ridiculous."

"I did it because I had to speak to you properly, away from the house."

She gave a dry laugh. "So you drugged me and carried me off?"

"That's a bit harsh," he said. "It wasn't a drug, and it wasn't meant to appear that way to you. I just had to get you alone."

Something fluttered inside her in response to his words, and she squirmed on the bed. "Well, forgive me if I think your tactics leave something to be desired," she blurted, annoyed that he could influence her so easily.

He shrugged, and there was humor in his eyes, as if he knew she wasn't really about to have him charged in court.

*Bloody cheek.* "Sergio will notice I've gone. He'll realize what you've done. He'll contact the police."

"You left him a note that said you thought it would be more professional to stay in a hotel overnight."

"You mean *you* left him a note."

Amusement twinkled in his eyes. "You're even more beautiful when you're angry, Katrina. Your eyes flash like gemstones."

She ignored his flattery. "Don't be ridiculous. That won't fool him. He's seen my writing . . . He'll question it. All he has to do is compare it to my notes in the study."

"My skills at forgery are more than adequate to convince my brother."

Damn him, he was so sure of himself. "I'll scream for help."

"That wouldn't be very good for our discussion. Besides, no one will hear you." He went to the door and rapped on it loudly. A moment later the sound of music filled the air from outside the room, some dreadful wailing radio station with a whole heap of interference.

Hell and damnation, he had an accomplice. Of course he had an accomplice: Raimunda. Katrina struggled to her feet and charged around the bed at him.

He captured her easily, holding her wrists aloft in his hands. "Nico!"

The humor left his expression, and his eyes darkened to black. It was as if the contact between them had changed the mood. His grip tightened, and his eyes blazed with sudden intensity. "There's something I must know. What Sergio said the other night. Is it true about you and him?"

Katrina swallowed. Her legs felt weak. The resistance in her began to dissipate. "It wasn't like he said it was. He flirted with me, yes, when it suited him."

He let her go. He didn't like that, and she saw both wounded pride and disappointment in his expression. Despite the setup here, that made her feel wretched. She reached out for him, one hand on his arm. She grappled for something to say. "But then so did you, didn't you, Nicolas? How do you think I feel about that? For all I know, I might just be another toy for you and your brother to fight over."

*There. It's out.*

Her heart beat wildly as she waited for him to respond.

He closed his eyes, his lips tightening. He turned away,

stared at the window. "I'm sorry, Katrina. Maybe you're right, maybe it started out that way."

"Too right it did. You didn't just bump into me on that street in Barcelona; you set out to influence me. You are using me every bit as much as Sergio is."

He looked back at her, and he looked so stung by her words she expected him to deny it all. He didn't. "I know that, and I apologize deeply."

He looked truly remorseful. He pushed his hand through his hair, a frown darkening his expression. "Something changed."

He glanced at her, as if it was beyond his own comprehension. "When I started out, I wanted to make contact, to talk to you. I didn't foresee it developing the way it has. Now . . . now, I want you." He paused, very deliberately, letting her feel the weight of his meaning. "I need to know about you and Sergio before I can move forward."

Her heart was beating so hard she felt dizzy.

"Is this why you brought me here?" She could barely get the words out.

"Partly." He shrugged.

Was it true? Had Sergio's words upset him? Did he really care for her? Was he interested in more than just the future of the collection? Was his attraction legitimate, even if his initial motives were suspect?

"I need to know," he repeated.

Perhaps she did owe him an explanation. "Look . . . Sergio flattered me. I liked the attention he gave me. I can't deny that. I'm not trying to give you excuses. I'm really not under any

obligation to explain myself to you; I just want you to understand that it's different with you. Because I . . ."

She paused, on the brink of saying something about caring
for him. And she did care for him, but it was too soon. Looking into his eyes with the words frozen on her lips, she saw
him acknowledge what was in her mind silently, with a gentle
nod.

*He understands me.*

She took a breath and continued. "When I first met Sergio,
I'd just been through a bad breakup; he made me feel better
about myself. My ex, he . . . he had an affair, and I felt unattractive, unwanted."

He spoke softly in Spanish, reaching out for her.

She put up her hands, halting him. If he showed her sympathy now, she'd buckle, and she wouldn't be able to finish. "Let
me explain. I needed to flirt with men. Sergio made me feel
good, whatever his reason. I'm an independent woman. I can do
what I want."

She stared at him, facing up to the challenge she found in his
eyes. God, he was possessive. It stirred fire in her to have a man
like him be that passionate about her. "But I can honestly say it
wasn't like you and me, truly. We never actually . . ."

Her glance automatically went to the bed, and then she
looked back at him, hoping for his understanding without having to go into sordid details. "With you, I wanted to do it all . . .
everything."

His eyes searched hers for the truth for several long moments, and then, finally, he nodded. She thought he was never

going to move, never going to speak, and then he hauled her against him, handling her roughly, kissing her passionately.

She melted, her lips parting under his. God, it felt so good. She had to fight her most instinctive urges in order to stand her ground. Breaking free, she put her hands up against his chest. "Let me go, Nico. I've said my piece, I've been honest with you, but you can't keep me here against my will."

He shook his head, his smile almost villainous while he eyed her slowly, deliberately, as if she were his and his alone.

Her innards trembled, her core burning for him. "Let me go, now, and I won't call the police."

"You won't call the police, especially if you listen to what I have to say."

It was as if her words had meant nothing; the discussion had not restored trust and equality between them. Infuriated, she thumped his chest with her fists, kicking his shins. "You know, I was getting to like you, feel sympathy for your situation, even. But your Neanderthal tactics have cleared the fog from my head."

"What is this word *Neander*—?"

"Caveman. You are acting like a primitive caveman." She made her hands into fists and thumped her chest, glaring at him.

"Oh, but you look so beautiful when you are angry." He gave a dark laugh and snatched her into his arms, lifting her with one arm underneath her knees, the other holding her upper body locked tightly against his chest. He dropped her back on the bed where she had started, and before she could even lift her head off the pillow, he was down with her, pinning her with strong hands around her upper arms, one leg thrown across the top of her thighs to stop her moving.

She was melting, her body on fire as he mounted her that way. The restraint felt too good. Her traitorous pussy salivated for his cock, her arms and legs aching to enclose him while he shagged her senseless. The effect he had on her was acute. His presence swamped her in heady carnal desire, dissolving her ability to reason clearly.

"I had to get you away. You wouldn't let me explain back at the house. Besides, we kept getting interrupted, and that was so very inconvenient." His glance dropped from her face, slowly cruising her torso, before returning to meet her angry stare.

"I preferred your responses the last time our bodies were this close together." Passion burned in his eyes. "When you begged me to take you, when you were so wet, so hot . . ."

She moaned, blinking, thrashing under him, denial battling with desire. "You surely cannot expect the same response; last time I was willing."

He wasn't in the least bothered by that. In fact, he seemed more interested in taking advantage of her.

"So you were. But you've just told me you wanted me, that you didn't want Sergio. You said you wanted it all, everything."

She swallowed. "I did want you, that doesn't give you any right to drug me and carry me off into the sunset."

Why did that make her think of some cheesy old romance movie? She kicked her legs, annoyed at the thoughts her current situation threw into her head. There was reckless behavior, and there was downright stupid behavior. One should not think of romance at a time like this, she told herself. She wasn't convinced. Maybe that was because of the darkly handsome, brooding man looming over her, the man that had seduced her so thoroughly.

"It was a gentle sleeping draught; Raimunda's friend mixed it for her."

"Gentle?" She gave a bitter laugh.

"*Mi amante dulce*, I'm sorry," he continued, his expression concerned. "It's a brew from the *tila* flower. She makes it for her insomnia, and Raimunda thought it might help you relax about leaving the house."

His soft rolling tones were too seductive. She couldn't trust herself for a moment.

"Raimunda had made it strong, and for that I am sorry." He shrugged. "But it is only an herb. I used to help them collect the flowers from the trees here in Castagona when I was a boy. It is not a harmful thing."

"It practically knocked me out," she declared angrily, trying to ignore the image that rose in her mind of him as a boy picking flowers for the old women to make tea. So different, so alluring.

"It was not meant to hurt you; I would never do that. But now that I see you like this . . ." His eyes darkened as he examined her stretched out on the bed. "I think it becomes you. I'd like to keep you locked up this way for much, much longer."

Oh, God, why did that arouse her so much? Why now, of all times, was her body responding to his threats as if they were invitations to pleasure? *Stupid woman,* she chastised herself. But he was smiling that smile, and he was watching her with those hungry eyes, looking devastatingly handsome as he moved his hips over hers, pressing his erection against her hip bone so that she knew how ready he was, how aroused he was.

"You can't keep me here," she repeated, her voice faltering.

He sighed. "Oh, but I can, and I know I can make you enjoy it."

"Threats," she blurted, unable to stop herself. That was the wrong thing to say.

"Threats, or promises?" He licked his lips, eyeing her again.

Katrina pursed her lips, annoyance flashing through her. But the annoyance she felt was more about the responses her body was giving to this situation. She was a professional art-valuation expert on a commission, pinned to a bed in a foreign country by a man who was contesting her client's actions, and she was aroused beyond belief. What the hell was happening to her? It was as if ever since she'd got hooked into this crazy situation with Nicolas, she'd lost all sense of reason.

He pushed up her top so that it bunched under her chin, his fingers brushing languorously over her lace-covered nipples. Infuriated, she wriggled and attempted to dent him with her elbow, which only made him laugh, a dry, husky sound that made her sigh inside. He moved his hand, slowly running it over the surface of her throat and then lower, down around the outside of one breast, slowly cupping it through her bra.

She tried to pull away, but he pushed her back onto the bed, pulling her top off over her head, then pinning her arms to the pillow.

He bent to rasp his tongue over the surface of her bra, where it sent a flame beneath the fabric, beneath her skin and into her breast. She couldn't voice an objection; her body wouldn't allow it. With Nicolas lying alongside her—toying with her, his large male body pressing so determinedly against hers, his mouth brushing over her skin—she was rendered speechless, helpless, a victim of her own desire.

Anger flared in her, futile anger. She rolled her hips away from him, turning her back as best she could. But he laughed softly, and his hand immediately went to the underside of her thigh. Pressing close against her back, he stroked his hand under her skirt, pushing it up to expose her G-string and her bottom.

"You want it; you know you do. No woman can look as pleasured as you did that night in the gallery and deny herself more of it. I admit how much I want you, Katrina," he coaxed, "I'm hard. You make me hard. This is because of you."

She had to count to ten to stop herself responding.

"You're so hot, damp." His hand was between her thighs, cupped against the fabric of her G-string. "I feel your need in the palm of my hand."

She lay still on the bed, her eyes pressed shut, mentally refusing to acknowledge him as his fingers moved the fabric aside and sank straight into the slick wetness of her sex, entering her with ease.

Her heart raced, her body clamoring for him.

"Tell me you don't want this, that you don't want me, and I will stop." He whispered the words close against her ear, huskily, his warm breath teasing over her skin, making her aware of him in every possible way.

Oh God, she wanted him, she wanted him badly, but she refused to move or speak, refused to give in to his demands and to her own lust.

His fingers moved inside her, and she heard the sucking

sound of her own wetness on his fingers as he drew them out and took them to his lips. From the corner of her eye, she saw him lick her juices from his fingers.

It was so primal, so bloody hot, that she bit her lip, lust making her crazy. Even though she knew she had to take a stand and walk away from this situation, she couldn't deny that she wanted him. She wanted to make this—whatever this was—about something other than the reason why they had met, and yet she could not have resisted him in that moment if her life depended on it.

He withdrew his hand from her, and she heard the sound of a condom wrapper. A moment later, his hand returned to the underside of her thigh, and the hard nub of his erection pressed into her from behind. When he pushed, pleasure rippled out from his cock, suffusing her entire nether region. He moved deeper, drawing a sharp gasp from her when he claimed her, thrusting deep and hard. Her position meant he was wedged against the front wall of her sex, and when he massaged a spot that made her pant, her breath caught on the extreme rush of pleasure it brought about.

He lifted her upper thigh, drawing it toward her body, parting her legs and grinding deeper still. Her groin was on fire, her body tightening and releasing of its own accord. Hot, electrifying friction built fast between them; he was riding her hard, and she loved it, her sex clutching at him. Dizzy with sensation, her emotions soared, her entire body carried on the rush.

He murmured in Spanish and then again in English. "You're so tight, so hot, your cunt is like a fist holding my cock. It makes me crazy."

She writhed on the bed, his raw words making her crazy.

Her nipples were hard inside her bra, chafing against it. Her clit was pounding, crushed as it was between her legs.

He thrust harder and faster, working his way into her as he neared climax. She could feel the head of his cock brushing her cervix, and wild strikes of lightning sensation reached her womb and beyond. Cries of ecstasy escaped her, and she gulped them back.

"Oh yes," he breathed in response to the sounds she made. "It's good. It's so right between us; you cannot deny that."

She pressed her lips together, biting into the lower one in case she blurted something that she would later regret.

Whispering words in Spanish, his voice husky and low, his hands moved around her hips. Firmly, but gently, he pulled her up and into a kneeling position, his cock barely leaving her before he thrust back inside her.

He held her hips, and she swayed, then put her hands on the bed to steady herself. His fingers locked on her, holding her steady, taking charge of her. Pressing her knees together with his legs outside of hers, he slammed into her from behind.

Her fingers locked on the pillows, and she stared down at them while whimpers escaped her mouth, her bottom tilting up, her hips moving of their own accord now, taking every lunge willingly, hungrily.

His cock had worked its way into that spot that made her feel wild and free, and she flung her head back. He cursed aloud in Spanish, his fingers tightening on her. His cock seemed to grow harder still, and she squirmed against him for ultimate contact, her sex stretched to capacity and sizzling with pleasure.

Her mouth opened as she reached her peak, release rushing through her, sparkling pleasure tipping into every nerve ending. She would have slumped forward, but he held her against him, his cock rigid and deep.

He whispered her name, then grunted heavily, his cock jerking as he came.

The power of the orgasm stunned her, and she trembled, and then reached back with one hand, covering his where it was locked around her hips.

He sighed her name when she stroked his hand, and his body shuddered against hers in the aftermath of release. Withdrawing, he removed the condom quickly, doing up his fly before rolling them both onto the bed, and then spooning her from behind.

She could feel his heart thudding against her back. Then he stroked her hair, and he whispered gentle, soothing words in his own tongue. Listening to them, savoring them, she closed her eyes and discovered that her lashes were damp.

Dazed, drowned in pleasure, she felt washed up and limp in the aftermath. It had been intense on a whole new level, so different from his measured lovemaking the night in the gallery. Hot and demanding, it reflected the dispute between them, and—above all—the passionate need for each other that overrode their circumstances.

He grew quiet and held her close, squeezing her gently, coaxing her to relax.

It felt good, so good, being nestled in his arms, in the afterglow. She was torn between the need to turn and look at her handsome lover, and the fear that this wildly passionate and strangely intimate moment would be lost if she did so. So she lay quietly, savoring the feeling of his arm around her.

*If only this could last forever,* she wished.

It couldn't though, because between them a wall still existed, even though that wall was the reason that had brought them together.

# 16

"What the hell do you mean she's gone?" Sergio demanded.

Elaine backed away, but he reached out and snatched her back by one shoulder, fighting the urge to slap her. "Elaine? Answer me."

"I told you, she's gone to a hotel for the night."

"Does Raimunda know where she went?"

"Raimunda's left food in the dining room and gone home early. The note was in the hall when I got back from Caldes." She gestured at the drawing room table. "It's over there; read it for yourself."

Sergio pushed her aside, then stormed over and lifted the note. He skimmed the contents. It was just as Elaine had related. Katrina was gone. What if Nicolas got to her again in the meantime?

"Why the hell has this happened? Where were you?"

"I went shopping." She shrugged. "Who knows, she might have walked out anyway."

Her remarks seemed far too glib to him, and he could see the insecurity in her eyes. He walked over to her, grabbing her as she tried to back away again. With one hand under her jaw he held her still. "You stupid bitch. You have one job to do, make sure everything runs smoothly here at the house when I'm not around, and you messed that up."

"Okay, I made a mistake leaving her here alone today, but I had to get out for a while." She squirmed in his grasp, dragging at his hands. "She'll be back; she has to finish the job. Her stuff is here. I checked the gallery, and her computer is still up there."

Sergio barely heard her words. He was contemplating how easy it would be to break her slender neck.

"I have to do everything myself," he whispered, his soul demanding recompense. His thumb was embedded beneath her chin, and he could feel her jaw working against it, the thrust of her tongue inside her mouth through the soft underside of her jaw. Her pale skin was so easily marked.

She gagged and then struggled for breath. "Sergio, no."

The look in her eyes was wild, she trembled, but there was a vivid warning there in her expression. "If you hurt me, I'm out of here . . . You know what that means. If I get nothing out of this after investing three years of my life, I'll make sure you get fuck all out of it, too." She spat the last words.

Her threat was real; he could see that. She could so easily wreck all their plans. Angrily, he let go of her, pushing her away in disgust as he did so.

She fell against an armchair and crumpled for a moment.

Straightening up, she tried to regain her composure. "I'm going to my room. For God's sake have a brandy and calm down. We can discuss this properly later and plan how to handle her when she comes back in the morning. You're in no fit state to think clearly right now."

She turned on her heel and headed for the door.

Stupid bitch, who did she think she was, ordering him around? In that moment, he realized that he'd begun to hate her. The sooner this was over, the sooner he could dump her. Right now, he couldn't take the risk that she'd mess up his plans, or—worse still—go to the police and expose what he'd done.

He despised her for making him feel so restricted; he hated being indebted to a con merchant he'd picked up in a casino. Cursing her, he screwed up the piece of paper in his hand and flung it at the door as it closed behind her.

*Lovely though it was, Katrina had to break the moment.* The need to move and see Nico's face had become overwhelming. Cautiously, she turned around.

He looked at her with searching eyes, his expression open and somehow tender, as if the fierce, rough lovemaking had broken down some artificial barrier between them.

She stared at him, her thoughts tumbling this way and that. God, he was gorgeous to look at. She ached inside, longing for their relationship to be simple. But it wasn't; it was very far from simple.

"Speak to me," he whispered. "What are you thinking?"

She gave a soft laugh. "I am wondering why I'm here, having fabulous sex with the disinherited son of the family I'm supposed to be working for. Am I crazy?"

He jerked back from her, his expression surprised. "Disinherited? Is that what Sergio told you?"

*That wasn't true?*

She drew back and considered him. She knew Sergio had lied to her; he'd told her he didn't know where Nicolas was or what he was doing, and yet he had threatened to ruin his career if he set foot inside the house. Had he lied to her about other things, too?

Nico shook his head and gave a wry smile. "No, Katrina. My father never disinherited me. Part of the family estate will be mine on my father's death. I have no interest in the business, so I receive no return from that, which is fair." He lifted one eyebrow. "Do you believe everything you are told?"

She flashed him a warning glance. "In the first instance, yes." She frowned. "Unless I'm given a good reason not to."

She peered at him, trying to piece it all together in her mind. "Okay, so you're not friendly with your father, but now you say you're not disinherited." She paused, and then laughed. "I admit it, I'm confused. What's the problem between you and your father?"

He eased up onto one elbow, his other arm still loosely around her. "It's rather simple, really. Unfortunately, we lacked understanding of each other. He is much more like Sergio, although not as shallow." He gave a wry smile.

She could see troubled emotions in his eyes, long buried.

"My father wanted me to work in the family business alongside Sergio. For them, the business and the family are bound together. I understood that. It wasn't what I wanted to do with my life, though. I wanted to go to the Institute of Performing Arts in Barcelona, practice, and maybe use what talents I had in teaching. My father thought it wasn't good enough, that art should be a hobby for me as it had been for him. He said I was 'wasting my life' pursuing it. I wanted only for him to let me do what called to me, maybe to be proud in some way. He refused me that."

Oh yes, there was hurt there, deep hurt. Katrina felt it, and with it there was a sense of loss in him.

"It didn't stop me. I applied for a scholarship under my mother's maiden name, won it, and worked my way through my degree. He suffered my presence here for a while, when my mother was alive, but when I qualified, I think he secretly hoped I would come back to the business. I didn't. Then my mother died, and Elaine arrived. That was the start of the end. He said he didn't want to see me again."

"But why would Sergio tell me that you were disinherited?"

"I have no idea. It has made you look badly on me, though, has it not? Perhaps that was his purpose."

"I suppose it did make me mistrust you. And, if Pocklington's had taken the goods to auction, the payment would have gone straight to his business account."

"Now you are beginning to see how he presented only what he wanted you to see."

"Did you know that Sergio and Elaine were . . . close?"

He nodded, and she could see he was pleased she was asking these questions. "Sergio brought her here to Castagona. They have always been close, although they tried to hide it. I soon learned that Elaine is a rather cruel, selfish woman. She tried to act differently with my father, and I think he was blind to her true nature because he didn't want to be alone. He missed my mother badly."

"It's your father I feel sorry for."

"Yes." His expression grew tense. "That is why I am here, why I try to get to the truth of his needs. It eats away at me."

His eyes looked haunted, and Katrina reached out for him, holding his shoulder, squeezing it gently. She sighed. "I thought . . . When I came here, I thought that the sale would help your father, but now I'm not sure of anything."

"I'm sorry, you have been badly misled by my brother."

Yes, there was deception going on here, in so many ways. Nicolas had used her, too. Could she really trust him? She wanted to, but she wasn't sure. If one brother had lied, she'd be stupid to believe that the other one was being totally honest. There was no escaping the fact that he'd seduced her for a particular reason. Bottom line, the job she was doing wasn't completely on the level. Worst possible scenario, it wasn't even legal. The fact that she might have to withdraw from the commission on behalf of the auction house made her heart sink. She'd promised her boss she'd come through, but he wouldn't want to be involved in something duplicitous, nor did she, even if it meant eating humble pie with Pocklington and looking like a fool in front of Henry Wallace.

Right now she needed to get some space, get her head together, and get in touch with her boss to discuss her concerns about the sale. "I'm sorry I haven't given you a proper hearing before now."

She sat up, and then stood, drawing away from him. "I need some time on my own to think this through."

"Katrina!"

"Don't try to stop me."

He reached out for her, but she stepped away.

Avoiding his eyes, she hunted on the floor for her sandals, badly needing to stand her ground for the sake of her sanity. Okay, she wanted the man, but she barely knew him, and although she wanted to trust him, the one thing her time here had shown her was that she couldn't even trust her own instincts. She had to get her head sorted, and she had to talk to someone outside of this family about the odd setup before it went any further.

Nicolas dropped back on the bed, cursing under his breath. Taking a deep breath, she resisted her instinct to reach out, to melt away the anger and hurt she sensed emanating from him. She simply *had* to think this through without either of the brothers trying to influence or threaten her. She also had a point to prove: that you can't just steal a woman away and expect her to fall into line. She was an adult; she needed to make up her own mind about all of this.

Spying her sandals lying abandoned at the foot of the bed, she reached for them and then unlocked and walked out of the door with them clutched in one hand, before Nicolas had time to reach out and grab her. As the door closed behind her, however, she glimpsed him out of the corner of her eye. He was staring fixedly at the ceiling, hands behind his head, his mood dark.

*Where am I?* Raimunda's house, in the village itself, that was it. The hallway she was standing in was small, with simple whitewashed walls. Two closed doors beckoned to her on one side, and one that stood ajar farther down the corridor betrayed its occupant by the sound of utensils being moved. Raimunda, no doubt.

Pushing her feet into her sandals, Katrina stepped over to the closed door and opened it as quietly she could. Another bedroom, Raimunda's. It was only marginally more furnished than her guest room. There was a crucifix over the bed and a colorful knitted blanket folded neatly on top of the simple bed-cover. She shut the door.

The other door led into a small sitting room, sparsely furnished. It housed two armchairs, an old television on a fold-out table, and two prints on the wall depicting sea views. Both prints were badly yellowed, and the varnish on the frames was peeling at the corners.

Raimunda came home here every night, after working up at the decadent surroundings of the Torre del Castagona? Katrina was angry about that bloody "cup of tea" nonsense, but this was sad. Then she remembered what Elaine had said, that she had told her to move out because of her affection for her husband, Jorge. Elaine had said it so smugly, too. Katrina really didn't like the new Mrs. Teodoro. Raimunda must have had to start a home from nothing, after many years of being a live-in housekeeper. Yet she was still devoted to the family.

She shut the door and headed back along the corridor. It looked as if she would have to go past Raimunda. She steeled herself and pushed the door wide open.

Raimunda was much as she had been the last time Katrina

had seen her, standing by a stove, pouring water from a kettle into a pot. The difference was the kitchen was tiny, as was the stove and the table, and she was preparing coffee, not tea.

Raimunda put the kettle down, rubbed her hands on her apron, turned off the radio, and then peered at Katrina. She clacked her tongue on the roof of her mouth, rolled her eyes, and shook her head. It was then that Katrina became aware that she was wearing only her bra and skirt.

"Oh, hell."

Panic hit her. *Have I even got my knickers on?*

Yes, her G-string was still in place, although it felt a tad damp. Her shoulders slumped, her will to get out of there slipping away. God, she was tired. She reached for one of the wood chairs at the table and dropped into it, suddenly exhausted. The drugged tea perhaps, or that humdinger of a tryst back there with Nicolas, or just . . . everything, catching up with her. She couldn't even remember when she'd had a decent sleep.

Raimunda looked at her, but instead of the usual suspicious glare, Katrina could see disappointment in her eyes. The woman looked almost tearful. What with that and Nico glowering at the ceiling back there in the bedroom, Katrina realized just how much these two had pinned their hopes on getting her away from the house to talk to her. She shuffled her feet, trying not to feel guilty.

*Hell, they drugged me. Why should I feel guilty?*

Even though she'd already decided that Pocklington's would have to pull out of the commission, she couldn't help being fascinated by the whys and wherefores of it all. Nico had said that

Sergio had no right to do what he was doing. What was he really up to, in that case? Elaine seemed okay with it. Elaine's role in this was suspicious, though. She was with Sergio.

Sergio had used seduction as a technique to get her out there. Nico had used her, too, but at least he'd apologized. She sensed deep down that Nico still loved his father, even though he claimed not to. Raimunda, as well, was devoted to this elusive man Jorge Teodoro. It was a pity he wasn't around to ask; that might clear up a few questions.

Raimunda glanced past her, waving her hands down the corridor and began muttering in Spanish, lifting her apron to dab at her eyes. She seemed to have decided that all had not gone as planned. She poured a mug of coffee from the pot and then gestured to Katrina. *"Café, señorita?"*

Remembering the "cup of tea," the irony of the invitation hit her, and Katrina couldn't help laughing aloud. It came out sounding slightly hysterical.

Raimunda shook her head, rolling her eyes again. She seemed to be apologizing and demonstrated that the coffee was not drugged by taking a swig, then offering Katrina her own cup.

Well, she wasn't about to drug her again. What would be the point in that? Katrina chuckled and nodded, taking the cup gratefully. *"Gracias, Raimunda."*

Raimunda nodded, standing by, and then color rose in her cheeks. Again, she looked tearful. *"Perdóname . . .* cup of tea."

Instinctively, Katrina reached out and touched her arm, nodding, indicating she understood. Raimunda seemed hugely relieved and immediately launched off on her monologue again. Katrina held the mug between both hands, sipping from it gratefully. The coffee was strong and heavily doused in creamy milk. It really hit the spot.

*She's lonely,* she realized, as she watched Raimunda talking to herself. She had devoted her life to a family she cared for, and then she was pushed out. Katrina felt sympathy for her, sadness, too.

*How did I get mixed up in this family and their crazy feud? Because I was reckless.*

If she hadn't been flattered by Sergio . . . If she hadn't followed *el diablo* that first night in Barcelona . . . *And now I'm sitting here, half-undressed in a stranger's house with a damp G-string to sort out and a grumpy lover to come to terms with.* She did want to come to terms with him. She smiled into her cup, thinking about what he'd said. "I want you." Simple words, but the way he'd said them had hit like a tidal wave, changing the rhythm of her heartbeat, altering her life forever.

It occurred to her with sudden clarity that choosing to be more adventurous meant she had to accept the consequences of that, take the responsibility for her reckless actions. If you let your boat drift with the tide, you have to deal with it when it gets stuck in the reeds. She'd been reckless, yes, but the unforgivable thing would be walking away from this mess without acting responsibly. She'd got herself involved; now she had to judge the best way to handle it. She wished she hadn't unwittingly made promises to Pocklington based on so little knowledge. She'd had a true wake-up call for life there.

She took another deep swallow of the coffee. It was clearing her head. It occurred to her that she was thinking more sensibly than she had since she'd arrived in Spain. How ironic, she thought with a wry smile. Now that her situation was a big tangled mess, her brain had finally kicked in.

Raimunda's gestures while she rattled on fascinated her. She kept punching herself in the chest and pointing down the corridor, presumably at Nico. Katrina guessed that she was putting in a good word for him or bemoaning the fact that the plot to get her on board hadn't seemed to work. Her body language indicated passion on the subject, and frustration, too. In fact, she was getting very emotional, and Katrina felt for her because she sensed this woman cared a great deal about Nico and about Jorge Teodoro, just as Elaine had hinted. If she cared about him and if she favored Nico, what did that mean? Her reactions seemed so genuine that Katrina wished she could understand what she was saying.

Raimunda shook her head sadly, and her eyes were filled with unshed tears. When she went for a second cup of coffee, she spilled some on her countertop. *"Merde,"* she said in exasperated tone, then covered her mouth with her hand.

*Merde?* Katrina's head snapped up. Raimunda had cursed in French. Katrina wondered if she was hearing things. This stoic Christian woman knew how to swear in French? It seemed so unlikely that she had to question it. *"Raimunda, parlez-vous français?"*

Raimunda glanced over her shoulder and nodded. *"Oui, naturellement."*

Katrina couldn't believe it. Why not, though? It often happened in the art world and the auction business. In European countries, with so many languages so close together, you could usually find some common ground with the person you were dealing with, even if it wasn't a first language for either party. She hadn't expected to find that kind of common ground with Raimunda, though.

The Teodoro housekeeper was now burbling away in French, apparently adept at the language. She explained that her late husband—God rest his soul—was a French merchant seaman. They'd met and fallen in love in Barcelona, where she'd been on a visit when she was only seventeen. It was only when Raimunda had got into this little tale that she realized she was conversing with Katrina, and that Katrina understood. Her words faded, and she looked across the room, openmouthed, as it hit her.

Katrina nodded. *"Oui, nous pouvons parler en français!"*

Raimunda stared at Katrina.

Katrina smiled.

Raimunda pulled up a chair, her eyes sparkling.

Katrina's heart lifted. Now she would hear the rest of the story.

# 17

*Nico had been glowering at the ceiling for a long time when the* sound of excited chatter coming from somewhere in the house gradually edged into his consciousness. It sounded like birds chirruping, hens clucking.

Women talking, he thought to himself with a wry smile. Who, though? He hadn't even noticed when the music had gone off and the chattering had commenced, but his curiosity was growing. The bleep of his phone interrupted his thoughts, and he reached over to the bedside table where he'd left it. "Kent, hello. Any luck with the rest of the places on the list?"

"Nada. Not a thing."

"It must not be a complete list of the nursing homes in this area," Nico said, his sense of frustration growing by the moment.

"Maybe. I've got some other information you might be interested in, though."

"Yes?"

"I was talking to my professor yesterday; you know, the guy who told me about your family. He said some other stuff about your brother."

Nico lifted his free hand in the air, incredulous. "What is it about this guy that he has to gossip about my family all the time?"

"Ha, I wondered about that, too, so I asked him straight out. Turns out he knew your brother when Sergio had just taken over your dad's company. The prof worked in one of the stores when he was a postgrad. Your brother had him fired. He didn't say what the disagreement was about, but he seems to think your brother was in a foul mood and took it out on him. Whatever, he holds a grudge."

Nico sighed. "It doesn't surprise me. I'm not the only person in the world who has a problem with my brother."

"That's just it. Thing is, the prof gets to wine and dine with some of the big financiers in Barcelona because of some family connection, and he said the rumor is that your father's company is in trouble, that Sergio has been making some very bad decisions . . . Sergio's trying really hard to keep it under wraps, but someone has leaked the info. Word is that investors are starting to pull out."

Nico was shocked. The company his father had built up had been so secure, as if it was set in cement. Someone would have to be very foolish or headstrong to have undermined all of his father's work. Despite the unexpected bad news, news that would have been devastating to his father, he had to laugh, wryly shaking his head.

"Nico? Are you laughing? Did you hear me right?"

"I did. It's a shock yes, but . . . Sergio is in charge, and failure couldn't happen to a nicer guy; you know what I mean?"

"Right." Kent sounded relieved, if a bit confused.

Nico drummed his fingers on his chin, his mind ticking over. "It explains why he needs to free up money from elsewhere."

"Yeah, that's what I thought," Kent said.

"I appreciate all your efforts. Maybe I can overlook two months' rent, huh?"

"This deal gets better all the time."

Nico grinned and was about to say his good-byes and hang up, when Kent spoke again.

"Wait . . . I'm curious, what are you gonna do?"

"Let my brother know that I'm on to him."

"Cool, I wonder how that will go down. Look, if you need any more help, just give me a call."

*"Gracias, amigo."*

"Good luck, buddy. Adios."

Standing, Nico felt much more focused, and his curiosity about the chattering he could hear grew. He noticed Katrina's top on the floor and picked it up, holding it in his hand as he followed the voices.

They were in the kitchen. Sitting on either side of Raimunda's table, the two women were talking animatedly in a language he didn't speak more than a few words of, French. He stood just outside the doorway for some time, observing, before they noticed him. It gave him the chance to study Katrina.

She looked as if she were at home in her own kitchen, half-dressed as she grabbed a coffee in the morning. That was a pleasing image, one he'd like to see every day. She alternated between wrapping her hands around the cup of coffee in front of her and reaching out to touch Raimunda on the arm with one hand when they shared laughter. Her eyes glowed; her hair was still gloriously messed from their lovemaking.

When she noticed him, her smile grew. "We've been chatting in French."

Raimunda said something, her head jerking in his direction. Katrina laughed, and they continued to chat on for several minutes, each interrupting the other excitedly. Nico felt sure it was a good thing, but he stared at them mistrustfully, nonetheless. She was supposed to be talking to him, listening to what he had to say. He hadn't been able to hold her, and yet here she was sitting happily in the kitchen chatting avidly with Raimunda.

After a while he stepped into the room and handed Katrina her top, which she pulled on.

"Isn't it wonderful?" Katrina said, looking up at him, her eyes sparkling.

"I don't know; I can't understand." He issued the response rather grumpily.

"You don't speak French?"

"French?" The absurdity of the situation had him firmly in its grip. "I've spent the past year trying to perfect my English. I've even shared my home with an American to help me master it. French is at the bottom of my list."

"An American? That explains the accent." Amusement sparkled in her eyes.

He frowned. "Accent?"

She blew him a kiss. "I'm teasing you. What accent you have is very attractive. You speak English wonderfully." Her eyes glowed at him, and Raimunda, too, looked at him with a proud twinkle in her eyes.

He felt strangely as if the two women had been discussing him, which he supposed they must have been. "Thank you. I've secured sponsorship to take the kids I work with to perform at European festivals, starting with the Edinburgh festival, but first I need to improve my English. I want to be able to lead them well."

"You work with kids now, like you hoped?" She looked fascinated.

"Yes, teenagers, in the city. I teach performance arts to the kids who wouldn't otherwise get the chance to understand the artistic heritage of our country."

She stared at him for the longest time. "I didn't know that about you." The expression in her eyes told him she had learned a lot from Raimunda.

"There's a lot you didn't know."

"I wasn't brought here as judge and jury, Nico." Her statement was delivered seriously.

It was true, and yet he had expected that of her after their first meeting. Why? Because of his sense of what was right and wrong in this situation, or something else? She was a professional hired to catalog an art collection, not to arbitrate a family feud. Why did he expect her to feel what he felt? Because he admired her. It struck him in that moment that he had foolishly expected her to see things through his eyes and feel what was in his heart. In some ways, many ways, she did.

"Nico, believe me, I want to do the right thing here, and I'm starting to get a better idea what's going on."

A faint sense of hope grew within him.

Raimunda, who had been biding her time while they spoke in English, butted in, speaking again in French. Katrina nodded at her, smiling, her glance shifting toward him every now and then.

He rested his back up against the doorframe, watching and waiting.

"Raimunda tells me you used to copy the artwork in your father's collection when you were a little boy."

He nodded.

"I found the paintings in the gallery. They were quite a mystery for me, until Raimunda told me the story."

"My father kept them?" He didn't know that; he was surprised.

"Oh, yes. They are very good."

She seemed to be waiting for him to say something on the subject, so he did.

"Thank you. For me it was a way to learn. I didn't want to be a copyist forever. I learned many things, but I wanted to go in my own direction."

"I see that now. What is it that you hoped to accomplish," she said, nodding down the corridor to the bedroom, "when you brought me here to discuss things?"

Her question was serious, but he could tell from the look in her eyes that she was thinking about what had happened between them just as much as he was. He wanted to take her back there right now, pin her down, and listen to those delicious muted sounds she made when she was pleasured, the sounds that made him want to lose himself inside her.

"I'm not sure anymore. I never expected to be so attracted to you, to want your approval, to want you to reciprocate my feelings. Then, in there, when you said you wanted to do everything with me. Well, I lost it."

"Nico." She lowered her gaze for a moment, and there was color on her cheekbones when she looked back at him. "I meant about the sale, the collection. Tell me now why you don't want it to happen. I'm listening."

"My concern is only that my father has agreed to this sale. I need to speak with him. If he is happy, then so am I. That's it."

"Well, that's my concern, too. I need his signatures on release documents, but every time I mentioned it to Sergio, he changed the subject."

Again, Nico felt badly that Sergio had manipulated her. Hell, they all had manipulated her, himself included. When she'd said it back there in the bedroom, he realized he'd been too swept up in the moment to register how she might have felt. Would he ever be able to make that up to her? He hoped so. He'd happily die trying.

"I haven't seen my father in a long time, as you know, but I would ask him myself. Problem is, I cannot locate him. Sergio would not tell me where he is."

"Is that what the argument was about yesterday morning?"

He nodded. She was observant and smart and caring. Even though they'd all lied to her, she wanted to do the right thing. Her uncertainty over how far to be involved was understandable.

Katrina was frowning, deep in thought. "You don't think Sergio has done something, like, really bad?"

She glanced at Raimunda and bit her lip.

Nicolas knew what she was thinking.

She locked eyes with him, speaking in a low voice as if not keen to say the words. "I mean like something . . . terminal?"

He shook his head. "It occurred to me, too, but I don't think so. If my father was dead, Sergio would not be able to sell the art collection."

She looked puzzled by that. "Why?"

"It was my mother's wish that the collection should be left to the national museums and galleries of Spain. My father agreed, and his will reflects their decision."

"Oh, my God." Her eyebrows had shot up, and she leaned forward in her chair. "So, unless your father has changed his mind about that, Sergio is acting against your parents' wishes?"

He gave her a sad smile. "Yes, you see it now. My mother was more emotionally involved in the collection than my father. To him it was always a financial investment. At the same time it was something they had done together, so he couldn't part with it himself. He spoke to Sergio and me about it. It was one of the things that drove a wedge between us. I was happy for the art to go to the national collection. Sergio wasn't."

Her eyes opened wide. "Really?"

He nodded, observing her reactions. This was bad news for her; that's why he'd been particularly reluctant to mention it before now.

Her eyes flickered with thought. "How do you know your father hasn't changed the will since you last saw him?"

"I can't be sure. He changed the will when Elaine came on the scene. I recently spoke to the family solicitor. He wasn't able to give me a proper answer, but he indicated that there hadn't been any changes to the section about the art collection since my mother's death. The business is Sergio's." He shrugged. "I did not expect to gain anything from the business. That wounded my father even more, though. He wanted me to want it. The fact that I didn't hurt him deeply, which was not my intention."

She listened, taking it all in. He wondered if he should have told her more before, but he'd needed to build the bridge of trust that had grown between them, and that Raimunda had helped along by adding in that final, vital link.

"There are financial provisions for the staff, and then the property is to be divided three ways: Elaine, Sergio, and myself." Again he watched for her reaction.

"And he said you were disinherited," she looked amazed.

"In terms of the business, I am. So that is not entirely untrue. But my father told me that despite our differences, the Torre del Castagona is my home. There are other properties, too. Deep down, I think my father believed it was something to draw me back, to force me to change my mind. He always hoped that I'd grow as hungry as Sergio for a cut, that I'd return to the family."

He smiled wryly. "He called me a lone wolf, but he said I'd return to the pack. Maybe he was right. I'm here now." He hadn't told anyone all this before, but now he knew why. He hadn't wanted to prove his father right.

She smiled back gently. "You're here to be sure the right thing is done." He could see she was working through all the information. "What I don't understand is why Sergio won't tell you where your father is."

"My guess is because Father has not agreed to sell the collection. He's a stubborn man. And . . . now I hear Sergio needs money. The business is in trouble; he's desperate."

She sat back in her chair, hands flat on the table, shaking her head. It was a lot to take in. "So you think he's got your father out of the way because he believes he can dupe me into taking the collection to auction without your father's permission?"

"I'm not sure, but it's a possibility."

She looked into his eyes, and he saw assessment there. "Yes, it is. He seemed very resistant to taking the documentation I had for your father to sign. He said he'd bring it to London later. I've seen enough of his behavior to understand how manipulative he is."

Nico felt a sense of relief, but they were only halfway there. He sighed, one hand rested up against the doorframe. "Where is my father? That is the unanswered question. I need to see him. Perhaps he has agreed to it, to save the business. I just want to hear that from his mouth. I would accept it then. I have a friend looking for him, but he hasn't found him yet."

Raimunda butted in, reaching across to pat Katrina on the arm. They exchanged words in French. Raimunda threw her hands up, shaking her head.

Again the irony struck him, the three of them were all speaking in different languages to each other, like a game of tag, but they were functioning as a team. At last.

When they finished chatting, Katrina stared at him, a deep furrow on her forehead, her eyes flitting about.

He wanted to kiss away the concern in her expression, tell her it was not a problem for her to be worrying about. He didn't want it to be, but of course it was; Sergio was trying to dupe her as well.

"Oh my God, Nico," she whispered, her expression changing, her eyes rounding. She spoke to Raimunda in French, rapid-fire, Raimunda nodded, and then shook her head as if denying something. Katrina spoke, and Raimunda looked confused but nodded again.

"Who is this man, Vincent?" Katrina directed the question at Nico in English.

"Vincent? I don't know who you mean." He could see she was onto something, so he quizzed Raimunda on the matter. Raimunda chastised him and reminded him she had mentioned the stranger in the house before. "Ah, yes, Raimunda had mentioned a visitor. She says he's a guest at the house, that Elaine said he was a friend of the family."

Raimunda added a comment in Spanish, to which Nico laughed.

"What?" Katrina asked.

"She said since he and you both stay in your towers, she has been carrying trays up so many stairs she is losing weight."

Katrina blushed. "I felt safe up there." She added something to Raimunda in French. When she turned back, she frowned. "Elaine told me he was a lodger, and rent was also mentioned." She looked at him meaningfully. "There are a lot of different stories flying around here."

"You think it's important?"

She was on her feet, her eyes bright. "I wondered if they

were lovers, at first. But that's not the case." She lifted her eyebrows and glanced at Raimunda as if she was about to say something else but then thought twice about it.

"He's a bit of a weird bloke," she continued, "comes across as very secretive, and he's almost always up there in the tower. I could see him from the gallery. Well, it made me wonder what he was doing there, and when I was talking to Raimunda about what happened, she described the day the ambulance came for your father . . ." She paused, staring at him, her expression disturbed. "Nico, she never actually saw him being carried into the ambulance."

Nico followed her logic. He double-checked with Raimunda, asked about the day his father had been taken. She shook her head. She definitely didn't see his father being taken out. In fact, it sounded as if the whole thing with the ambulance departing had been timed for when she was arriving at the house for the day.

"What, you think he never left?" he asked Katrina.

"There's a chance, if it's some sort of scam, isn't there?"

Raimunda butted in, demanded to know what they were saying. He explained quickly in Spanish and asked her whether she thought his father could be in the guest apartments at the Torre. Her eyes rounded, and she immediately shook her head, but he could see the doubt in her eyes even as she thought it over. She kept shaking her head, but then she lifted her shoulders and gave a funny little shrug. When she finally replied, it was to say that this man, Vincent, had been a resident there from a couple of days before the ambulance came. He'd kept her away from the tower, it was true, but still she could not believe it. It was hard for her to admit; he could see that.

Katrina was looking at him, agitated that she couldn't keep up with the conversation. This three-way dialogue had him switching gears into English faster than he'd ever done before. "Raimunda isn't convinced, but she agrees that it might be possible."

"She won't want to admit it, because she hasn't realized, you know." There was compassion in her eyes, and he loved her for that.

"Yes, it would be hard. Not much escapes her, but if they convinced her with an ambulance, staging a show as evidence . . . She also said that Vincent was brought in a couple of days before the ambulance came."

"Had your father been ill before that?" Katrina asked.

He nodded. "Raimunda had already been in touch with me. She said my father was sleeping a lot, and she heard Sergio saying that the old man didn't have long."

"Bloody hell, that Sergio is all heart," Katrina said with a look of disapproval.

She appeared so haughty, so sternly British, that he wanted to hug her.

"Do you think he could really do something like that?"

He shrugged, but only because he didn't want to bad-mouth Sergio anymore until it was proven. He knew that Sergio was perfectly capable of cold-hearted acts, if it meant he got what he wanted.

"Well, if you've been unable to find him, and Sergio won't tell you where he is . . ." She shivered. "How dreadful, if it is true, to think of him being kept there, a prisoner in his own home."

"I'm going up there now. I'm going to find out."

"No," Katrina said, closing on him. "Let me go back. I can say I changed my mind about staying away and that I want to get an early start in the morning."

"It's not safe. We don't know who this man Vincent is."

"Yes, but at least I'm welcome in the bloody house."

She had a good point there.

"Nico, if I can at least check first, why risk it? Your brother will have no qualms about stitching you up if he finds you there. If I go back in, I can at least check if that guy Vincent is still around and whether we can get access to the tower. If they find me, I can always say I meant to go to the other tower to do some more work, and I got lost. I'm covered; you wouldn't be. I'll find out who is about, and then you can come in as well."

"You would do that for me?" Nico's chest felt strangely tight, but he was worrying most of all about Katrina, the risk she might take. Sergio was capable of anything. He had brought Elaine in to help manipulate his father. If Katrina were in danger, he would never forgive himself. There had to be another way to check it out. He turned away from her to gather his thoughts.

He felt her hand on his shoulder. "Nico, what is the matter? Let me check it out. Whether he is there or not, I will cancel the valuation, and I'll help you to find him before I leave."

She was saying all the things that he had hoped she would say; yet all he could hear was the fact that she would be leaving. *Of course she will be leaving; deal with it.*

The way she looked up at him, with such sincerity, made him wonder why he hadn't met her at another time. She was so fresh and alive, both passionate and compassionate. She had so many worthy qualities.

"Trust me, I can easily find out what's going on in there. We'll know today."

Reluctance weighed heavy on him, but he had to know. "We'll go up there, but not yet, not before dark. It will be safer that way."

# 18

*"Tell me again why you want to undress me?"*

Katrina's eyes closed, and she caught her bottom lip between her teeth, savoring the feeling of him undressing her. His fingers undoing the zipper on her skirt made her pulse trip, and then he pulled it down her thighs, dropping it on to the bedroom floor. He sat down on the edge of the bed and kissed her on the curve of her belly just above the line of her G-string, making her shiver with pleasure. He stroked the outline of her buttocks, his hands so sure of her body, familiar now.

"You will see," he murmured. "It will be more practical." Glancing over her, he sighed. "Although the actual undressing is making it very hard to resist you."

His hands were on her hips, his thumbs sliding beneath the band of her G-string. He looked up at her, his eyes dark with passion.

Her body trembled in response. "Nico, it's almost dark; we'll be able to go soon."

"You've had enough of me already?" His question was teasing.

He already knew the answer; his expression told her that. He just wanted to hear her say it. Her hand went to his hair, and she pushed her fingers into it, scrunching the thick texture of it as she shook her head. "No, I haven't had enough of you yet."

"I'm very glad to hear that," he responded, one hand moving to pull her G-string down the length of her thighs. "Because I want you, Katrina Hammond."

He pulled her down onto the bed, swapping their places so that she was on her back and he was kneeling on the floor, his gaze on her pussy.

"Nico!" Delighted laughter escaped her. She wanted him, but she wanted to resolve this huge issue that was hanging over them. Then . . . then what? Would their connection be over? She wanted to be with him and experience him in every mood. Her throat felt tight, her emotions both elated and constricted in her chest. She propped up onto her elbows.

"Nico, I know why you are doing this . . . You're trying to distract the both of us from what we're supposed to be doing now, what we've agreed."

"Just a taste, please," he breathed over her skin, easing her back down on the bed with one hand. He kissed her below her navel, his hands pushing her thighs apart so that he could move between them.

She gasped, amazed but thrilled.

He stroked two fingers through the moist folds of her pussy

and then touched one finger against her jutting clitoris, stroking it ever so lightly. Deep and heavy waves of sensation spread out from his fingertip, escalating as they moved through her pelvis, as if he had touched her everywhere inside, through the conduit of that most tender spot.

His mouth moved down across her abdomen, and then he reached forward to bury his face deep between her thighs. She moaned and writhed beneath him, and then her breath caught when his tongue made contact with her clit. Sensation charged up across her body from his lips, her entire skin alive to his touch. He engulfed it with his mouth, his tongue moving rhythmically. Then he ran his tongue down one side of her sex folds and up the other before riding back and forth on her clit again.

When she moaned, he drew back, gazing down between her spread legs with eyes filled with admiration.

"You are so sensitive here." He blew on her exposed pussy.

The warm air moving across her aroused skin made her wriggle and squirm, breathless laughter escaping her mouth. "Nico, please, you're torturing me."

"Torture?" He adopted a mock serious expression. "But I don't want to do that. I only wish to bring you pleasure."

Moving back into place, his mouth closed over the tingling nub of her clit, making her sigh with relief. Eyes closing, she melted into the bed, made weak by his intimate assault. His hands moved up and over her body, outlining her hips, her waist, and then he squeezed her breasts possessively through her top. His hair brushed against the sensitive flesh of her inner thighs, making her crazy. Breathlessly, she rolled her head to one side and opened her eyes to look to him.

The image of those powerful arms reaching over her was so essentially male that she clenched and melted inside, and a moment later fluid dribbled down between her buttocks. When his tongue plunged inside her, she cried out. He swirled until she whimpered. Reaching out, her fingers fleetingly touched his head, and then she gripped at the sheets on either side of her. He flashed his eyes at her from between her thighs, which made her blush, and she looked away.

"No escape," he whispered. His tongue moved up the crease on one side of her sex lips, around her clit, and down the crease on the other side, tantalizing her.

"Nico," she pleaded, desperate for release.

He inserted two fingers inside her, curving them around the front wall of her sex, just as his mouth covered her clit again, his tongue flicking over it.

Wham. Her climax rattled through her like a freight train. She felt hot, a deep spasm inside, then another, a shot of pure bliss blossoming in her clit. Her lower body juddered, her hands clutching at the bed.

When she gathered herself, he was stripping off his jeans. He took one look at her expression and laughed. "I'm getting changed; that is all."

He gestured like a true Latin at that point. She rolled onto one side, propped herself up on her elbow, and watched as he pulled a bag from beneath the bed. He unzipped it and extracted a pair of particularly sexy looking black leather pants, the pants he had been wearing the morning he and Sergio had argued.

Tugging them on, he gestured for her to sit up. He had to

gesture again, to snap her out of the spell she was under watching him. The view was too good. His gorgeous, fit thighs and his tight buttocks encased in soft black cotton mesmerized her as they disappeared into the snug black leather pants. She sat up on the edge of the bed and observed him doing the buttons over his fly. His strong hands moving over the bulge there made her wet all over again. "I could watch you getting dressed and undressed all day."

"The feeling is mutual," he said as he dropped into a squat. He lifted one of her feet and slipped it into his abandoned jeans.

"I'm wearing *your* jeans?"

"It will be more practical than your skirt."

He looked so sexy there at her feet, and when he encouraged her to stand and pulled the jeans into position over her hips, she closed her eyes, savoring the feeling of his hands dressing her.

Reaching into his bag again, he lifted out her phone and tucked it into her pocket, before he pulled the belt tight, and then tighter again, before doing it up, hauling her toward him with a jolt.

"My phone," she murmured, putting her hand over it.

"Yes, you said you were expecting a call, so I brought it."

"Oh, that call. It was about a shipping date for the collection." She looked at him. "I'll cancel it in the morning."

He nodded, and then he looked at her very seriously. "What did you mean when you said you knew why I was trying to distract the both of us?"

It took a moment to realize he was referring to what she had said before he started kissing her in intimate places. "I meant there is a part of you looking for excuses not to go up to the house and resolve this."

He frowned, his hands moving to her arms. "Why do you say this?"

Did she know him well enough to guess at this, and to know how he'd take it? He looked very serious, but he was stroking her arms gently as he encouraged her to talk to him. He did want to know.

"The rift between you and your father, you aren't sure whether you want it healed or not . . . Am I right?"

His hands paused on her arms, and his lips tightened. For several long moments he didn't respond. "Maybe," he eventually replied. Then he gave a deep sigh. "Yes, I suppose I have been torn. There is no reason for me to care, but part of me still does. I believe, perhaps, it is loyalty to the memory of my mother."

Her heart went out to him. "Nico, I understand how hard it is. It's far easier to analyze someone else's relationship with their parents than it is your own, believe me." She gave a wry smile, thinking about her own awkward relationship with her mother. "I can see that you have to know, but that part of you resents that. It's not wrong; it just makes it harder."

He stared at her, his gaze searching hers. "You are the most intuitive woman I have ever met."

It wasn't what she was expecting him to say just then. "I'm flattered, but really . . . I am trained to notice things, to question the history and origin of things. Those skills sometimes came into play when I observe people, as well as art."

She reached out and kissed his lips, eager to soften his

expression. "The history you have with your father will still exist, no matter what; deep down you are connected. Things might get easier between you when you see him again; on the other hand, they might never be resolved. What's important is that whatever piece of you is still invested in this family needs to know where he is. We must find out. Now."

She wasn't expecting what she saw in his eyes right then, either. Yearning. For her. Oh God, it touched her so deeply inside. She longed for him, and when he took her in his arms and kissed her, deeply, she held his face, her chest aching with emotion. Was it just this odd situation they found themselves in? Was that what had forced them to know each other so quickly? Would their attraction fade, once this was over? That thought scared her. She hoped it wasn't the case.

He pulled back, and nodded. "*Sí.* Let's do it."

*Outside, Katrina stared at the motorcycle in disbelief.* "I've never been on a motorcycle. I'm not sure I can do this."

Nico grinned and handed her a helmet. "It's easy. Just hold on to me, and you'll be fine. You might even enjoy it."

Now she understood his leathers and the need to change clothing. She stared at the motorbike again, dubiously. Then an odd thought hit her. *How did I get here?* She had vague, incomplete memories of him holding her in his arms, being carried, Raimunda checking on her. But how? Horrified, she pointed at it. "You didn't bring me here on that when I was asleep, did you?"

"Yes," he replied, deadpan. "We pulled your skirt up around

your hips, Raimunda tied you to my back, and when we drove through the village, everybody came out for a look. We told them that you did it for a dare."

She felt slightly queasy. "Oh my God, Nico!"

He strode up and held her, his expression serious for a moment, before breaking into a smile. "Beneath that passionate exterior, you're a very sweet-natured, trusting woman, Katrina Hammond."

He reached out to kiss her, and suddenly that was all that mattered.

"Paco, the gardener, drove us here in his car," he said as they drew apart. "It's barely roadworthy, and it was not the most comfortable journey, but I assure you that you were comfortable and your honor was perfectly safe."

Relief coursed through her. She'd always been particularly gullible, but she didn't realize he'd cottoned onto that already. "I should slap you for goading me like that."

"You should perhaps slap me for a lot of things."

They were silent a moment, staring into each other's eyes. She had a way to tease him back. "So Paco drove us here. I bet you didn't you know that Paco is gay."

The expression on his face told her he definitely didn't know.

"Gay? Paco? Are you sure?"

"I saw him and Elaine's houseguest together."

Nico looked at her questioningly, and she nodded emphatically.

"You don't suppose that he told Vincent about you bringing

me here?" she asked, suddenly aware that Paco was the only member of the household who seemed to be involved with both sides.

"He is Raimunda's nephew. He wouldn't dare to cross her. Besides, Paco doesn't say very much."

"Makes you wonder how he and this guy Vincent got together."

"We didn't say very much when we first got together," he reminded her with a wink.

Something about the way he said that, and the way he was looking at her made her feel deeply connected to him. "No, we didn't, did we."

Again they stared into each other's eyes.

"Come on," she added. "Let's go. If I'm right . . . Well, we need to get a move on. It's been too long already."

"Practical, too. You're quite a woman."

She stared at the motorcycle and then climbed up behind him, easing herself into the space available, the helmet dangling from one hand as she held on to him around the waist and got into position.

"There are footrests." Nico nodded to the jutting metal bars.

"I got them," she replied and adjusted her position.

"Hey, Nico," a voice called out, and she heard a wolf whistle. A man walked by, calling something out to Nico in Spanish as he passed. He had three bottles of cerveza under one arm and a couple of DVDs in the other.

Nico waved back in greeting, responding with laughter in

his voice. "An old school friend," he explained when the man had gone.

Nico had friends in the village, even though he lived in Barcelona now; that didn't surprise her. She wondered if Sergio did. "What was he saying?"

"He was admiring the view. You ready?"

"Yeah," she said distractedly, flattered, but noticing again how frustrating it was not being able to understand the language. As she did, she also realized that lack of skill was important; there was a reason for it. She shook her head. "You know what I've just realized? The reason Sergio wanted me for this job wasn't just because of my skills with French art, it was because I didn't speak Spanish. If I had done, I would have figured him out much sooner."

"You're probably right. Helmet." He pulled his on, and she did the same.

The engine roared into life. Katrina felt the power throbbing up through her body. She clutched him around the waist and squeezed him tightly to let him know she was ready to go. He nodded and drove the motorcycle out onto the road and through the village.

Katrina looked at the lights in the windows of the houses as they passed, the sound of music that came from the bar at the heart of the village, and wished they were part of that more normal life right then. Although she wanted to sort this out, she didn't particularly want to go back to the house. Strange, how it had turned out. She'd been removed from there against her will today, and now she didn't want to go back. Now, she knew the full story—well, more of it—and she was determined to find out the rest soon, for Nico. Above all, for Nico. She clung to him, resting her face against the leather of his jacket.

Out on the road that wound up to the Torre, he put his foot down, and the motorcycle sped away from the village. The thrill of the ride kicked in. She hugged close to the bulk of Nico's body, her spine tingling as much from that as anything. She felt the air rush around them, lifting the tails of her hair where it stuck out of her helmet, wisping them around her neck.

This experience was so far from anything she'd ever have in her ordered life back in London. She would never be riding pillion on a motorcycle if she were at home. She supposed it was something she could do, but her life had been set on a different course since the Teodoro brothers had entered it. Although she regretted that she had flirted with Sergio, she wouldn't be here now, with Nico, if she hadn't. Life had a strange way of unfolding, sometimes, but it made her see that she didn't have any regrets about being more adventurous. Not if it meant that the man she clung to now, in the dark night, wanted her.

When they reached the private road to the house, Nico slowed the motorcycle down and flicked the headlight off. Katrina gripped onto him tighter, wondering how he would see. He would know the route well, and she guessed he'd done it this way before. They passed along the road securely until they neared the house, and she could see light glinting through the trees and the tall, metal fence. Maybe now she would find out how he got past the security system.

Without warning, he pulled the motorcycle off the road, and they bumped over some rough ground before they came to a halt.

"We go from here on foot," he said after he took his helmet off.

She nodded and did the same, climbing off the motorcycle reluctantly. She'd taken to riding pillion. Or maybe she was just taken with the heat of his body against hers. She smiled at him when she removed her helmet. "You were right, I did enjoy it."

"That's good, because I intend to take you away from here by the same method, as soon as possible." He winked at her.

That made her feel good. She wanted to leave here with him. She looked around the spot, listening to the insects humming in the night. He'd stopped just before the pillars and fences that marked the perimeter of the grounds. "So, how do we get in?"

"There's a path." He gestured into the dark undergrowth that grew at the side of the nearest pillar. "It's very overgrown, but if you stay behind me, you'll be safe. I know the path well; there's an old gate up at the side of the house. Raimunda used to use it before they put the security system in. It's not in the loop."

"How does she get up here from the village?"

"Most days she walks; sometimes Paco drives her. The women she brings in to help with the heavy work one day a week also share a car, so she gets a lift then."

"She walks all that way?" Katrina shook her head. "It must have been so different before she had to move out."

He nodded, and his raised eyebrows showed her that he didn't approve. "It is wrong, too, because my father has provided for her. If the Torre is ever sold, there would be enough money for her to buy a house in the village. I think he was pressured into making her leave, but as it is, she lost her home, and she has to rent until such time as this place is sold or my father passes on, or both."

"Elaine said she didn't want Raimunda there, that she felt Raimunda had a crush on your father."

Nicolas gave a dry laugh and shook his head. "That isn't true. Raimunda was devoted to my mother, and she looked after everyone else out of loyalty to her. They were like sisters."

That was so different from the impression that Elaine had given her. Did Elaine know the truth? Had she twisted it to suit what she wanted, or was she really ignorant, kept in the dark by Sergio?

Nicolas gestured again at the path. "Come on, before I change my mind and go in there myself, through the front gates and right under the surveillances cameras."

"No, we need more time before they know I'm back," she said, with more surety than she felt. Looking into the gloomy, overgrown area he'd indicated made her think of wild animals and insects, and her skin reacted to the very suggestion of going in there, goose bumping, making her want to step back onto the road. If she'd just managed to ride pillion on a motorcycle for the first time, she could face a quick hike through the bushes. She didn't want to let Nico know it creeped her out; otherwise he'd think she was a wimp and wouldn't let her go into the house alone. They didn't need another fight between him and Sergio right now; it might stop her getting to the tower. It was important that she did this; they needed to find out the truth.

She watched as he pushed the motorcycle out of view, turning it so that it was facing the road, ready to leave. Did he think they would have to make a quick getaway? She didn't really want to think about that. Nico took her helmet from her hand and hung it together with his from handlebars of the motorcycle.

"Come on." He grabbed her hand and led her into the dark, leafy furrow.

Darkness swamped them.

Katrina swallowed when she felt the first brush of foliage against her arms. Stumbling behind him, she wished she had proper shoes on, rather than the open-toed sandals she'd put on that morning. The foliage brushing against her made her squirm, and already the toes of one foot were wet with something that felt distinctly gloopy. Walking boots and a full bodysuit were the order of the day up here, and she was in a flimsy top, borrowed jeans, and sandals. She shivered and blinked into the gloom up ahead. "How far is it?"

"Not far. Stay with me."

He kept hold of her hand, pulling her tightly against his back. The path—such as it was, more of a trodden niche—was on a slope. Nico had to push against the dense undergrowth to progress up the incline. The sound of the insects seemed to be louder than ever, and Katrina realized grimly that was because they probably made their home in here. Strange scuffling noises sounded nearby, as if something was scurrying through the undergrowth. She yelped, then coughed to cover it up, and tried not to dwell on what that creature might be. Whatever it was, she didn't want it near her.

"Still with me?"

She could hear the humor in his voice.

"Uh-huh." She didn't want to open her mouth properly, lest something land in it.

She rested the fingers of her free hand against the leather on his back, barely resisting the urge to jump onto him at every unfamiliar touch on her skin and hair.

"Watch out for the—"

Katrina didn't catch to rest of it.

"Nico!" Something spindly and sticky had latched onto her arm. The thing had got her hair and was lifting it up and tugging. She froze. "It's got me. Get it off me, please."

"It's sticky branches, that's all. It doesn't mean to catch you. It wants the insects." He plucked it off her and then kissed her in the darkness, his mouth brushing across her cheek to meet with hers. "I'm the one who wants to catch you," he breathed huskily as he drew back.

"You did that already," she replied, forgetting all about the insects and the sticky branches and the wild creatures of the night. She snuck her arms around his neck, snuggling closer inside his leather jacket. "You did that with your mask and your cloak and your trident, *el diablo*, back in Barcelona."

"Is that how I did it?" He gave a soft laugh, and then she felt his mouth against her hair.

"Uh-huh." She could feel his heart beating, and hers seemed to move in time with it. She felt safe there in his arms.

"We're almost there; come on." She sensed him smiling in the darkness as he urged her on.

She was smiling, too.

A faint chink of light appeared on the right-hand side, and when they got closer, she saw that they were near the side of the house. Light from the windows reached through the lawns and shrubs to illuminate the way. Nico pushed open the old gate, and it creaked heavily on its hinges.

He darted over to a tree with her in tow. "Okay. I'll wait here." He gave her a slip of paper. "This is Raimunda's code to the back door, the entrance into the kitchen. If you follow the path around to the left, you'll come to it. Have you got your phone on vibrate mode?"

"Yes." She patted her left hip pocket and pushed the piece of paper into the right. "Is this where we synchronize watches?"

"Oh yes, and I'm giving you five minutes."

"Five minutes?" She shook her head.

He frowned. "That's long enough to check if this Vincent man is still in the tower."

She didn't want to tell him that Vincent kept the tower locked. She'd thought of a way to deal with that. "It will take me that long to find my way in from the kitchen. Make it ten minutes, and I will at least be able to find out who is in there. You never know, if they believe I'm not coming back, they might all have gone out for the evening."

"Maybe." He did not look convinced. "If I don't hear from you in ten minutes, I'm calling the police and I'm coming in there after you. I mean it."

His expression showed there was no point in arguing.

"I'll speak to you or send you a text message in less than ten minutes, I promise." She winked at him.

They checked watches, and then he kissed her again, holding her flush against him for several seconds before releasing her. She could feel the need and the reluctance in his every touch. That alone gave her strength.

# 19

*Jogging across the grass, Katrina told herself that she wasn't* being reckless; she was being brave. This was about setting wrongs right, and she needed her nerve for that. She was acting as a scout, a spy, and she wanted to do it well. The Katrina of a week ago wouldn't have done this kind of thing. What a turnaround. But then she had finally met a man who made her feel confident, sexy. There was no denying that.

Heading for the first window, she followed the wall to the left as Nico had suggested. Glancing in as she passed, she saw a reception room she hadn't been in. It housed a grand piano and a card table. The lights were all on, but no one was there. Following the building around, she passed the dining room. Again, the lights were on, but there was no one in there, either. Had they gone out to dinner? Peeping in, she saw that the table had the remnants of a meal on it. Her heart sank.

She braced herself and jogged on until she reached the door. Pulling out the piece of paper, she squinted into the gloom, moving it in her hand to catch the light of the moon. Entering Raimunda's code, she held her breath. The door clicked open. Stepping inside, she recognized the kitchen from earlier that day. In fact, the tea tray still sat on the table, the chair she'd been sitting on pulled out from the table. So much had happened in between then and now.

She moved on, feeling her way through the gloomy kitchen, unwilling to turn on any more lights. Cutting through the dining room, she found her way to the reception hall. The house was quiet, almost too quiet. If Elaine and Sergio were still awake, they weren't in the main function area of the house. She looked up the stairs, noticing how all the emergent bitterness and secrets made the place seem less airy and spacious to her. She wanted to head straight for the tower, find out if her hunch was right, and get it over. If she got caught, she would say she'd come back from the hotel in the dark and got lost looking for the art gallery. Her laptop was still up there. *I'm a wandering houseguest,* she told herself, *confused in the night and in the wrong tower.*

She crept up the stairs, glancing left and right as she did. Occasionally one hand went to her hip pocket where the phone was safely ensconced. She turned the stair, passing the now-familiar Klimt paintings.

If she did make it into the tower, what would she find? Raimunda had said Jorge was frail and that he'd been ailing for a long time. Was Sergio capable of murder or of covering up a death to suit his purposes? The question entered her mind just as she reached the corridor where the bedrooms were located. The thought creeped her out, and she didn't want to entertain it any longer. She was taking responsibility for her actions; she owed it to the owner of the property she had come in to value. That in itself was enough of a reason, without even thinking about her motivation to show Sergio she wasn't some idiotic woman he could wrap around his finger, and prove to Nico . . . Prove what? She smiled. Prove to him the very same thing, but for different reasons.

She passed the first few doors quickly and then paused when she saw that the door to Sergio's room was slightly ajar.

*Bloody hell.*

She gritted her teeth and counted to ten before darting past the door. The sound of voices reached her, it was Sergio and Elaine, and they were arguing. She heard her name being mentioned.

Her heart thudded; she wanted to get away from them, but curiosity gripped her. She hid herself in the shadows of the curtained window just beyond the doorway and listened. It quickly transpired that they were arguing about the fact that she'd gone missing.

"If you hadn't scared her, shouting your mouth off at Nico and dragging her around, she'd still be here doing her job instead of sleeping in a hotel somewhere." Sarcasm rang in Elaine's voice. "You went too far and freaked her out. You told me she would be easy to convince, and this would be straightforward."

Elaine's tone was angry and vindictive. "I'm tired of waiting, Sergio, and I'm tired of being messed around. Right now I feel like walking out of here with the two Klimts you promised me and getting on with my life."

So that's why he wouldn't commit the Klimts to the auction. It wasn't that he wanted them at all; it was because he'd promised them to Elaine. Katrina smiled to herself as the missing pieces of the puzzle fell into place. She should have known. Sergio had no interest in the art, not any of it.

"But you promised me so much more than that," Elaine added, "and I'm still waiting."

"How can it possibly be so hard for you to be patient when we are this close?" Sergio shouted in response. "You've got everything you could possibly want here, and you aren't the one dealing with angry shareholders on a daily basis. If I hadn't offered you this opportunity, you'd still be struggling to pay off your gambling debts."

Katrina's eyebrows shot up. So that's how Elaine had got muddled up with Sergio and this scheme of his. She glanced at her watch. Three minutes had already gone by. Nico would be on his way up here if she didn't get a move on, but still she wanted to hear what was said.

"That's charming, that is," Elaine shouted. "When we met we were just about equal on that score. Now stop being so bloody hotheaded and figure out what we're going to do about this mess."

Katrina was riveted. Sergio was a gambler? Well, she supposed he had to be, to run the risks he was running now. It would certainly be an explanation as to why his business was suffering, and it was another reason for him to want the funds that would be released from the sale of the collection. It had never been about his father's care at all. But, if she was right and Jorge was in the tower, how coldhearted the pair of them truly had to be, living here in this house while they kept him prisoner. She glanced away, determinedly, about to set off.

"I've already taken action," he snapped. "As soon as I read her note, I contacted another valuation expert: Henry Wallace."

Katrina froze when she caught Henry's name.

"I should have used him in the first place rather than expect a woman to do the job without getting skittish and fretting over nothing. A man would have been clear-sighted, motivated by the profit involved."

Sergio was bringing Henry in? For a split second she felt annoyance, and then she realized what would happen. Henry would walk in here thinking he'd been brought in to sort out her mess, and then he'd find out the real truth, that it was some sort of scam, and she'd already wised up to it.

"Well let's hope you are right on that score," Elaine responded. "When is this man of yours due to arrive?"

"He's on his way. Once I told Wallace she wasn't doing the job quickly enough, he said he'd come over and sort it out immediately."

*I bet he did.* Katrina silently cursed Henry; she could just picture him gloating over the idea she'd somehow slipped up.

"What about Katrina?"

"What about her?"

"The note said she would be back in the morning."

"Her boss will take over; she'll just have to do as he says."

"But Sergio, she was getting suspicious; even I could tell that. Aren't you worried she'll call you on this?"

Sergio mumbled something, annoyed. "It was Nicolas—he got to her." He sounded frustrated.

*Yes, and that's not all. I figured out your master plan, Mr. Teodoro.* Katrina squared her shoulders, facing him off in her imagination. She glanced at her watch and saw her time was running out. She'd heard enough. Heading farther down the corridor, she crept toward the arched doorway that led to the guest apartments in the tower.

She took a deep breath as she hid in the shadows beyond the doorway and then reached into her pocket for the pebbles she'd picked up outside Raimunda's. The first one she threw at the door missed by a mile and bounced along the floor ineffectually. So much for making Vincent believe that his lover was trying to lure him down to the corridor. She cursed herself for being a poor shot. She tried again, and the second was right on target, making a loud sound against the door.

She counted the seconds. No response.

"Oh, to hell with it," she said aloud, ran over, rapped on the door, and then ran back into the shadows, holding her breath.

Her heart was beating very hard, but for some reason all she could think of was being told off by her mother for doing the very same thing when she was seven years old, playing with the neighborhood kids, knocking on doors and running away for a lark. Her mother had spotted her and was furious.

The coincidence prompted a chuckle, and that calmed her down, but the sound of a key rattling in the door to the tower made her gulp that chuckle down.

The door sprang open, and Vincent stood in the doorway. There was a bright light behind him, and she could see that he was wearing shorts and a T-shirt. He was barefoot, his hair awry as if he had been asleep. She folded herself back into the corner behind him, willing him to look everywhere but there.

"Paco?" He whispered the name into the gloomy corridor, and then said something in Spanish under his breath.

Despite the tension, Katrina congratulated herself internally. How keen would he be to find out if it really was his lover lurking out here?

He hovered around the doorway for a few moments, and then wandered along the corridor toward the central staircase, glancing about as he did so. He hesitated when he got to the door that was ajar. Katrina smiled. This house was full of secrets, and each of its occupants had their own. He listened for a moment, then sped up and shot past the door, moving to the staircase beyond.

*Now is my chance.* Her feet suddenly felt like lead, as if they were glued to the floor. *Hurry,* she urged herself, peeping out, making sure that he was still heading in the opposite direction. She took a deep breath and darted through the open door and into the tower. How far could she get before he came back? Nico had told her the layout was different from the tower that housed the art collection. She glanced at her watch. She didn't have long before he'd be on his way behind her. All she had to do was find out if Vincent was in here alone or not. Glancing into the room ahead of her, she saw a casual seating area where a TV flickered, the volume turned low. Beyond it, a door stood open. It looked like a bedroom, but she couldn't see from this vantage point.

She heard a sound behind her. Vincent was on his way back

already. She had hoped he'd have a good long wander in search of his lover. She didn't have any choice; she darted up the staircase, rounding the top into the gloomy darkness on the half landing, just as he walked back into the seating area below. He paused at the doorway, glanced back. Relief hit her as he walked on. A moment later the TV got louder.

She was stuck in here now, had to see it through. Slumping against the wall, she took a moment to gather herself. As she did, she became aware of a chink of light on the wall above her. The room on the floor above was illuminated. Climbing to her feet, she pulled the phone out of her pocket and tapped in a text message for Nico.

*In tower. Give me 2 more mins.*

She pressed Send. Shoving the phone away, she crept on and up to the next level. The door there was slightly ajar, allowing a narrow beam of light into the landing area. She could barely breathe as she approached it and pushed it open. The phone in her pocket vibrated, but she barely registered it, transfixed as she was by the image before her. Her hand went to her mouth.

A single lightbulb in a Perspex shade gave the room a clinical feel. It was stripped of furniture, save for the bed. Next to it stood a drip feed, and the figure lying on the bed had a mask over his face that was attached to an oxygen tank nearby. Her hand was glued over her mouth, her stomach rolling. The man was Jorge—she recognized him from the photo—and he looked sick; he should be in hospital. He needed medical attention, and fast, and yet they were keeping him here.

Or was that the point? Were they keeping him here—here in the last place anyone would look—so that he couldn't argue against the sale of the collection?

Her stomach churned again as she crept closer. She'd been a blind pawn in their game, the crucial agent that would see this horrible thing through. Elaine had to know. She was a cold person, but was she really this evil? The first time Nico had come to her here in the house, he'd said that Elaine was mercenary. She hadn't believed him. Now she had proof.

His skin was so pale, it had a parchment quality about it; he looked almost corpselike. Acting on instinct, she remembered what little first-aid training she'd had. She reached for his hand, checked for his pulse. It was faint, but he was alive. She stroked his hand, and his eyes flickered open, at first unfocused. He blinked and looked directly at her. His mouth moved under the mask, and his free hand lifted from the bed. He was reaching out for her.

Compassion and dismay hit her in equal measures, and she had to swallow it down. She took his hand, put her other hand to her lips, hushing him. She winked, hoping he would understand. His fingers clutched at hers, feeble, but she felt his faint squeeze all the same.

She reached into her pocket and pulled out her phone. How long would it take the police and an ambulance to get up here into the hills? A shiver went through her. As she went to send her message, she heard a noise. Her hand was snatched from behind. *Vincent.*

Her blood ran cold, and she screamed. The phone dropped to the floor and skidded across the room. Her arm was wrenched behind her back. She screamed again, just as a thick male fore-arm moved under her chin and her head was jolted back. Would anyone be able to hear her? Would she even want Sergio and Elaine to find her there?

Vincent spat words at her in Spanish, and for once she was pleased she couldn't understand. Struggling against him, she fought for breath, but his arm tightened against her throat, mak-ing it impossible to breathe or swallow. Her arms grew limp, self-preservation setting in. He hauled her with him as he moved closer to the bed, powerfully strong. Her stomach knotted.

With one hand over her mouth, her body contorted in his grip, he ducked down and pulled out something from beneath the bed. Horrified, she stared down at the strap Vincent pulled out and flung over Jorge's body. He was going to tie him down?

Nauseated, she realized she had to act, and fast. What did she have to bargain with? Nothing came to mind at first, but then she remembered that there was something. She had to break free. While he fiddled with the strap, she took her chance, lifting her heel to slam it back against him. She hit his lower leg, and he reacted. His grip loosened, and she struggled free.

"Paco," she shouted, as she stepped away and faced him, backing away toward the spot where her phone lay on the floor. It was her lifeline. "Paco and Vincent."

He froze, and then muttered something vehement.

*Oh hell, what was the word for lover?*

*Amie? No, that was French.*

"Amante." It came to her suddenly; her memory of Nicolas whispering it to her had lodged it there. *"Paco, amante!"*

Oh yes, that disturbed him. Anger flared in his eyes. Vincent spoke at her in Spanish, his lips contorting in anger. Back when she'd seen him with Paco, she'd thought he was much more worried about discovery than Paco had been, and he was. Why? She glanced down at his left hand. Yes, he was wearing a wedding ring.

She ducked down, snatched her phone up from the floor, pointing at his ring finger to keep him occupied. *"Amante."*

She had a split second to realize he didn't see her comment as a bargaining tool but as a threat. Then he launched himself at her again.

She screamed and ducked, heading for the door.

He snatched at her hand, but she wrenched it free. Staggering toward the staircase, she felt him close at her back. When his hand moved around her waist, she instinctively turned on her heel and spun out of reach, facing him. The floor seemed to shift from under her.

Too late she found that the top stair was only halfway beneath her feet. Her body wavered. A nasty laugh contorted Vincent's face, he said something and then reached out and pushed her shoulder with one finger.

"I don't know what you're laughing at, you bastard," she shouted, as she grabbed his wrist.

*If I go, you're coming with me.*

She never got the words out before she fell.

With her fingernails embedded in his wrist, Vincent was taken unawares and was caught up in her momentum. She fell several steps, then bashed hard against the wall with one shoulder. Vincent's weight fell heavily over her legs. She'd hit the wall and broken his fall, hauling them both up short of the full drop.

Blinking into the half darkness on the stairs, she struggled out from under him. It dislodged his body, and he fell farther down the stairs. Staggering to her feet, she clambered over him, forcing herself to step on his back to get past. She caught sight of him reach out for a banister as she did. He dragged himself up just as she stepped onto him, which sent her tumbling again. She shut her eyes and tried to put out her hands, but her forehead hit something, and she lost any chance of breaking the rest of the fall.

She heard a whimper in the distance and then recognized it as her own voice. Silence descended for a moment; then she heard Vincent groaning somewhere behind her. How far away? She opened her eyes, found herself lying awkwardly on the floor at the bottom of the staircase. The door to the room with the TV was to her right, just inches away. Dizzy and suddenly cold, her hand automatically went to her forehead. It throbbed unbearably where she had hit it in the fall. When she looked down, there was a dark patch on her palm. Blood. She stared at it, uncomprehending, for a few seconds and then jolted into action. She slid forward onto her hands and knees with great effort and crawled forward toward the door to the corridor. Turning the key and snatching at the door handle, she pushed it open with all her might and crawled out into the corridor.

She heard Vincent's stumbling footsteps behind her, and her heart sank. She scrambled forward but was jerked bodily from the floor moments later and gasped as she was lifted into the air, Vincent's hand clamping over her mouth as she tried to shout. She heard him bellowing out in Spanish, and she picked out Sergio's name as he yelled down the corridor.

The corridor blurred, and she struggled in Vincent's grip. Her head was thumping, and she was having trouble focusing. Even so, a fast-moving image caught her attention. Blinking, she stared down the corridor. Was it her imagination, or had she just seen a dark shadow cross the corridor at the far end?

## 20

*Time had never gone so slowly for Nico. He stared at the* second hand on his watch, willing it to go faster so he could keep his promise to Katrina. It simply was not going to happen. As soon as she left, he had begun to wonder how foolish he was to be convinced to let her go in there alone. When he was with her, looking at her upturned face and the earnestness that he found in her eyes, he figured she could probably convince him of anything, no matter how dangerous or foolish.

The discovery drew a wry smile from him. It meant something. He already knew he desired her, and that he craved more than what they had already shared, much more. But now he also had to accept that he cared for her in a way that meant he didn't think straight.

As a result, he never did wait out the five minutes. After two minutes, he got out his mobile phone. He was about to send her a text message telling her he was on his way in, when he gave up that idea as well, and set off, jogging along the same path that she had followed to the kitchen entrance.

He punched in the numbers on the keypad at the door, a sense of urgency rising in him all the time. The door clicked open. He went inside and closed it quietly, taking barely a moment to listen for sounds. All was quiet downstairs, even though many of the lights were on. Doors were open, as if the inhabitants had just stepped out for a moment. Where was Sergio? He made his way through the kitchen and into the dark hallway beyond. At the bottom of the main staircase he could hear distant voices coming from the bedroom corridor. He'd mounted the first step when the voices suddenly grew louder.

"Stop ordering me about. I've had enough of it." It was Elaine, and she was at the top of the stairs, shouting back over her shoulder.

Nico stepped back into the dark hallway and merged into the shadows, listening to Elaine's footsteps clatter down the first set of steps. He moved slightly so that he could see her. She was on the half landing, and she appeared to be taking one of the Klimt paintings down from its place there. She leaned it against the sculpture in the center of the landing and went to retrieve its partner as well.

*What the hell is going on?*

Where was Katrina?

"Elaine, put them back. You're not going anywhere right now." It was Sergio, shouting angrily from above. Elaine ignored him but seemed to be struggling with the fixture on the second painting.

Nico didn't understand what was going on here, but it didn't seem to involve Katrina. She must have made it past them. His phone vibrated in his hip pocket, and he pulled it out. Making sure he was concealed in the shadows, he read the text message.

*In tower. Give me 2 more mins.*

He stared at it, then at the time. Perhaps luck had been on their side, and this man, Vincent, was out for the evening. He pushed the phone back into his pocket.

On the landing, Elaine had managed to free the second painting and had lifted both of them, clutching them against her chest. The frames were heavy, and she struggled to keep them together and balanced. Knowing Elaine, Nico assumed that cocktails would have been involved in this little drama, and that she wasn't thinking straight. Wryly, he thought to himself that he didn't hold out much hope for the paintings remaining intact, which normally would have concerned him, but right at that moment, all he cared about was Katrina's safety. Once again, he cursed himself for allowing her to walk back into this situation.

"No way. This is my insurance," Elaine shouted back up the stairs. "I'm packing them in a suitcase tonight, and if you threaten me one more time, you can say good-bye to me *and* the paintings."

Holding the paintings like a shield, she marched awkwardly back up the stairs. The sound of arguing still reached Nico when she disappeared out of view. He waited until the voices faded to be sure that neither of them was coming back, then cautiously made his way up the staircase, following in Elaine's steps. At the top of the stairs, he paused. They had gone into a room. From the end of the corridor, he could see that one of the paintings was leaning up against the wall outside Sergio's room. The door was open, and the sound of discussion came from inside.

Just at that moment, there was a scream and a loud, clattering noise from beyond.

*Katrina?*

He moved to one side of the arch leading down the corridor, craning his neck. Had the noise come from the area of the tower? Was the other guy, Vincent, in there after all? He couldn't see anything in the gloom at the other end of the corridor and was about to make his way down there when the door burst open, and Katrina crawled out of the doorway on her hands and knees. A heavily built man stepped over and pulled her up from the ground, lifting her easily with one hand clutching her top. He clamped one hand over her mouth, holding her dangling from the other like a fish on a hook. It was too far away to see her expression, but her forehead was stained with blood.

Anger speared through Nico's chest. The man, who was built like a real *gamberro*—a thug—pulled a switchblade from his pocket; pointing it at Katrina, he then bellowed out in Spanish, alerting Sergio that the Englishwoman had discovered his father.

*Katrina was right. He is here in the house. He never left it at all.*

Nico clenched his jaw.

The *gamberro* lifted his head.

Nico flattened against the wall. Stunned and angry, he had a split second to make a decision before Sergio appeared. The *gamberro* was toying with Katrina now, no longer looking down the corridor. Nico couldn't risk walking down there, in case he used the knife on her. He needed to contact the police before alerting Sergio or the *gamberro* to his presence. On the opposite side of the corridor, the night breeze at an open window stirred the curtains, drawing his attention. He would go via the balcony.

He darted over and stepped behind the curtain, climbing quickly onto the windowsill. He paused for a second, straining to hear. He heard Elaine's voice.

"No, Sergio. Don't do it."

*Do what?* Nico was torn. Go back in, or approach from outside and have the element of surprise on his side? If he went to his own room, it would put him in a better position to make an attack, and once he made it as far as the first balcony, he could alert the police out of earshot. Without pausing for breath, he took the leap from the solid frieze he was standing on across to the first wrought-iron railing.

Moving faster than he ever had, he was on the first balcony moments later. He phoned the police, giving the briefest of details about a dangerous hostage situation, and the code that would open the electronic gates. That done, he headed on. Clambering across the network toward his father's room, he moved as fast as he could, angrily cursing himself for allowing Katrina to go back in there. If she ever forgave him, he would make this up to her. Reaching out, he moved across to a fixture, swinging onto it monkey-bar style.

The joint made a grating sound, and then his body jolted and swung loose, one hand losing its grip immediately. The right-angled fixture had come free of the wall and was hanging out, attached at only one end. Holding on with one hand, he dangled precariously. His other arm thrashed wildly as he tried to reach up. It was loose before, he remembered too late. Anger gave him strength, and he latched one hand higher and onto the bottom of the next section of metalwork. Pain shot through his shoulder from the overreach. He let go of the loose fixture and swung around, both hands on solid struts again. Moments later, when he barely clambered onto his father's balcony, he heard the metal fixture crashing to the ground.

Would they hear that inside? Squinting across at the balcony of his old room, he saw that the doors were shut. He tried the handle on the door to his father's room. Thankfully, it clicked open. Inside he made his way stealthily across the room from memory, but even in the darkness he saw that a chair was overturned and the bedcovers were strewn on the floor. Had it been this way since his father was removed from the place? Knowing Raimunda, she had been unable to bring herself to restore order here until she knew he was coming back to it.

The door was locked from the outside. Cursing silently, he put his head against it. He could hear arguing. There was still a chance. Reaching up, he felt along the side of the doorframe until he reached the picture rail, and dipped his fingers into it, moving slowly along it. Within moments, his fingers had settled around a dusty key. He lifted it and thanked whoever was watching over him.

It was Sergio's fault that this was here. He had twice locked

Nico in a room and done God knows what with the key, denying it when quizzed by their parents. It was his usual sort of prank as a youngster. Their mother had a knack with the truth though, and although Jorge sided with his eldest son, she secretly hadn't. An extra key was cut for every room, and she hid them in the picture rail, where he could find them if he stood on a chair. Nico was the only one who knew this, and the fact that he would miraculously escape when Sergio locked him in infuriated Sergio to no end.

Which, no doubt, it would do all over again, right about now. Unlocking the door, he opened it a crack. He would be level with Sergio's room, not as close to Katrina as he hoped, but much closer than he had been before. He heard Elaine wailing, and when he peeked, she was kneeling on the floor, picking up the overturned Klimt painting that had been standing there. The frame had broken on one side, and in her rush to pluck the flailing wood free of the canvas, she jagged her wrist on a sharp edge.

"Leave the fucking painting." It was Sergio, and he was nearby.

Nico flattened against the wall, craning his neck to peer farther down the hallway through the gap in the door. As he did, he saw Sergio gesture. There was a gun in his hand. Nico's gut balled, his teeth grinding as the implications flashed through his mind.

Elaine had cut herself. She was angry, and her face was wet with tears. A moment later Sergio was gone—in Katrina's direction. Elaine cursed him.

Nico opened the door, preparing to step out.

"Sergio, think about what you are doing," she shouted, struggling to her feet. Then her head turned, and she noticed Nico in the doorway. Her eyes were wild as she looked at him, but she was thrown by his appearance. She glanced back at Sergio and, as her mouth opened, Nico stepped out of the doorway and pushed her aside, quickly darting down the corridor after Sergio.

Sergio was shouting, so he didn't even notice Elaine's latest wail of dismay behind him, but Nico knew he'd realize soon enough. At the end of the corridor he could see Katrina being held by the *gamberro*. He had one hand on the back of her head, pushing her forward so that she was at arm's length; the other hand held her arms behind her back.

Sergio was pointing the gun at her.

The *gamberro*'s expression changed, and Nico knew he'd seen him coming. He had split seconds to make this work. He leapt on Sergio's back, just as his head began to turn. Nico grabbed at the arm holding the gun, but Sergio pulled away, and it fired a shot as he did so. Behind them, Elaine screamed.

Anger barreled through Nico, and he grabbed Sergio's hand, crushing it inside his.

The gun fell to the floor.

Sergio staggered under his weight, and Nico kicked him in the calf muscle as he leapt back to the ground. Turning him around by the shoulder, he drove Sergio up against the wall. Sergio's eyes were filled with hatred.

Nico fixed him there and then took a moment to look back down the corridor. He had to know if Katrina had been hurt. If anything happened to her, Sergio was a dead man.

Relief hit him hard and fast. Katrina was on the floor, on her hands and knees, wavering unsteadily. Next to her, Vincent lay crumpled on the floor, one hand on his shoulder where a large bloodstain was seeping through his T-shirt. Nico released a long-held breath and turned back to Sergio. "If you had hit her, you wouldn't have lived to see another day."

Sergio struggled in his grip, glancing down where the gun lay on the floor, a desperate look in his eyes.

"Don't even think about it," Nico instructed. Holding him up against the wall with one hand, he hit him square on the jaw. Sergio's head jolted and made contact with the wall, and Nico watched with grim satisfaction as his brother's eyes closed and his body slumped to the floor. "You've had that coming for a very long time."

He heard Elaine whimpering on his left-hand side. She was standing there, bewildered, staring down at Sergio. When she looked at Nico, she began to back away.

"The police are on their way; don't even think about leaving," Nico instructed, and lifted the gun from the floor, showing it to her to indicate that there was no way out.

She nodded her head, clutching her injured hand to her chest.

Nico darted down the corridor. He kicked the *gamberro*. He was conscious, but there was no fight in him. Then he dropped down beside Katrina, who was now sitting on the floor staring up at him.

"He's in the tower, your dad. He's up there; go." She nodded her head in the direction of the apartment.

Nico shook his head and took her into his arms. "One moment. First I need to check on you." He smoothed her hair back from the wound on her forehead, examining the injury. "It looks as if the bleeding has stopped, but we need to be sure. Are you hurt anywhere else?"

"Some dents and bruises, nothing else, at least I don't think so." She looked at him suspiciously. "You didn't wait for the agreed time, did you?"

"No, and I'm very glad."

In the distance, he heard sirens. Glancing down the corridor, he saw that Elaine had bolted and was running toward the staircase.

"The police will get her. If not now, later. She won't get far." He glanced back down the corridor, still watchful. Sergio didn't move.

He wanted to check on his father, but he had to be sure Katrina was safe, too. Once the police were in the house, he could leave her. Even though the immense sense of relief he was experiencing had slowed down his heart rate, and his anger was subsiding, there was still a heavy weight lodged in his chest, and it was because of the woman in his arms. "If anything had happened to you, I couldn't have lived with myself."

Katrina stared up at him for a long moment, and then she smiled. She reached her hand around the back of his head, gently drawing him down to kiss her lips. Only then did he recognize the weight in his chest as fierce passion for her. As her lips parted, and she reassured him that she was going to be okay by giving him a long, luxurious kiss, his passion began to burn and flame.

# 21

*A bilingual policeman took Katrina's statement while she was* being treated in an ambulance in the driveway of the Torre. Vincent had been removed from the house on a stretcher, accompanied by police officers. From her vantage point in the driveway, she saw Sergio being taken away, handcuffed, later on.

She'd been lucky; she was going to have bruises just about everywhere, but there were no signs of concussion. Her head wound was superficial, and the medic dressed it and made sure her responses were good. When he let her leave, the medic handed her a leaflet. It was in Spanish. The police officer told her it was a list of things to look out for after head injuries. She stared down at it. If it was the last thing she ever did, she was going to learn to speak Spanish.

Shakily, she climbed down the ambulance steps. As she did, she saw Elaine being escorted back toward the house, a policeman on either side of her, restraining her when she spat foul insults and struggled against them. She'd never looked more like the snake she was, her decorum completely shattered. Katrina watched as they took her to a police van. What would happen to her? she wondered as Elaine was forced into the vehicle. She hadn't wanted to face the police. Did she have a previous record? They would find out everything eventually; the last pieces were hovering now.

The lawns in front of the Torre del Castagona were buzzing with activity. Three ambulances were still pulled up in the driveway, and a half dozen or more cars. It looked so different from the day she had first arrived. Light spilled out of all the windows and the door. There seemed to be noise and police everywhere.

She walked slowly toward the house, watching the activity, half-nervous about what would happen next between her and Nico, half-relieved that the problem that had brought them together and hung between them had been solved. An ambulance crew had been inside with Jorge for some time. She could only assume Nico was with them. She had insisted he go to his father after the police arrived. At first he wouldn't leave her, but when the medics arrived on the scene and began attending to her, he finally did as she asked.

Looking out beyond the activity on the driveway, she could see that a small crowd of people had gathered. Police were holding them back. Occasionally a flash would go off, and she could hear voices calling out to the police, asking questions. Were they villagers, or had the story reached the press already?

Katrina smiled to herself and opened her phone to check the

time. Thankfully it was still working, despite the battering it received earlier. It was past midnight. She called Pocklington's work number and left a message on his voice mail, telling him the collection was being sold without the permission of the owner and the auction should not be announced. In conclusion she said she would speak to him properly tomorrow.

That's when she noticed that there were two voice mails on her phone. The first was from Lucy about the shipping date, and it had been left earlier in the day. She recalled the phone vibrating when she'd been in the tower. She'd assumed it was Nico, but now that she looked at it, she saw the later voice mail was from her mother.

She played it.

"Hello, Katrina. I guess you are still away. Let me know when you get back from Spain. I've got cards and a present here from Auntie Joanna and your uncle Bill. I expect you are out partying. Happy birthday for tomorrow."

*Happy birthday?* Katrina counted the days back while she shut her phone. Yes, it was her thirtieth birthday tomorrow. She'd forgotten all about it. She'd forgotten all about everything while she'd been wrapped up in the strange goings-on at the Torre del Castagona and her affair with Nicolas. It had turned out to be the strangest commission she'd ever have. She'd never forget the place, and she'd definitely never forget Nicolas Teodoro.

It was then that she caught sight of someone familiar, a man standing on the driveway behind the entourage of cars and ambulances, staring up at the house. A bewildered Englishman. "Oh, my God, Henry."

Standing amid the chaos in the driveway, he had a briefcase in one hand and an overnight bag in the other. He was staring at the entrance, his path blocked by the jostling crowd who were being held back by a line of policeman.

Katrina couldn't help smiling at the image of her bewildered ex looking like a fish out of water in the midst of a police investigation. It served him right, but after everything that had happened, she felt kind of sorry for him. She made her way through the crowd, waving at him.

"What the hell is going on here?" he asked.

"Oh, attempted murder, attempted fraud, you name it . . ."

"Good grief." He looked horrified.

Katrina quelled a laugh.

Henry scanned the scene again and then looked back at her. His eye twitched, as if he suddenly remembered their connection and why he was here. A defensive expression took up residence on his face. He gestured at the house. "They called me in to help with the valuation. Speed things up a bit."

He looked uncomfortable, as well he might.

"As you can see, you aren't needed. If you had cared to get in touch with me to discuss it, I could have told you that and saved you the trip."

"I didn't think," he mumbled.

"You did think, but you were thinking of yourself, as usual." She sighed, but in all honesty she felt no animosity toward him now. She'd moved on over the last few days; she'd changed. There was nothing between them anymore, and that meant there was nothing to say.

She shrugged. "That's irrelevant now. There isn't going to be a Teodoro collection sale for Pocklington's. I've left a message for Mr. Pocklington to inform him of that."

Staring at her, he frowned. "I see."

"The items were meant to go to public galleries in Spain," she added.

Henry would look bad over this back at the office, she realized. Not as bad as she would for making promises she didn't know if she could keep, but he'd look every bit as misguided for racing out here at the eleventh hour. She didn't have the heart to make him feel any worse about it than she could see he already did.

Pushing back her hair, she gave him as reassuring a smile as she could muster. "I'm sorry you had a wasted trip."

Frowning, he peered at her. "What happened to your head?"

"I came into contact with a wall and a staircase, head-on." He looked so appalled that she had to laugh. "It shook off a lot of dust," she added, still amused.

He gave an unsure smile and then glanced back at the house.

When she followed his gaze, she saw that medics were finally carrying another stretcher from the house. Relief flooded through her at the sight of Jorge. He was no longer wearing an oxygen mask. He was still hooked up to a drip, but this was a drip that she trusted a whole lot more than whatever Vincent was pumping into him. Nicolas was walking alongside the stretcher, close to the side of his father, whose face was turned in the direction of his son. When they got to the ambulance, Jorge reached out for Nico's hand, and Nico bent over to listen to what his father was saying. He was clearly lucid enough to speak with his estranged son, and that warmed her heart immensely.

Henry's voice reached her.

Forcing herself, she drew her attention away from Nicolas and Jorge for a second. "I'm sorry, what did you say?"

"I said I asked the taxi to wait when I saw all the police cars. Do you want to grab your stuff and come back to the airport with me?" It was a peace offering.

"Thanks, but no thanks. I have to stick around, but I do appreciate the offer." On the spur of the moment, she reached up and gave him a quick kiss on the cheek. "Good-bye, Henry," she added, as she walked back to the house, and it felt final in a way far beyond the moment.

When she glanced over her shoulder, she saw that Henry was staring after her, but when he was caught looking, he headed back down the drive toward the gates and the waiting taxi.

By the nearby ambulance, Nico was still talking with his father, but they seemed to be saying their good-byes now. Would they be able to bridge their differences? she wondered. It made her think of her mother and their differences. What would she think when she found out her daughter had made a huge error in her job, an error that meant she would probably lose that job?

A fresh start wouldn't be the end of the world, would it? Her mother might not see it that way, but for her own part, Katrina felt quite liberated by the idea. Excited, even. She had to show her mother that life wasn't always about taking the safe path. She also needed to put her straight about what happened with Henry. She was ready to do it now. During these last few days she had faced unknowns, and working her way through them had made her strong. That had brought about good things, as well as bad. But she felt ready to face both.

Instinctively, she turned back to where Nico was. They had lifted Jorge's stretcher into the ambulance. Nico was standing there at the foot of it, hand raised in greeting to his father. As soon as the ambulance doors closed, he headed over to where she stood.

Katrina watched him approach with nervous anticipation, suddenly on tenterhooks. She wanted to run into his arms, but each step closer he took unsettled her. He had done what he needed to do. His problem had been solved, and she had served her purpose. What would happen between them now? Would that be over, as well?

"Hey, beautiful, how are you feeling?"

He took her into his arms, examining her head and then tucking her in against him for warmth.

She rested her head against him for a moment, closing her eyes gratefully, the contact bringing a sweet rush of happiness. "Okay. A bit shaky and sore, but that's it." She drew back and looked at him. "How about you?"

He shrugged one shoulder and looked at the ambulance that was driving slowly down the driveway. "Relieved, mostly. Come, you must sit down."

They walked over to the small wall that enclosed the shrub border and sat down, surveying the scene.

"I am glad this is over," Nico said. "I am so sorry that you had to be dragged into it."

"That wasn't your fault. I don't regret anything; please remember that." She reached up and touched his face, unable to stop herself from doing so. "What did they say about your father? Will he be okay?"

"They'll have a better idea when they run more tests, but I think so. They're taking him to a hospital in Barcelona, so I'll be able to visit tomorrow. The police know that guy, Vincent. He used to be a nurse in a psychiatric hospital, but he lost his job. He already has a file."

"That doesn't surprise me." She gave a little shiver, and Nico held her closer still. The feeling of his body against hers was too good. She could sit there all night, just for the feel of it. "Was your father able to tell you anything about what happened?"

"A little. He said that Sergio tried to get him to auction off parts of the collection, but he refused. Then he caught Sergio selling stuff secretly. That's when Sergio turned."

Katrina nodded. "There were items missing from the storage sections. I only knew because I used your mother's ledgers."

Nico looked pained. "I expect those things are gone for good. She would be so upset; she was collecting it all for Spain, in her heart."

Katrina nodded, unable to speak for a moment. She could see and sense that goal from the ledgers now, and from the care that Señora Teodoro had taken over the collection. Her final wishes had been her life's goal. "It mustn't have been enough for Sergio. Did your father know why he needed the money?"

"He'd run up huge personal debts. Apparently he had neglected the business for a long time, maybe ever since he took over from my father. Things were going badly. He wanted my father to invest the money from the collection into the business to keep it afloat. He needed to underpin the company with his personal money or start selling the major share hold. My father said he would rather end up without a euro to his name than go back on his word to our mother."

She could see the pain in his eyes, and there was regret there, too, now. She reached out for him, cupped his face, and smiled at him. "You stopped it happening."

"He said he was sorry that he had pushed me away." He said the words simply, almost disbelievingly.

She nodded and kissed him gently.

"Thank you for helping me, for being this clever woman who unraveled this mess."

She glanced up at the house. "I felt the secrets and the ghosts as soon as I went in there, but I had no idea how truly bad it was."

"Nobody did, except them. Not even Raimunda guessed. It sickens me, what Sergio did."

"What will happen to him?"

"I asked the police. He'll be charged because of his actions tonight. More than that will depend on my father, whether he will press charges."

She could see that troubled him, so she didn't quiz him anymore. She looked again at the door to the house. There were still police moving around inside, collecting evidence, she supposed. "I have to get my stuff, but I really don't want to go back in there."

He kissed her forehead. "You don't have to go in there. I'll get your things. We will stay at Raimunda's tonight. We need to tell her that my father is okay."

"Yes, that would be good."

"And tomorrow, we'll go to my place in Barcelona."

She smiled, unable to withhold her pleasure at his statement. He said it so naturally; she couldn't imagine arguing with him, even if she wanted to. And she definitely didn't want to.

"You don't have to rush back to London, do you?" He locked eyes with her as he asked the question. That's when she knew that he wanted to address what was between them as much as she did.

"No. I don't even know if I'll have a job to go back to."

"I'm so sorry."

She shrugged. "I'm not sure if I am." Looking into his eyes, the statement hung between them, then the corner of his mouth lifted.

"Good. I want to keep you in Spain." Again, he said it so simply but so firmly.

Her stomach fluttered. "That's funny, I was just thinking that I really must learn Spanish." She lifted the leaflet that she'd left on the wall. Showing it to him, she chuckled. "It's been so frustrating not being able to understand." She winked at him. "Hey, I could claim a few days compassionate leave after harassment by a client and his brother."

"Come here and let me harass you some more." His free hand cupped her bottom.

An odd sense of wistfulness came over her. "Have you got time to harass me some more?"

"Plenty, for you."

"I have to stay around for the rest of the week anyway, in case the police need to talk to me again."

The expression in his eyes grew warm again. "Good; now everybody is happy."

"Yes." She snuggled in against him. "Although I've never had to deal with the police before."

"It'll be okay. I'll be there with you; don't worry."

"Thank you." That sounded so good. Had anyone ever really been there for her like this, before now? "You know, after this whole situation, I feel so duped by Sergio and Elaine. I'm not sure I want to sell people's art collections anymore."

"What would you like to do instead?"

She shrugged. "I have skills I could use elsewhere. Maybe try for a gallery post or help people to exhibit their own art. I don't know."

She'd changed. She wasn't the same woman who had followed the safe path in life, and the world felt fresh and new and exciting as a result. "One thing I know for sure is I'd like to learn to understand those Spanish words you whisper when you are about to come."

She glanced up at him.

He held her tighter still, smiling. "I will teach you; I wouldn't trust anyone to do the job as well as I can."

He winked at her.

She rested her hand on his chest, moved it gently over his heart. "I'd like to get to know you better, Nico."

"That sounds good, but I think you know me pretty well already. You figured out things about me that I didn't know about myself. I admire your intuition, Katrina Hammond."

She knew what he meant: that he cared for his father even

though he'd thought there was nothing between them, that his battle with Sergio had just grounds, and that he wouldn't have pursued it if he hadn't been concerned for his father's safety. Unlike Sergio, Nico was not motivated by money or the need for the kind of power that went with it.

"In fact, I like a lot of things about you."

"You do?" Her heart burned in her chest. She knew what this meant. She wanted him, she cared for him, and he felt the same way. Over the past week she had discovered how strong she could be, how responsible and independent. Even so, she wanted to share it with someone, and this might be the someone she wanted.

His forehead puckered. "You're making this very difficult. You know what I'm trying to say."

She gave him her best come-hither look and breathed her response. "I do?"

He broke into a soft laugh, and kissed her, his lips lifting hers before he answered her. "Katrina. I want more of you, I want to know everything about you."

"But the way we met, all of this, it's all been so odd."

"Does it matter how we met?"

With those words, the whole world melted away, and there was only him, only him and her. His lips met hers again, and the reasons why didn't matter anymore.

"I guess not," she replied, as they drew apart. A naughty thought occurred to her. "It's my birthday tomorrow."

"It is? Well, then, we must celebrate. What would you like to do?"

"When I was in London, my friends asked me that, and I

didn't know what I wanted to do to mark the occasion . . . but I do now."

"Name it, and I'll make it happen."

Looking into his eyes, savoring the feeling of his arms around her, she knew what she wanted for her birthday. She knew exactly what she wanted. *El diablo.* Just like that first night in Barcelona.

## 22

*A spotlight flashed on, breaking the hushed air of expectancy in* the small theater. The light was focused on a dancer, a slim, striking girl who was wearing a dress somewhere between traditional and contemporary. It was long and fitted in the torso, but where there would be ruffles on a traditional flamenco dress, this one ended in wispy layers. Her eyes were beautifully made up to accentuate her elfin looks. Her polished black hair was tied back, her lips parted as she responded to the music.

Katrina had expected traditional guitar music to accompany the dancer, but, as with the dress, there was a modern twist. There were two male guitarists, one on either side of her, scrawny teenagers with attitude. They were both playing electric guitars, which gave a big, rock-edged sound for the dancer to follow. It was obvious she loved what she was doing, and her performance was filled with exuberance. Her heels pounded, filling the stage with infectious energy, a wave that moved through the near-empty theater and captured Katrina in its spell.

Nico was at the side of the stage, watching the dress rehearsal, overseeing the teenagers he worked with. Katrina could see him from the back row of the small theater, where she waited for their time together. Her admiration for him had multiplied. Seeing him work with the young people, she felt as if she saw a whole new world through his eyes. It was inspirational. She knew for sure that she didn't want to sell art anymore—she wanted to work with the people who created it.

Nico. Since their doubts about each other had disappeared, a whole new level of intimacy had begun to evolve. When they'd finally turned in and gone to Raimunda's guest room the night before, he'd held her close all night long. She could barely sleep because of the happiness that simple thing brought her.

As the song drew to a close, the small audience of young people and their friends and supervisors clapped and cheered. Nico came onto the stage and spoke with all three of them in turn. She noticed how effortlessly he interacted with each performer, squeezing the shoulders of the young men approvingly when he talked to them, bowing to the dancer, making her blush. He was easy and proud in turns, genuine, like a father. That stirred a new emotion within her, something deep and essentially female.

Her admiration and curiosity about him grew by the moment, and she felt privileged to have been here to observe. When Nico looked in her direction and gave her a wave and a subtle smile, her stomach fluttered with anticipation and pleasure. It was her signal that it was time to leave. She stood up and slipped out of the theater by a side exit.

Out on the street, a keen sense of anticipation mixed with the positive vibe she'd got from the rehearsal. There was a waxing moon in the sky, and although autumn weather had finally arrived, the streets were still filled with activity in the popular evening hours. Katrina threw her shawl around her shoulders and moved quickly toward Las Ramblas.

He said he'd find her there. That thought alone thrilled her. She moved through the busy heart of the city, following the streetlamps, remembering the first night they'd played a game like this. She tried to pace herself, strolling through the performance and mime artists, heading toward the place where the avenue was filled with flowers and birdsong, and pretty multicolored birds lured the attention of the passerby.

She paused to watch a young family posing for photos with a mime artist. The performer was dressed as a statue, everything from his hair to his bare feet and the robe he wore colored gray white, rendering him like some ancient noble brought to life. For minutes at a time he would stand with his eyes shut and his hand extended, then he would shift and move to a different position, to the delight of the children, sending them running in fits of giggles and pointing fingers.

She was smiling over it when she felt a shiver down her spine. Nico was here; she was sure of it. What was it about him that she sensed his presence? She walked on, treading the side of the busy avenue where the bars spilled light and music onto the pavement, the smells and sounds of cafés adding to the spectacle.

He appeared ahead of her quite suddenly, emerging from an

alleyway and walking across her path onto the main thoroughfare. He paused, casting his cloak back over his shoulder, waiting for her to follow. Her heart beat faster as she trailed him,
watching him merge with the other performance artists on Las
Ramblas.

He approached a seated tourist who was having her portrait
sketched. He exchanged a few words with the artist, then moved
over to the tourist and put his hand beneath her hair, drawing
out a flower, which he showed her, then tucked it behind her ear.
The woman smiled in delight. The artist clapped and then began
to add the feature into his drawing. *El diablo* moved on. As Katrina passed, she looked at the flower in the woman's hair, a soft
red bloom that added a new dimension to her coloring.

*El diablo* was weaving his way through the crowd, and she
hurried on, anticipation urging speed into her footsteps. When
he took a side street, she clutched her shawl around her shoulders and darted after him. The street was cobbled, the shops
there shuttered for the night. The streetlights were few and far
between, and she couldn't see him. Walking on quickly, her
heart beat hard as she looked into the gloomy doorways. When
she was halfway down the short street, she turned and looked
over her shoulder.

He was at the end of the street, behind her. He must have
been in one of the first doorways as she passed; the idea of it
sent a delicious shiver over her skin. He watched her, and she
could just make out the smile on his face in the shadows.

She headed on, knowing that he would follow.

Oh, how that turned her on, knowing that he was pursuing
her, and this time he would capture her and hold her tight. She

kept her pace even, looking ahead, but with her head cocked to hear when he might approach. The street turned a corner and opened out into a square. It was a more residential area. Which way should she go?

She glanced over her shoulder. He was nowhere to be seen, and then she felt a rush of air and movement on her other side and turned to see him pass behind her, overtaking her again. His stalking shadow made her restless and hot.

He moved quickly across the square to the opposite side. She couldn't take her eyes off him; it was as if static clung in the air between them, hooking them up to each other. When he reached the end of a street there, he stopped and leaned up against a wall about ten feet down that street.

He was still as a statue, but he hadn't hidden from her view, not this time. As she stepped closer, her breath came quicker. What would he do when she passed? Her spine tingled with anticipation, her body humming with it. She clutched her shawl loosely, her hips rolling as she walked, the essential woman deep inside her instinctively aware of her mate so close by, so filled with male power.

As she approached, he looked directly at her. She walked slower, and her shawl slid down from her shoulders to rest on the crook of her arms. He watched, his expression inscrutable. When she stepped on and passed him, he made his move. He circled her, causing her to stop. She swayed. He circled her again. This time she turned to face him as he did so, their dance of desire closing all the time. When he captured her into his arms, she gasped at the sudden contact, her head dropping back as she awaited his kiss.

His lips on hers made her melt against him, her body growing hot and her core turning to liquid fire. His hands on her body were powerful, demanding, and he shunted her up against the wall, his body rigid with tension. His tongue plied into her mouth, teasing her, making her crave the hardness of his cock plunging inside her as well. She trembled in response to him, and he growled low in his throat. Clutching her against him, he rolled her body against his, turning, moving them both farther down the street, away from the streetlights and into the shadows.

She gasped for air, clutching at his shoulders as he wedged her against a solid surface, dizzy with sensation. The wall behind her was overhung with trailing flowers, and she felt the brush of them against her hair. He drew her closer to an old gate set in an arched niche. In the streetlights, she could see the trailing flowers were red and purple, like the one he had given the woman on Las Ramblas. Had he passed here earlier? Had he planned their route?

He moved her, easing her into the niche of the gateway. There in the shadows his hand latched around the top of her thigh, and he lifted her leg against the outside of his hip, grinding his erection against her groin. She could feel how hard he was, how ready, and the need to lock their bodies together rocketed through her. Breathlessly, she put her hand against the wall to steady herself.

He smiled and reached over the top of the gate and into a narrow gap, where he released a latch. The gate yawned open. Drawing her in against him, he stepped through the gateway. Peering in, she saw a private courtyard filled with huge potted plants, a jungle of them, at the center of which there was a trickling fountain lit from below the surface of the water.

She held back when he urged her on by pulling gently on her hand. She shook her head. "We can't, not in here."

He didn't respond but instead stalked back and lifted her into his arms. Her shawl slipped away onto the ground. She didn't care. Pushing the gate closed behind them with one foot, he carried her through the courtyard to a stone bench set beneath an arbor. She clutched at him and squinted through the foliage, over to where the house stood. "Nico, we might get caught."

Sitting down with her in his lap, he sought her neck, kissing her there. "I don't care. I can't wait any longer to be inside you."

The feeling of his warm breath on her skin shoved rational thought from her mind. His hand was under her skirt, stroking her thigh. Beneath her, she could feel the hard bulge of his erection. Could they really get away with doing it here? If they were quick, maybe it would be okay. The heady scent of flowers hung in the air, intoxicating her. She moved fast, lust making the decision for her. Hauling her dress up around her hips, rolling from one buttock to the other to do so.

He growled.

"I want you, too, now." Her need for him was total, and she turned to face him, sitting in his lap with one leg on either side of his hips. She didn't care if they were trespassing. She had to have him; fast, furtive sex here in this place, before they were discovered.

"Oh, yes, that's good," he said, his hands moving under the bunched fabric of her skirt to cup her bottom with his hands.

He kissed her in the sensitive spot at the base of her throat, and when he looked up at her, the moonlight caught his expression. He was as desperate as she was. "I adore you, Katrina."

With one hand still against her bottom, his other hand stole between them to stroke her pussy through the sheer fabric of her panties. He squeezed her mons, cupping her, his thumb gently crushing her clit inside its sensitive nest. She groaned aloud and rocked her hips, showing him that it was good, nodding, her lips parted as she breathed his name. "Nico, inside me, now."

"Like this?" He ran his finger under the fabric, stroking the sensitive folds of skin beneath.

Her sex clenched, and she clung to his shoulders, her need for him making her body shift, constantly rolling back and forth against him for contact, her bottled-up desire frothing and spilling over. "Please don't tease me. I need you now."

She shuffled back in his lap and plucked at his belt urgently. He let her undo it. Awkwardly, hurriedly, she pulled his buttons open and freed his cock. It jutted out, reaching for her, hard and hot against the palm of her hand. She stroked it, reveling in its combination of rigidity and satin smoothness. With the other hand, she reached down, plucking the last of his buttons open so that she could stroke the full length of him and cup his balls.

He groaned, turning his face up to the sky, his eyes closed. She stroked her fingers over the head of his cock and felt it ooze for her. Her body responded in kind.

"When you touch me, it makes me loco," he said, shaking his head as he fumbled for his pocket, pulling out a condom.

She nodded, unable to form words while she pulled her panties to one side, ready for him. Her clit throbbed and burned when the fabric moved across it, and she rubbed it with her fingers while he rolled the condom onto his erection. When it was done, he smiled at her, and she saw his eyes flash in the moonlight.

She climbed over him, ready, oh so ready to slide down onto his cock. With her hands on his shoulders, she savored that first feeling of entry, the way the head of his cock stretched her open, gliding against the slippery walls of her sex, filling her as she eased down onto him. Her body clasped him eagerly, and his erection thrust right up against her cervix as she settled on him. The sensation was so acute, so longed for, that she moaned with relief. Her hands locked around his neck, and she began to roll her hips back and forth, her toes just making contact with the ground when she leaned forward, giving her leverage. The head of his cock massaged her so very deep inside that the contact caused pleasure/pain ripples around her sensitive cervix. Her womb throbbed with it.

The skin on her back raced with self-awareness, her senses honed for the sound of a passerby. What if they were discovered here? The danger made her needy and desperate. At the same time, she was overwhelmed with the need to mould herself around him, to hold him inside her forever. The combination was incendiary. Throwing her head back, she moved faster. Sweat dampened her skin, urgency overcoming her.

His hands held her buttocks, guiding her, her anchor as she closed fast on climax. His head was flung back, the muscles in his neck corded tension. "I'm going to come," he whispered.

She rode him hard, fast, and fierce, so hungry for this man.

She was so close, and she ground down onto him, pleasure laced with pain spearing through her in her release. When his cock jerked against the neck of her womb, another wave of sensation hit her, making her weak. Her legs vibrated, her torso shuddering as her core went into spasm. She struggled for breath, rolled forward, leaning over his shoulder, clutching at him with weak fingers, whispering his name over and over.

His hands on her back felt so sure, so solid. He stroked her, kissed her, and she felt cherished. She savored that feeling.

They stayed that way for several moments, and then she thought of passersby again and moved, reluctantly. He lifted her free and moved her onto the bench beside him. While he stripped off the condom and did up his fly, she wilted onto the bench. Resting her fevered cheek against the cool stone, she closed her eyes as her body leveled. When she opened her eyes, she could see lights twinkling in the windows of the house at the end of the courtyard garden. She sat up, put her hand on his arm, gripping him. "Nico, we ought to go."

"Not yet."

She gave him a look. "Look, Nico, I realize you can insinuate yourself anywhere with utter stealth, but I don't think I could run if my life depended on it right now. Let's get out now before someone catches us." She laughed breathlessly.

"Nobody is home, except us." He smiled at her, tracing his finger down her breastbone, where the skin was still damp. "This house belongs to my family."

"Oh. You tricked me." She glanced at the surroundings with fresh vision, laughing at herself. *I should have known: the flower.*

"You wanted to be dangerous, yes?"

She pouted, but he was right. He'd been so observant, remembering what she liked, what thrilled her.

He put his arm around her. "When I visited my father this afternoon, we talked about you. He is very grateful for what you did for him; as am I."

"I didn't do much of anything," she interrupted, feeling embarrassed, "but I'm glad he's able to talk a little more."

"Yes, he's going to be okay. He insisted I bring you here to stay, so that you might enjoy Barcelona in comfort." He glanced at the house. "Sergio has put the property up for sale, but my father wants to look at things again, when he is well enough. I don't think he wants to go back to the Torre. He might sell it and move here. This was my parents' first home. I was born here."

"Will you help him make the decisions he needs to?"

Smiling, he touched the tip of her nose with his lips, teasingly. "Yes, I will."

She looked back at the house, a tall, impressive mansion set between others of a similar style. It had gabled windows that opened out onto miniature balconies. The style reflected that of the Torre del Castagona, but in city mode. She saw that now. The ground-floor door that she could just make out through the courtyard garden was embellished with glittering mosaic tiles that caught the moonlight, twinkling like stars. It was like a secret hideaway here in the city, and she couldn't help being curious about the interior.

Nico was watching her.

She smiled up at him. "I was enjoying Barcelona anyway; being with you is enough."

"That makes me happy." His voice was hoarse.

She reached out to touch him, and he kissed her fingers. "Besides," she added, "I like your apartment. I tried to sleep this afternoon, but all I wanted to do was enjoy the view across the rooftops."

"I'm glad you like it. However, I want you to myself, for as long as I can have you," he looked at her meaningfully, then smiled, "and Kent is there. As much as I like him, he can get in the way between a man and the woman he desires."

*I want you to myself, for as long as I can have you?*

Her heart beat hard. It was hanging between them, a heavy sense of longing, a need to affirm what was happening here. It would be so easy to step apart in a couple of days, to walk away. Both their lives had a purpose and volition of their own. To make them continue to cross and intertwine for longer than these few days was something they both had to want. It was there, a powerful tug.

"For as long as you can have me?" she queried cautiously.

He nodded. "Will you consider coming back to Spain?"

"I'd love to, especially if you want me to."

"Of course I want you to. I want to keep you here forever." He growled and frowned. "Katrina, do you understand what I'm saying? I worry I'm not expressing myself well in English. I want you to be my woman."

The way he said it and his sudden insecurity about expressing himself drew a deep, contented sigh from her. She stroked his hair. "You couldn't have expressed it any better; believe me. I would love to be your woman, Nico Teodoro."

"You have no idea how happy that makes me." He mumbled

in Spanish and kissed her nose, her cheek, and her ear. Then he sought her mouth, kissing her deeply. She melted into him, wrapping her arms around him, embracing him totally. Instantly, her passion flared, her body eager to be bonded together in passion again.

"Let's go inside," he murmured.

"Wait. I have something for you. I meant to give it to you earlier." She reached into her cleavage and pulled out the small satin object she had hidden there inside her bra, handing it to him.

He unfolded the satin eye mask that he had worn that first night during the festival, staring at it with a smile. "You kept it."

"Of course I kept it. You know, that night, I wished you weren't Nicolas Teodoro; that you'd been just some man in the street I could have been with, properly. But if that had been the case, I might never have seen you again. I wouldn't have wanted that."

"*Sí.*" He lifted her into his arms, carrying her toward the house.

"When I leave London and come back to Barcelona," she teased, "I'd need to find a little apartment . . . something to share with a lover, maybe."

"What about something in the city, overlooking the rooftops?"

"Sounds good."

"I think I know a place, but I hear the landlord gets grouchy when his *inglés* lover isn't close by." He nuzzled her. "But when she's around, he's not so bad."

"I'd give him a try out, for sure. I don't think he sounds so bad," she replied. "In fact, I bet he's an *amante caliente.*"

He paused at the doorway, staring down at her with amusement and admiration. "A hot lover. Who taught you that one?"

"When Kent woke up, I introduced myself, and I asked him to teach me some phrases, just in case the opportunity presented itself to use them." She stroked her hand over his torso possessively.

"Kent? That makes sense." He rolled his eyes, nudged the door handle open with his knee, and then paused again on the threshold. "Katrina, you do realize I'm loco for you?"

"In that case, it's just as well I learned to say *te amo*, Nico," isn't it?"

His eyes shone. "I love you, too, Katrina Hammond."